A Homecoming in Shady Springs

Shady Springs Book Two

Sarah Anne Crouch

Sarah Anne Crouch

Scrivenings PRESS
Quench your thirst for story.
www.ScriveningsPress.com

Copyright © 2025 by Sarah Anne Crouch

Published by Scrivenings Press LLC
15 Lucky Lane
Morrilton, Arkansas 72110
https://ScriveningsPress.com

Printed in the United States of America

All rights reserved. No part of this publication may be reproduced, stored in a retrieval system, or transmitted in any form or by any means—for example, electronic, photocopy, or recording— without the prior written permission of the publisher. The only exception is brief quotations in printed reviews.

Paperback ISBN 978-1-64917-456-7

eBook ISBN 978-1-64917-457-4

Editors: Amy R. Anguish and Linda Fulkerson

Cover design by Linda Fulkerson—www.bookmarketinggraphics.com

Scripture quotations are from the ESV Bible® (The Holy Bible, English Standard Version®), copyright © 2001 by Crossway Bibles, a publishing ministry of Good News Publishers. Used by permission. All rights reserved.

All characters are fictional, and any resemblance to real people, either factual or historical, is purely coincidental.

NO AI TRAINING: Without in any way limiting the author's [and publisher's] exclusive rights under copyright, any use of this publication to "train" generative artificial intelligence (AI) technologies to generate text is expressly prohibited. The author reserves all rights to license uses of this work for generative AI training and development of machine learning language models.

To Michael, my college sweetheart and best friend forever. Life is better with you by my side.

1

AUGUST, FRESHMAN YEAR

No one sent Henry Mullins packages in the mail. Except for his Halloway University acceptance, he hadn't received a letter since the eighth-grade.

Henry did not get packages, of that he was sure. He didn't get boxes of cookies from home or well-wishes from friends and family. So, why did his heart lift when he saw the bright yellow slip of paper inside his mailbox?

Was it possible? Had his parents sent him something for the first day of his first year of college? Definitely not Dad, but maybe Mom. Even if it was just some socks he left behind when he went to school, he'd be happy to receive something from them. Anything to say they missed him or were thinking about him.

"Oh, look. You got a package!" Jason snatched the canary yellow slip from Henry's hands before he even had a chance to read it.

"Shouldn't I be the one to take it to the post office?" Henry tried but failed to grab the paper from his best friend.

"It's highly unlikely they're going to check to make sure it's really you." Jason held the slip out of Henry's reach. "We look so much alike, anyway."

This was not true. At six feet and four inches, Jason dwarfed Henry and most other people. Henry often wished he had Jason's height and easy confidence, but he was grateful for the scraps of attention he got from the girls who flocked to his tall friend. Henry was usually able to leverage his good looks and wit to charm young women once they finished fawning over Jason.

"Maybe it's a care package from home." Jason winked at him.

Henry allowed a bubble of hope to build for just a moment. What if? No. Mom and Dad had been happy to send him away, and they certainly weren't missing him. But maybe, just maybe, he was wrong.

Henry shook his head. "Jason, you and I both know it's more likely that *your* parents sent me something than mine."

Actually, that did make sense. Jason's mom had always felt a little sorry for Henry. What if Nancy Jones had sent him a box of something?

"Hey, there, Angie." Jason draped his lanky frame over the desk of the campus post office.

"Hiya, Jason." The cute blonde behind the counter fluffed her already quite fluffy hair, and her cheeks grew pink.

"Could you get this package, sweetheart? It's for my friend." He dangled the paper above her head.

Angie giggled as she attempted to take the slip before Jason pulled it out of her grasp. Jason handed it to her and winked. Henry rolled his eyes.

Angie turned to the shelves behind her and grabbed a brown box. "Here you go. See ya later." She waggled her fingers at them.

"Sure thing." Jason hoisted the package on his shoulders as Henry trailed behind. He always had to work extra hard to catch up to his giant of a friend. "How about you show me your new digs?"

"They look about the same as everyone else's." But Henry led the way to his dorm room anyway. Walking through the student center, Jason said *hello* to about twenty different people, guys and girls.

"Hey, J, wait up." A lanky man strode over to where Jason and Henry walked. Raymond Williams was Jason's roommate and fellow athlete. The two friends matched each other in height, but Jason's fair complexion stood out in contrast to Ray's dark hair and sepia-toned skin. Their personalities were opposite but complemented each other somehow—Raymond was cool and quiet, Jason energetic and always the life of the party.

"Do you know *everyone* on this campus?" Henry asked.

"You'll be the same way next year. Trust me." Jason laughed and nudged him in the ribs, or at least he would have if Henry had been any taller. As it was, Jason's elbow came to Henry's shoulder.

Though Henry and Jason had been best friends since junior high, Jason was a year ahead of him. They'd known each other as long as Henry could remember. Shady Springs, Arkansas, was such a tiny town, one couldn't live there long without knowing everyone and their grandma, as Jason's older sister always said. But the boys hadn't had a reason to spend any time together until they both played junior high basketball.

The year before Henry graduated, Jason took a basketball scholarship at Halloway University. Henry visited Jason in his dorm room on campus that fall. He'd had such a good time, he didn't even mind the terrible ache in his neck from sleeping on the floor. Before Jason, Henry had never gone to church, let alone entertained thoughts of attending a Christian university. Now here he was, a college freshman with an academic scholarship, walking across the Halloway University campus with his best friend.

Henry smiled as he scanned the scene outdoors. The front lawn, a wide expanse of green grass and tall oak trees framed on four sides by red brick buildings, was one of the places he loved most at Halloway. Despite the heat, and the fact no one was allowed to wear shorts until later that evening or on the weekends, the morning was beautiful. Dappled sunlight filtered through the trees. Alone or in pairs, students sat on the white swings dotting the grass. Water gurgled happily from the fountain at the far end of the lawn.

He led his friends to a red brick dormitory and through a long hallway of linoleum. "Home sweet home." Henry flicked the light switch in his cinder block box of a bedroom and let Jason inside.

"Cool." Raymond and Jason smiled and nodded politely.

It wasn't much. A bed with sheets and an old quilt, a shelf full of textbooks, a Shady Springs High School coffee mug full of pens and pencils, and a hand-me-down typewriter on the built-in desk against the wall.

"Nice curtains." Raymond gestured to the dusty blue valances hanging from the two windows in the room.

"Frank's mom bought those." Henry's roommate had been embarrassed by his parents and all the fuss they made. Henry brushed off Frank's discomfort nonchalantly, but not before he'd charmed Mr. and Mrs. Thomas into taking them both out for dinner.

"Let's see what's in this thing." Jason plopped the package onto Henry's bed and swiped his keys across the tape on top. "Ooh." He grabbed something small from inside.

"It's … very … pink." Henry gaped in confusion at the contents of the box. Pink tissue paper was wrapped around several small parcels. A pink card rested at the top of the pile. And pink confetti was sprinkled over the top.

Henry's gaze shot up, suddenly aware of Jason and Raymond watching him. His face must have turned the exact color of the inside of the package. He shook his head in disbelief.

Jason rummaged through. "There's candy and cookies. Some pencils. Here's a note." He opened the bubble gum colored card. "Uh-oh."

Henry yanked the paper from Jason's hands. "Let me see that." His stomach dropped. Henry spun the package around and looked at the name on the top. He groaned. "This isn't my mail."

"Yeah. I figured as much." Jason barked out a laugh.

Raymond snickered, one side of his mouth upturned. "Oh, man."

"How did this happen?" He turned to the others in confusion.

"Remember in orientation when they talked about campus mail?" Jason asked.

"Sort of ..."

"Well, you have a box buddy. Someone who shares your mailbox."

"Why?"

Jason shrugged. "Growing enrollment, I guess. They have too many students and not enough mailboxes." He waved his hands, gesturing around the room. "Decided to spend money on air conditioning instead of adding more boxes."

"So, this girl and I share a mailbox. And I accidentally got her mail."

"I'm sure this sort of thing happens all the time. It's no big deal." He pulled the card back out of the box. "Besides, it looks like she's a really great girl."

"What do you mean?"

"I think this is a care package from her church. They all signed the card. *We miss you—Hope you're having a great time. Come home to visit soon* ... Sounds like they really like her." Jason chewed loudly.

"What are you chewing on?"

"Nothing." He swallowed, his Adam's apple bobbing.

Henry slapped himself in the forehead. "Did you just eat her candy?"

"I took it out before I knew it wasn't yours. It's not like she'll ever find out."

Henry shook his head. "No more stealing from my box buddy. I'm going to need to do a lot of sweet-talking to get out of this."

"Yeah," said Raymond. "You've gotta share a mailbox with her for four years. Assuming you pass your classes."

At the mention of class, Henry's pulse raced. "Oh, no. It's almost time for Bible."

"Better get a move on, kid. We'll watch your stuff for you."

"Not a chance." Henry grabbed the package. "I'm taking this back to the mailroom. There's no way I'm leaving you in here with all that candy." He gestured to Raymond and shoved Jason out of the room, then locked the door. "Walk me to class?"

"No, sorry. I'm going in the opposite direction. See you in the cafeteria at lunch. Noon." Jason pointed finger guns at Henry and took off beside Ray, their long legs carrying them twice as fast as normal-sized humans.

Henry sighed. "Now I've just got to get to class on time and figure out how to get this package back to ... Catherine Hodges. Whoever that is."

2

AUGUST, FRESHMAN YEAR

Henry squeaked into the classroom just as the bell rang. He'd hoped he would have time to run Catherine Hodges's package over to the post office, but he would've had to make it there and back to the Bible building in five minutes. Then, he spent two minutes going to the wrong side of the building. All of that meant he carried the box under his arm as he tried to find a seat to squeeze into. He'd prefer a spot in the back of the large room, but only the second row was available—much closer than he'd like.

The room buzzed with the nervous energy of thirty Freshmen on their first day of classes. The man who must be his professor walked up and down the aisle with a stack of syllabi. He handed out several per row, each student taking one and passing it on.

When Henry got his copy, he scanned it until he found the list of test dates and due dates. For people like Jason, who had grown up going to church their whole lives, a class on the New Testament would not be a difficult prospect. But for Henry, who had only read the Bible for the first time a few years ago, it was daunting.

"All right, folks." The professor strolled back to the front of the room. He waved his hands to quiet the students. "Let's get started. Welcome to Honors New Testament. I'm Dr. Cooper."

Wait, what? Honors?

As a requirement for his scholarship, Henry had been placed on a special academic track. He just didn't realize that New Testament would be one of his honors classes. How could he possibly pass an *advanced* Bible class?

"Before we begin, I'd like everyone to stand." Chairs scraped as the students rose. "Great. Now, please lift your left foot off the floor."

Some students giggled, but as Henry looked around, he saw everyone balancing on one leg.

"Wonderful, thank you. I just wanted to make sure we got started on the right foot."

Several low groans could be heard around the room, but Henry let out a loud burst of laughter. A girl giggled from somewhere to his right. Henry poked his head around to see who it was and found a short young woman with curly brown hair. She turned, maybe to see who shared in her laughter, and gave Henry a shy smile.

Henry's anxiety eased a little as he slipped back into his seat. At least the professor had a sense of humor. Maybe he'd also have a lot of grace for his students.

"I know a lot of you might be wondering what an honors Bible class will require of you. I'll admit, this will likely be one of your more rigorous classes this semester. You can't just skate by without reading or studying, like some of your friends."

Henry shook his head. He definitely hadn't been counting on breezing by in any of his classes.

"But I promise, you will get out of this course what you put into it. And I hope by the end of the semester, you will find it has been one of your more rewarding educational experiences."

It would be an experience all right.

"Now, I encourage a lot of discussion in my classes. And in

order to feel comfortable doing that, we need to get to know one another. I'd like to go around the room and introduce ourselves. Just give me your name, your hometown, and a favorite hobby."

Dr. Cooper looked at the front row. "Let's start here."

The curly-haired girl from earlier spoke. "My name is Catherine Hodges, but my friends call me Cate."

Henry gasped. He cleared his throat to disguise the sound, looking around to make sure no one noticed. His box buddy.

"I'm from Wichita, Kansas. Oh, and I like to read."

Henry didn't hear much else as the next person took a turn. Well, at least he figured out how to find Catherine. Or Cate, assuming she would ever consider him a friend.

The next step, Henry decided, was to figure out how to give Cate her package without burning any bridges. If he was going to share a mailbox with this girl for four years, he needed to make a good impression.

One by one, guys and girls introduced themselves. When it came to Henry, he only had to think a minute. "Henry Mullins. I'm from Shady Springs, Arkansas. And I enjoy photography."

In a few minutes, the rest of the students had shared. Henry realized he hadn't actually caught more than a couple names. He needed to pay better attention if he wanted some friends to study with in the future.

"All right, let's see how I can do." Dr. Cooper rubbed his hands together and pointed to the first row. "Cate, Heather, Kevin, Nichole." He proceeded to name each and every student in the room. Henry whistled. A few students clapped, impressed. It helped a little to know that his professor at least cared enough to learn his name.

Next Dr. Cooper walked them through the syllabus. There were reading assignments every day. And it was a daily class. There was a mid-term, a final test, and a research paper due before Thanksgiving. Henry took a deep breath. He'd only finished his second class of the day, and he already felt as if he were drowning.

After the last bell rang, Henry quick-stepped over to Catherine's seat, the package under his arm.

"Hey, Catherine—Cate!"

Her curly hair bounced over her shoulder as she turned to face him. He hadn't noticed before, but she had beautiful brown eyes and a smile that made his heart stutter. "Hi, um…"

"Henry. Henry Mullins. I know we haven't officially met yet, but you're my—I mean, we share a mailbox." He gave what he hoped was a disarmingly handsome smile.

She raised one eyebrow. "Oh? I had forgotten about that." She stuck out her hand. "Nice to meet you, Henry."

"Thanks, I hope so. I mean, you too." *Real smooth, Henry.* He grimaced. "I don't know how to tell you this." He held out the box. "I accidentally picked up your mail."

"What?"

He laughed. The whole thing was pretty ridiculous. "It was actually my friend Jason. We saw the slip and didn't even think about checking to see—"

She took the package from him. "But it's been opened."

Henry leaned against the back of her chair. "Right, like I said, we—"

"And it looks like someone went through all the stuff inside." She looked up at him, confusion and anger written all over her face.

"It's so crazy. I didn't realize at first that it wasn't mine."

"But my name is written all over the outside. And on the card. And I'm sure it was on the slip of paper from the post office." Her eyes flashed, and her cheeks grew crimson.

"Yes, you're totally right, and I'm so sorry." He ran his hands through his hair and gave another of his patented Henry smiles. "I guess I didn't read any of those things. I mean, I read the card—"

"You read my card?"

"Sure, that's how—" Henry stopped suddenly when he saw the look on Cate's face. She was no longer confused. She was flat-out angry. Did this girl have absolutely no sense of humor? How could he possibly get himself out of this mess? "Don't get upset."

"Okay. So, you neglected to read the notice from the post office." She ticked off each point on her fingers. "You somehow conned the mail room into giving you my package. You opened the box and rifled through *my* things. And you read the card which was written *to me*."

"Wow. When you put it that way—" Henry shrugged. "I'm really sorry. It was an honest mistake."

"There's nothing honest about this whole thing." She shook her head. "I hope mail fraud won't be a regular occurrence with you."

"No, I'll be much more careful in the future. Promise." He held up his hand.

"I certainly hope so." She tucked her syllabus inside a folder and tapped the folder and her notebook sharply on the table before stacking them on top of the box.

"I guess I'll be seeing you around." Henry moved her chair out of the way so she could exit the aisle.

"It would seem to be unavoidable." She marched off.

"Bye, Cate." Henry couldn't tell if she heard him. Probably not, since she didn't turn or say anything back to him.

"Rough first day?"

Henry turned to see Dr. Cooper at the front of the room, collecting papers into his briefcase.

"I'm sure she'll cool off … in a few days." Henry looked around the classroom. While he and Cate had been talking, all of the other students had left. Only he and the professor were there now. "Actually, I was hoping to talk to you."

"Of course. What can I do for you, Henry?"

Henry smiled, glad to know Dr. Cooper still remembered his name. But that didn't change the fact he needed to get out of this class. "I don't belong here."

"Are you not an honors scholar?" Dr. Cooper tilted his head.

Henry sighed. "I am, but I can't pass this class."

"Why not?"

Henry spread his fingers and looked down at his hands. "I've only ever read through the Bible once. I just started going to church a few years ago. There's no way I can keep up in an honors Bible class."

Dr. Cooper nodded. "This class is required for all honors scholars. You need it to keep your scholarship."

"But isn't there another course I can take? Or maybe a remedial Bible class?"

"Remedial Bible." Dr. Cooper laughed. "We don't offer that, and you wouldn't need it anyway."

Dr. Cooper gently gripped Henry's shoulder. "You have the scores and the grades to show that you do, in fact, belong in this class. You're not the first recent convert to come here and, Lord willing, you won't be the last. I've taught plenty of students who have never cracked open a Bible before." He smiled. "If you keep up with the reading and come to me anytime you have a question, you'll be just fine."

Henry nodded, though he was still unsure. "Okay."

Dr. Cooper clicked his briefcase shut. "I mean it. I want you to visit during office hours next week."

"Yes, sir." Henry wondered if office hours were like the college version of detention. Either way, he could use whatever help he could get.

So far, college was shaping up to be much harder than he'd expected.

3

PRESENT DAY

"I love the smell of funnel cakes." Catherine Mullins inhaled deeply and turned to her daughter, Madeleine.

"And kettle corn. Mmm." Maddy smiled back at her, shifting her weight.

Both women were laden down with art prints and frames, carrying Maddy's unsold paintings back to her car after a long day at the Shady Springs Harvest Festival. Booths and tents lined the walkways of Spring Park, and the sounds of banjos and fiddles floated through the air. The crowd had thinned significantly, but dozens of families still stood in line for fried treats or icy lemonade. Many had already made their way over to the square-dancing exhibition taking place on the other side of the park.

"Did you have a good day?" Catherine asked as they hiked through the field-turned-temporary parking lot.

"It was great!" Madeleine beamed as she set down her load and unlocked the car trunk. "Much better than last night. I'm sure the next couple of days will be a little slower, but I've more than made up for the cost of reserving my booth. I even had some repeat customers from last year."

This was Maddy's second time selling her art at the Harvest Festival. After spending a summer painting a mural for the small church in downtown Shady Springs the year before, Maddy had decided to split her time between her hometown of Kansas City with her mom and her aunt's house in Shady Springs, Arkansas. It didn't hurt that her boyfriend of a year, A.J. Young, also lived in Shady Springs.

As if summoned by Catherine's thoughts, A.J. appeared behind her, his arms full.

"You got all that, A.J.?" Catherine carefully leaned her frames against the car so she could take a couple from him.

"Thanks, Ms. Mullins. I think we've about got everything now."

"Catherine. You've got to start calling me Catherine, especially if—" Clamping her lips suddenly, she cut her eyes to her daughter. She breathed a sigh of relief. Maddy was fiddling with something in the driver's seat and didn't seem to hear anything.

"I've got the last of it." Maddy's father, Henry, joined the rest of them at the car. He gave Catherine a smile, and she nodded her head in return.

"Here, let me help you, Mr. Mullins." A.J. and Henry unloaded the rest of the prints and frames into the trunk and the backseat.

"Are you two going to stick around a little while?" Henry shut the last car door and turned to Maddy.

"What do you think, A.J.? Want to walk around a bit?" She turned her face up to A.J.'s, slipping her hand into his.

"Of course. Would anyone care to join us?" A.J.'s tone of voice was inviting, but his eyes, peering over Maddy's head said otherwise.

"Oh, no. You two go have fun." Catherine waved them off, leaning against the car in an attempt to look casual.

As soon as they were out of sight, she turned to Henry. "Did you bring the camera?"

"Of course. It's in my car. Did you text Clara?" He pulled car keys out of his pocket.

"Not yet." Catherine whipped out her phone and typed a brief message to her sister. "Done. Let's pick up your camera and meet her by the lemonade stand."

They walked in silence for a few minutes. "How're you feeling, Cate?"

"What do you mean?" Catherine turned to him.

"I mean, how do you feel about …" Henry gestured broadly.

She nodded, understanding. "I'm okay. I mean, it's a little bittersweet, but I like him. She could do a lot worse."

"I like him too. He's a good guy." Henry stopped and looked at her, his eyes narrowed. "Does he seem—?"

"Familiar? Like maybe we've seen him before somewhere?" Catherine had wondered the same thing since she met A.J.

"Yes!" Henry's face lit up. "I'm glad I'm not crazy." He shook his head and kept walking.

"No, I see it, too, but it's not possible for us to have met him before. He just moved to Shady Springs four years ago, and his family is all in Little Rock."

"Hmm." Henry clicked his key fob, and a nearby sedan beeped.

"New car?"

"Yeah … well, new to me, at least." He retrieved a camera bag from the trunk. "My old clunker finally gave up the ghost."

"Still went with red, I see."

"Of course." Henry grinned at her, and her heart skipped. That dumb smile of his always got her. "When I saw they had one in red, I had to buy it."

Catherine gave a tight-lipped smile. She hoped her pink

cheeks didn't give her away. Even after all their years apart, she couldn't shake her attraction to Henry. It didn't help that she had never been in a serious relationship with anyone else after him.

They trekked through the field together, toward the lemonade stand where Catherine's sister, Clara, waited.

"Cate! Henry!" Clara waved her arms.

"It's good to see you, Clara." Henry enveloped Clara in a warm embrace, and Catherine's breath caught. Was that ... jealousy?

"I was thinking if we cut through the field on the west side, we should be able to get close enough without being spotted."

"Sounds like a plan." Henry patted Clara on the back, and the three headed off together.

"Well, I *thought* this would be a shortcut." Clara's gaze roved over the booths standing in their way. Vendors packed away wreaths of tulle, carved wooden signs, and bars of goat milk soap.

"Come on, let's go across here." Catherine led the way to a large empty tent.

"How have you been, Henry?" Clara patted him on the shoulder as they walked.

"Good, Clara. Really good." Henry beamed at her. "I was booked solid for wedding season. We're getting ready for some fall sessions at the studio, and I've got an agreement in the works with a pumpkin patch nearby. I'm going to offer a package deal with a mini-session for families."

"You said 'we.' Have you been able to hire some help?"

Although Cate knew he'd taken a long hiatus from his photography to work through personal issues, Henry had made an impressive amount of progress in a short time with his business in Fayetteville.

"Yes, I have an assistant now, Leah. She's taken a lot off my plate. And if we keep growing, I might be able to hire a second photographer."

"That's great, Henry." Catherine turned to smile at him. Was that a faint blush in his cheeks, or just her imagination?

They hunkered down against the trunk of a large oak tree. "Did A.J. say what he'd do to give a cue?" Henry asked.

Catherine barely noticed the rough bark of the tree against her back as she turned to face Henry. His blue eyes peered into her own. Somewhere in the back of her mind, she registered that he'd asked her a question, but all she could think about was how his cologne still smelled the same. She willed her heart to slow down.

"Yes, he's going to stop close to that bench." She pointed to a green park bench a few yards away. "Then, he'll kneel."

Henry nodded, but he blinked. Did he look sad that their daughter was already old enough to be getting engaged? Or was she projecting her feelings? He turned away from her, pulling his camera out of his bag.

"Look, there they are. *Shh, shh.*" Clara patted their arms.

Catherine, Henry, and Clara peeked around the tree trunk at the sight before them. Maddy and A.J. strolled along the path, completely oblivious to anyone else.

Henry lifted the camera to his face, kneeling on the grass. "Cate, would you grab my bag? I'm going to move closer in a minute." He spoke without looking away from the viewfinder.

"Of course." Catherine shouldered the strap of his heavy equipment bag. How many times had she done that same exact movement in the past? A dozen times a hundred?

"I'm going to try to sneak around behind them to get a different angle from my phone," Clara whispered in Catherine's ear.

"Good idea." Catherine settled back behind the tree and leaned to find a good vantage point.

Henry snapped a few shots. "Could you grab my other lens?"

"Uh, sure." Catherine reached into the bag again. There were two lenses, both black, and she wasn't sure which was the right one. "Is this it?"

Henry glanced away from the camera. "No, that's the macro lens for closeups of the ring. The other one."

"Right. Here you go." She grabbed the other lens and handed it to him.

"Thank you." His fingers brushed hers as he took the lens.

A jolt. Electricity zipped all over her skin, not just where she'd touched him. "Sorry about that."

Henry cleared his throat. "It's no problem. I'm not always great at communicating."

That was an understatement if she ever heard one. "Well, I used to be more helpful. It's just been so long ..." She trailed off.

"*Shh, shh.* Listen." Henry turned back to his camera, and Catherine took in the scene in front of her. Her stomach roiled. She'd thought she was ready for this, but now she wasn't sure.

4

PRESENT DAY

Madeleine and A.J. sauntered over closer to the tree where Catherine and Henry were hidden. Behind them, Clara crouched on the other side of a bench. She peeked out, holding her cell phone. Catherine could just make out A.J.'s voice.

"Madeleine Mullins, since the moment I met you, I knew you weren't like any woman I've ever known."

Catherine held back a chuckle. Their meeting had been memorable. Maddy had attacked A.J. with a wooden prop sword, thinking he was an intruder. Thankfully, A.J. had a great sense of humor.

"At first, I convinced myself we weren't supposed to be together. I tried my hardest to keep you at arm's length as just a friend. But the more I tried, the more I fell in love with you." A.J. pushed a lock of hair from Madeleine's forehead. He reached for both of her hands and took a shaky breath. "Madeleine, you're one of the greatest blessings God has ever given me. This past year with you has been the best year of my life, and I don't want it to end." A.J. knelt on one knee.

Catherine looked over to Henry. He glanced back and caught

her eye. Bittersweet nostalgia welled up inside her. She gave him a small smile and wondered if he was thinking of the same night she was remembering.

"Mrs. Lewis?" A couple of teenagers walked by the bench where Clara was hiding.

Clara waved a little and shushed, but it was too late.

"Aunt Clara, what are you doing there?" Maddy turned around, her forehead wrinkled in confusion.

"Mr. Young?" One of the boys saw A.J. kneeling on the grass. His eyes grew round as he took in the scene before him. "Oh ... oh! Uh ... see you later!" He grabbed the hand of his girlfriend and quick-stepped away, looking over his shoulder repeatedly.

A.J. shook his head and chuckled. He sighed as he smiled up at Maddy, pulling something shiny from his pocket. "Madeleine Jane Mullins, would you marry me so we can spend the rest of our lives together?"

A pregnant pause hung over them. Maddy's eyes widened as she took in the scene before her: a kneeling boyfriend, a brilliant ring, an aunt waiting in the wings and still holding up her cell phone. She searched the nearby trees, very close to where Catherine and Henry stood. Her face was drained of color. She took a couple breaths.

"Um, yes. Yes!"

Catherine let out a sigh. For a moment, she'd been worried that Maddy might turn A.J. down. But that would be crazy. She and A.J. were perfect for each other. And they'd been dating over a year, which was long enough for everyone to start asking when they'd finally tie the knot.

A.J. picked Madeleine up and swung her around. Clara squealed as she popped out from her hiding spot and ran over to congratulate the couple. A.J. jumped in surprise, clinging to Madeleine to keep her from falling on the ground. He set her down carefully and waved to Catherine and Henry.

Catherine jogged over from behind the tree. "Congratulations!" She scooped Maddy into a hug. "I'm so happy for you, sweetheart."

"Thank you, Mom." Her expression was still dazed and unfocused, presumably from all the excitement. "I thought you might've been hiding nearby."

"Yes, we were watching from over there." Catherine gestured to where Henry still stood with his camera. She reached for Maddy's fingers. "Now, let me see that ring."

"Wait, the ring!" Maddy clapped her hands to her mouth. "Where did it go?"

A.J. held up his palms, empty. Everyone looked down at the grass.

"It has to be here somewhere." Catherine knelt to the ground. All four of them searched carefully, picking through each blade of grass.

"Ta-da!" A.J. brandished the ring in triumph. He slipped it onto Madeleine's finger. "Now, it's official."

"And I promise to be very careful with it." Maddy tilted her head as A.J. kissed her.

"You're sure to take better care of it than I have. I'm glad it's in your hands now." A.J. gave her another peck on the lips.

Henry strolled over to join the group.

"Did you get that craziness on film?" Catherine asked.

"Every bit of it." He waved the camera.

"How about some group shots, and then I can take a few of the couple?"

"Sounds great." A.J. used his long arms to pull Clara and Catherine in for a hug.

Henry took photos of Clara, Catherine, A.J. and Maddy, and then some of just the ladies.

"How about some of you, too, Henry?" Clara beckoned him over. "Lend me your camera, and I'll see what I can do."

"Oh, I don't—" Henry stammered.

"Come on, Dad. What's the worst she can do to it?" Maddy laughed.

Henry made a face as though he were thinking of all the possible terrible fates that could meet his beloved equipment.

"All right, fine. Come over here, and I'll show you what to do." Henry pointed out which button to press and how to frame the shot. He lifted the shoulder strap over Clara's head and gingerly placed the camera in her hands before joining the others.

"Say cheese!" Clara shouted.

Catherine caught Henry's eye and chuckled. "Cheese!"

"Just a few more." Clara's finger clicked away at rapid speed.

"That's enough, Clara. I don't want to lose our light." Henry gestured for Madeleine and A.J. to sit on the nearby bench. "Now, just the two of you. Let's get some good shots before the sun sets."

Catherine slipped her arm over her sister's shoulder. "What a perfect night."

Clara smiled at her. "I was thinking the same thing. And once they get married, I can add another couple to my list of successful matches."

"That's right. You did push them together a little, didn't you?" Catherine bumped her sister with her hip.

"I might have planted the idea in A.J.'s head. And talked Maddy up every chance I could get. And given him a picture of her."

"You did?" Catherine chuckled. "You're ridiculous."

"It worked, didn't it?" Clara crossed her arms. "A.J. saw how pretty she was and was smitten with her right from the start."

"I'm sure her winning personality had nothing to do with it." Catherine rolled her eyes at her sister.

"Maybe." Clara smirked.

Once Henry finished taking pictures, A.J. and Madeleine said their goodbyes. A.J. had made reservations for dinner in Fayetteville, and the couple looked eager to celebrate in a more private setting.

Catherine sighed as she watched her only daughter walk away, hand-in-hand, with her fiancé. Madeleine had been her whole life for more than two decades. She'd have a hard time adjusting to this new development.

Once the happy couple left, Clara spoke. "I'm just going to grab some things from the grocery store. Henry, you're welcome to join us for supper, if you like."

Henry glanced at Catherine, eyebrows raised. She shrugged her assent.

"Um, sure. I'd like that." Henry smiled.

"Great. I'll see you in a few minutes."

"Need any help packing up everything?" Catherine glanced around at all of Henry's photography equipment set up on the grass.

"Sure. That would be nice."

They worked together quietly. Catherine still remembered how to break down the tripod, although she didn't know where anything went in his bags.

Out of nowhere, Henry sighed. She knew he probably didn't even realize he had, but that sigh always meant he had something on his mind.

"What are you thinking about, Henry?"

"I guess A.J. asked for your blessing before he proposed." Henry spoke without looking up from zipping his bag.

"He did." Catherine nodded. "I told him he didn't need my blessing, but I was happy to give it anyway."

Did Henry's thoughts mirror her own? If things had been different, if Henry had never left, A.J. would have asked Henry for his blessing too. They would have given it together, as a team.

"He kind of did need to ask." Henry stood and met her gaze.

"What do you mean?" Catherine folded her arms over her chest. "Madeleine has a mind of her own. If she wants to marry him, she's going to do it, with or without permission from me."

Henry tilted his head. He had a gentle expression on his face, almost pitying. "She has a mind of her own, but her heart is tied up in you. If you didn't support her marriage, I don't know if she could go through with it. I just wish ... I wish I could have been a part of it too."

"Well, it doesn't matter anyway." Catherine waved him away and began walking toward the parking field. "I do support them because I believe they really love each other. And I'm hoping they'll have a great marriage. Not like ..." She stopped.

"Not like ours?" Henry kept walking, barely glancing her way.

"Well, yes." Catherine rubbed her forehead and continued on to the pathway. "Surely you don't want her to have what we had."

"Not the bad parts, no." Henry ran his fingers through his hair. "But there were some good parts. Some of it was pretty great."

Catherine's heart flipped as Henry met her gaze. She remembered the great parts too.

"I was thinking about us when A.J. was proposing. About when you proposed to me twenty-five years ago." Catherine lowered her eyes as she walked.

"Me too." His voice was heavy with sadness and something else. Was it longing?

"A.J. is a sweet boy, but his proposal doesn't hold a candle to yours."

Henry laughed, a rich melodious sound that thrilled her heart. "It was a little much, probably."

They chuckled together, hiking through the field until they got to Henry's car.

"I'm just over here." Catherine pointed to her own vehicle a few yards away. "See you at Clara's?"

"I'll be there." He waved before climbing inside.

Catherine smiled to herself. It was times like this that almost made her forget why she and Henry had been separated for eleven years.

Almost.

* * *

Dinner with Henry should have been uncomfortable, but it wasn't. Perhaps because of Clara's presence or the celebratory energy of the night, the three of them chatted and ate happily just like they used to. They were clearing the dessert dishes when A.J. and Maddy pulled into the driveway.

"Hi there, honey." Catherine pulled her daughter into a hug once she crossed the threshold of the living room. "Let me see that ring again." Madeleine showed off the bright sapphire. It was a beautiful piece of jewelry.

"Did you two have a nice dinner?" Henry shifted on his feet, his hands in his pockets.

They passed around hugs and congratulations, lingering in Clara's cozy living room. When the sky had grown dark, and fireflies blinked their love letters to each other in the yard, A.J. and Henry headed out for the evening.

The three women retired to the kitchen to clean up.

"That was something I haven't seen in a while." Madeleine sat at the counter in Clara's kitchen, a mug of tea in her hands.

"What's that?" Catherine brushed a strand of hair behind her ears.

"You and dad together. It's a little weird." She quickly amended her statement. "Good, though."

Aunt Clara hummed as she washed dishes.

"I'm just trying my best to forgive and move forward. And

part of that is allowing your dad to be there for the big moments in your life." Weaving Henry back into the tapestry of their lives had been difficult at first. But Maddy needed her father, and Catherine needed to forgive him.

"That was a surprise. Having everyone there." Madeleine frowned, lost in thought.

"I'm very happy for you two. He's such a sweet boy." Catherine patted her hand before joining Aunt Clara at the sink. She picked up a dish towel and dried the pots and pans as Clara finished.

Madeleine hopped off her chair to put a saucepan away in the cabinet. The three women worked together wordlessly, moving in choreographed circles around each other.

"What're you thinking about?" Clara gently elbowed Maddy in the ribs.

"Oh, nothing. Married life."

Catherine snorted. "That's certainly not nothing." She huffed as she passed Madeleine the last of the dishes. "It's going to take me some time to get used to you being married."

"Well, you'll have a nice long engagement to prepare. A.J. and I are thinking about Christmas of next year."

"Good. That will give you plenty of time." Time for premarital counseling, time for moving out of the house in Kansas City, and time for planning the beautiful wedding her daughter deserved.

Madeleine bit her lip. "What were your engagements like?"

Catherine stopped in her tracks. She found herself smiling. "Your dad went all out for our engagement. You've heard the story before."

"Didn't he hire out a band?"

"It was an a cappella quartet, but live music, nonetheless. It was all very romantic." Henry had always been good at the grand gestures. It was the smaller day-to-day tasks that he had a hard time with.

Clara sighed. "George proposed on a camping trip with friends. The stars were out. It was summertime." She trailed off, lost in the happy memory.

"Were either of you nervous? You know, about a lifelong commitment and the magnitude of marriage?"

Clara furrowed her brow, but Catherine spoke first. "I probably should have been, seeing as how things went later. But no. I was just happy that day. We'd been talking about marriage for such a long time, I knew he would propose eventually."

"George and I had a whirlwind romance, but I hoped he would propose. We were ready to get married almost from the beginning."

Catherine smiled at her sister. "I remember." The couple had met when Clara moved to Shady Springs to help out with Maddy. She was a colicky baby, who seemed to have difficulty with everything from nursing to bathing. Clara came to Arkansas for her sister, but she stayed for George. He was a dear, sweet man who was taken too soon by cancer. Catherine was happy to remember some of the golden times before his diagnosis.

Madeleine nodded and twisted her hands behind her back. "A.J. told me he's found a graduate school he likes."

Was this the reason for her daughter's unrest? She seemed awfully introspective for a woman who just got engaged. Maddy should be grinning and glowing. Instead, she chewed her lip, her gaze unfocused.

"Are you nervous about moving away?"

"A little, but I know he's wanted this for a long time."

"Don't worry." Clara squeezed her arm gently. "Grad school will only be a couple years. I'm sure you'll both be just fine."

Madeleine nodded and gave a weak smile.

"So, when do we get to start planning the wedding?" Clara grabbed Maddy's hand and pulled her into the living room. "We need to find a dress!"

"Isn't this a bit early?" Maddy protested but followed her aunt.

A bit late, according to the clock. But she'd much rather miss some sleep than miss out on wedding excitement. "Don't get started yet. Let me grab a notebook!" Catherine called from the kitchen. She was sure that nothing would cure Maddy's worries like planning a wedding. She'd be just fine in no time.

5

AUGUST, FRESHMAN YEAR

"Thanks for letting me know. I'll be sure to keep applying."

Henry shook hands with the head librarian. Yet another faculty member who didn't want to hire him. He rolled his shoulders and looked at the list in his hands. So far, he'd crossed off the education resource center, the business computer lab, the bookstore, and now, the library. He was either too late applying or too inexperienced for the job.

A rumble in his stomach alerted Henry it was almost time for lunch. Before he headed to the cafeteria, he hoped to stop by his mailbox and maybe the student resources office.

While he was inside the library, the dark storm clouds he'd seen earlier had let loose in a torrential downpour. "Oh, great." The sidewalk was already flooded. Henry stood under the narrow awning in front of the library and craned his neck around, looking for a dry path to the student center.

Nothing.

He briefly glanced at the small pile of umbrellas just inside the front doors. Nobody would know if he "borrowed" one for a quick trip across campus. He shook his head. No, he'd just have to make a break for it.

Henry gulped in a deep breath and darted through a sheet of rain pouring off the awning overhead. In moments, he was soaked through. He raced to the art building and opened a side door. Henry wiped his feet as best he could and squeaked his way down the hall.

He poked his head in an open door. It was a gallery.

Henry once had grand dreams of studying art when he was younger. He'd hoped to move to New York or Los Angeles after high school. But when the reality of how much a move like that would cost—let alone the expense of a fancy art school—sank in, he knew he'd have to stick closer to home.

An art degree didn't guarantee a paycheck. Henry didn't have a trust fund or even a savings account to fall back on. He'd start life in the real world with a small mound of college debt and needed a steady income right away. So, he settled on a business degree, with the hopes of finding a somewhat lucrative job after graduation. He'd study numbers and finance and computer systems. And then he'd be able to support himself, maybe a family, and keep taking photos on the side as a hobby.

The walls inside the small gallery were a bright white, offsetting the brilliant, beautiful photographs hung there. A look at the information card up front told him they were pictures from a summer mission trip to Kenya taken by a handful of students and faculty.

Henry found himself lost in a sea of greens and browns. One print in particular grabbed him and wouldn't let go. A man, a small hat perched on top of his head, sat and stared straight into the lens. His eyes pierced right into Henry's soul.

His stomach growled again. Time to get going and stop dreaming about what might have been.

Henry raced across the space from the art building to the student center. When he stepped inside, goose bumps popped up all over his arms from the blast of AC. The cool air smelled like hamburger meat and pizza. Henry waved to Mike from his English 103 class, who was on his way out. Jason had been right —Henry was already greeting multiple people every time he trekked across campus.

When Henry walked past the lobby, he was blasted by a wall of sound and colorful T-shirts. Jason had warned him that club activities were starting soon, but he hadn't been prepared for this mass of people and energy. There was laughing and jostling and something that sounded like singing. A small cluster of guys were stomping and slapping their knees in a way that was rhythmic and made him want to join in.

Henry skirted around the outside of the clubs. He dodged and wove between giggling girls and back-slapping boys until he reached the back stairs. He'd just have to take the long way to lunch today.

The upstairs hallway was much quieter, and Henry was finally able to breathe easy. He chuckled to himself. College was turning out to be pretty wild. Now, he just had to figure out how to make his way over to the cafeteria.

Henry turned down one hallway and then another and found himself at an open door labeled "The Talon." Must be the offices of the student newspaper.

"Come on, Greg. Pick up, pick up!"

Henry knocked on the door. He poked his head inside and saw a young man holding a phone to his ear, frantically tapping a pencil on a desk. "Hey, do you know how to get to the cafeteria from here?"

The boy looked up at him, annoyed. "It's that way." He jabbed a finger in the direction Henry was headed. "Just go straight 'til you hit a stairwell."

"Thanks." Henry lingered in the doorway. He hated to leave a guy in trouble. "Hey, are you all right?"

"Yeah. Just can't get ahold of my cameraman." He tugged his

fingers through his hair. "And our photography editor is out of town." He waved his wrist in the air, pointing to his watch. "Greg was supposed to be here an hour ago, and no one is answering their dorm phones."

"I could take pictures for you."

The young man froze, then looked him up and down. "What's your name?"

"Henry. Henry Mullins."

"Henry, I'm David." He ran over to another desk and grabbed a camera bag from a drawer. "You ever use a whatever-this-is before?" He unzipped the bag and showed Henry the contents.

Henry nodded. "We used a similar camera for the yearbook in high school."

"Really? Okay. Great. I need you to go downstairs and snap some photos for my article while I interview people."

Henry reached for the camera, but the young man pulled his hand back quickly. He narrowed his eyes at Henry. "I need good group shots. Clear focus. Get happy people having fun. Get something interesting."

"Got it." Henry gently took the camera and pulled the strap over his head.

"All right, now let's hurry. Club open house is only supposed to last thirty more minutes."

Henry shifted the weight of the camera in his hands, getting a feel for it. His stomach growled, but he didn't care anymore.

Following the sounds of the crowd, they raced down the hall and toward the stairs.

Henry poked his head behind the lens. *Take off the lens cap, dummy.*

Snapping off the lens cap, he found a shot of two girls together. With an adjustment to the focus and the aperture, the photo would turn out just right. There. *Click. Click.*

"What was that?" David tapped him on the shoulder.

"I got some pictures of those girls in the blue T-shirts."

"Okay. I'm going to get their names." He darted through the crowd, calling back. "Keep it up."

Henry wandered around the student center. He had missed the young men stomping, and he was afraid that nothing else interesting was going to happen. Then, yelling began to his left.

A swirling mass of orange swooped in. Henry ducked out of the way as an unsuspecting young woman was swarmed by about twenty other girls.

Click, click, click.

"Great shot." David whispered from right behind him.

"Thanks."

"Okay, now come with me. I've gotta ask people some questions."

Henry listened in while David interrogated some of the nearby upperclassmen. He snapped a few more pictures.

"Save the film, man. You're a little trigger happy, you know."

"Sorry." Henry fiddled around, adjusting the focus.

"Thank you, ladies." David waved to the girls, then patted Henry on the back. "I think I've got all I need. Come on, Henry Mullins. Let's take a look at that film."

Upstairs, David took the camera back from Henry. He fiddled with the settings.

"You know what you're doing?"

"Not a clue." He turned the camera upside down.

"Maybe you should wait for your photography editor."

"You're right." David set it down, grabbing his pen and notepad again. "Can I give him your name?"

"Who? Why?"

"Our editor." He shoved the notebook toward Henry. "We'll print your name in the paper beside the photos you took. And if these are any good, maybe you can fill in for Greg."

"I'd like that." Henry scribbled down his name and dorm

phone number. He added his campus mailbox just in case. "I'd be happy to take pictures for *The Talon* anytime you need someone."

David looked over the paper, satisfied. "We normally take applications in the spring, but I'll talk to our editors and see if they'd like to put you on the staff."

"Cool. Great. Thanks, David."

They shook hands.

"Thanks to you, Henry, we're going to have a photo to run next week. You saved my hide."

"Glad I could help."

Henry headed back downstairs. He smiled to himself. Turns out he didn't need to give up his photography hobby just yet. But he did still need some lunch.

6

PRESENT DAY

Catherine let out a long sigh. She was home. Her days as a nurse practitioner were often long and difficult, but this week had been especially busy. When Maddy graduated from high school, Catherine had taken an additional job at the hospital as a PRN nurse. Picking up extra shifts when she was needed was good for her. It kept her mind stimulated and helped pay for Maddy's very expensive art school. But Catherine's body couldn't always keep up with her crazy schedule, and she wondered if maybe the time had come to settle into something a bit slower. Maybe move closer to her sister.

As she rifled through the mail, a letter caught her eye. An invitation to a retirement party in honor of Dr. Nathan Cooper.

Wow. That really takes me back.

There had been many years when Catherine and Henry would drive back to Halloway, sometimes with a tiny Madeleine in tow, to visit former professors and classmates at Homecoming. But Catherine hadn't felt like revisiting old memories in a long time.

How had the Coopers even found her address? Probably

from the alumni office. Somehow, Halloway University was always able to track her down—usually to ask for money.

Catherine tossed the rest of the mail in the recycling bin but turned the card over and over in her hands. It looked like the reception would take place at the Coopers' house during Homecoming at Halloway.

Dr. Cooper had chosen to ask for donations to a scholarship for preachers at the Halloway School of Theology—the same graduate program Madeleine mentioned A.J. liking. She decided to write a check even if she wouldn't attend.

Catherine pinned the invitation to her corkboard along with the assortment of pictures and appointment cards already there. *Maybe I'll go.* She hadn't seen the Coopers in such a long time, and they'd always been supportive of her during college. *Perhaps it's my turn to support Dr. Cooper for once.*

The thought of returning to campus alone, when so many memories there were tied to Henry, sent a wave of melancholy across her shoulders, constricting her chest. She could ask Henry to go with her, but people would assume they were together. *I bet Clara would come with me if I asked her. She probably received an invitation too.*

Clara had attended the Coopers' Bible study a few years after Catherine and Henry. Like so many other students, Clara had bonded with the Coopers. Thinking of all the lives the couple had touched boggled her mind. *I wonder how many marriages Dr. Cooper officiated. And how many of them actually stayed together.*

Her feet propped on the ottoman and a mug of hot peppermint tea on the end table, Catherine pulled out her phone to check her missed messages.

Call me when you get a chance.

A text from Henry. She dialed his number, choosing to ignore the emotions swirling inside at the sight of his name on her phone.

"Hey, Cate." He sounded happy to talk to her. Catherine could almost envision the smile on his face.

"Henry, what's up?"

"I just put the finishing touches on the photos of the proposal from last weekend. Can I email them to you?"

"Sure, I'd love to take a look at them." Excited, Catherine opened her laptop and waited for the message to appear. She clicked on the file that he sent and grinned. Dozens of gorgeous pictures of Madeleine and A.J., in golden evening light, popped up on her screen.

"Oh, these are beautiful, Henry." She scrolled through photos of A.J. proposing and the group poses of the ladies. Catherine chuckled to herself when she saw some of Clara's ridiculous poses. "That Clara can't take a serious picture to save her life."

"And she always blinks at the exact wrong moment." Henry laughed. "You have no idea how many shots I had to delete."

"Oh, look." Catherine came to the pictures of Henry, Catherine, Madeleine, and A.J. "It almost looks like we're a family."

Henry was silent on the other end.

"I'm sorry. I didn't mean—" *Here I go again, sticking my foot in my mouth.*

"It's all right. I've just been thinking about what things could have been like." He sounded wistful.

"If you hadn't left us?"

"Right." Henry took a deep breath. "A.J. would have asked me for my blessing too."

Catherine waved her hands, though she knew Henry couldn't see her. "Oh, we've already talked about this. Madeleine didn't need my permission."

"I know. That's not what I mean."

Catherine sipped her tea. "What do you mean, then?"

"I missed so much. And now I'm afraid I'm going to keep

missing out, even though I'm back in Madeleine's life. I'm worried it's too late. Things will never be the same again."

"They won't."

Henry huffed a breath of air on the other end of the phone.

"You know that, Henry. I don't think you fully realized it when you left. But you knew it would be incredibly difficult. That's why you waited so long to reconnect with Madeleine."

Henry sighed. "You're right. But is there really no hope? Can things ever be somewhat normal between Maddy and me?"

Catherine took another drink while she thought. She didn't want to torture Henry, and she wanted Madeleine to have a good relationship with her father. "I have an idea."

"What?" Henry sounded desperate, ready to latch on to anything.

"How about we throw Madeleine and A.J. an engagement party? In Shady Springs?" She carried her mug back to the kitchen and grabbed some paper and a pen.

"That's a great idea."

"We can get Clara to help us, but we will co-host as Madeleine's parents." Catherine doodled on the paper while she waited for Henry to reply. Would he balk at the thought of sharing so much time with her?

"Do you think Madeleine will mind me doing that? Hosting a party for her? As her dad?"

"You *are* her dad." She tapped the pen, her anxious energy like a motor inside of her.

"I know, but I haven't been a real father to her for so long."

She shook her head. "So, start now. Take small steps, and before you know it, you will be bouncing happy, chubby grandbabies on your knees."

Henry laughed. "Are you really ready to be a grandmother?"

"Yes!" She grinned. "But don't tell Madeleine or A.J. They'd be mortified."

Henry hummed happily. "I'd love that too. I want them to be ready, of course."

"Of course, of course. But ..."

"But grandkids would be really terrific."

"Right?" Catherine laughed.

They chatted a bit about specifics, and Catherine jotted down potential dates that worked for both of them.

"Okay," Henry said. "Talk to Madeleine and Clara and let me know when you have a final day for the party. I'm close by, so I can talk to restaurants or caterers, whatever you want."

"Thanks, Henry. I think this will be really nice."

"Thank you, Cate." Henry took a deep breath. "Thank you for helping me. Thank you for everything."

There was so much weight to that word, *everything*. It encompassed a decade of emotional baggage and pain between them. Catherine had endured so much, but she knew forgiving Henry was the only way to free herself from the pain.

"You're welcome, Henry. I'll talk to you later."

Now, how was she going to find time to plan an engagement party while working two nursing jobs?

Flipping through the calendar, Catherine checked dates and circled a couple weekends that might work with her schedule. She jotted down a list of possible locations and caterers. *How many people might show up to this party?* Most of Madeleine's friends from college and high school lived in Kansas City. Four hours was a long way to drive for a party. But she and A.J. were close to the teens in the youth group and some of the young adults at church in Shady Springs. And A.J.'s family would probably want to drive up from Little Rock.

She grabbed her phone again and dialed Clara's number. It was a good time in the evening to talk to Clara. She'd probably finished grading and prepping for class tomorrow but wasn't quite ready for bed yet.

"Hello, big sister." Clara's voice rang out happily on the other end.

"Hello, little sister." Catherine smiled to herself. Talking to Clara always made her feel better, no matter how hard her day had been. "I have a question for you."

"What's that?"

"Henry and I would like to throw an engagement party in Shady Springs for Maddy and A.J."

"Ooh!" Clara squealed. "I love that! Can I help?"

"Yes, that's what I was hoping."

"I accept. Consider me officially on board."

"Henry volunteered to do the legwork to find a caterer if we can pick some dates that work for us. We'll have to run it by Maddy and A.J., of course."

They conferred briefly about which weekends worked and which restaurants they should try. Catherine took notes on her pad of paper.

"So, you and Henry have been talking a lot." Clara's tone of voice suggested there was more she was thinking.

Catherine hesitated to give in to her sister's pestering. "Yeah, I guess."

"I mean, he came to Maddy's proposal, and now you're planning a party together."

"Ye-es." She dragged out the word slowly. Catherine thought she knew where this line of reasoning was going, and she was not okay with it. She still needed to figure out how *she* felt about this new proximity to Henry.

"So, is there anything I need to know about?"

"What do you mean?" She took a sip of her peppermint tea, grown lukewarm on the counter from neglect.

Clara huffed. "Well, are you two getting back together or something?"

"No!" Catherine almost choked on her tea. "We are *not* getting back together."

"What *is* going on then?"

"I've forgiven him. I'm trying to forgive him." She rubbed her forehead. "It's a long process."

"You can forgive him without hanging out all the time and planning events together."

"I know that, but he wants to be a part of Maddy's life. And I want her to have a relationship with her father."

"But you're not getting back together." She sounded a little disappointed.

"No. Forgiving him and jumping into a relationship with him are two separate actions. I can move on without becoming his wife again."

"Sure. Of course." Clara trailed off.

A long pause.

"What? What are you thinking?" Catherine remembered now how infuriating her sister could be.

"I agree with you. One *could* possibly have an amicable relationship with her ex-husband without any romantic entanglements."

"But?"

"Oh, it's probably nothing."

Catherine slammed her hand down on the kitchen counter. "What, Clara? You're driving me crazy."

"It's just the way he looks at you." Clara sighed. "I think he's still in love with you, Cate."

Catherine dropped her pen. Still in love with her? "That's not true. You must be wrong." She knew she still had feelings for Henry, but there was no way he felt the same.

"I wouldn't be so sure. He's got that look, the one he had when you brought him home from college the first time." Clara laughed. "I think he's still got it bad for you, Cate. Just like when we were teens."

"I'm sure you're wrong. And even if you aren't, it doesn't change anything."

"Really? You don't have any feelings for him still?"

Catherine couldn't lie to her sister. "I mean, I wouldn't say I have *no* feelings for him. We were married more than a decade, after all. It's hard to let that go."

"Yes, it is." Clara's voice quieted. She'd experienced grief of her own when her husband, George, passed away.

"I am not planning to get back together with Henry." Saying it out loud reminded her of the truth. "He hurt me, Clara. I'm working toward forgiveness, but I can't go right back to the way things were before."

"No, I guess you can't."

Clara and Catherine talked a bit more before Clara had to go to bed.

"Gotta hit the sack. I have an early morning tomorrow. Chemistry Club is meeting, and I'm bringing snacks."

"Ooh. You're such a nerd." Catherine chuckled.

"You know you love me."

"I do. You go get some sleep. I'll call you tomorrow after I've talked to Maddy."

"Sounds good. Talk to you tomorrow."

Catherine clicked her pen while she thought. She drew loops around the top of the page. She needed to call Madeleine, but she couldn't get two questions out of her mind. Was Henry still in love with her? And, more importantly, was she still in love with Henry?

7

AUGUST, FRESHMAN YEAR

Henry rubbed the meaty flesh of his left hand. Dr. Cooper had been talking for forty minutes straight, and Henry could barely keep up. He wouldn't be surprised if a plume of smoke began to rise from his pencil. Slowly stretching his neck, Henry worked out the kinks, grateful that Dr. Cooper had to take a breath every once in a while. Henry would need to reread these notes later to make sure he'd absorbed all the information he'd written.

A quick glance at his watch told him only five minutes were left in the class. Dr. Cooper seemed to sense the time was winding down as well. He walked to the front of the lectern and addressed the students.

"As you all know, your research project is due in four weeks. I'm going to need those of you who have not turned in your topic yet to get that to me next Monday. If you need some ideas, I'd be happy to help. And if you need some sources, I've left a list of books down at the library. Just check in with the front desk, and they can help you out.

"As always, I have office hours Monday, Wednesday, and

Friday. I'd love for you to come by anytime." He tapped his watch. "Okay. Class dismissed."

A small cluster of students formed at the front of the room. Henry assumed they all had their research ideas ready to be approved. He hadn't even started thinking about his yet. Guess he'd better get to work.

Dr. Cooper had asked him to come to office hours this week. Henry had been stalling, nervous about how the meeting would go, but now was as good a time as any. He'd never been one to disobey a teacher, and he didn't have another class for a couple of hours.

Henry took his time packing his pen and paper into his backpack as he waited for the last students to head out the door.

"Dr. Cooper? You asked if I'd come to office hours this week." Henry stepped up to the front of the classroom.

"Yes, Henry. Let me pack up my things, and we can head over." He snapped shut the lid of his briefcase and led Henry out of the room.

"I'm just down the hall here." The Bible building had a row of classrooms on one side of the building and a row of offices on the other side. Dr. Cooper's office was sandwiched between a couple of other Bible professors. Several comic strips decorated the door on the right. The office to the left had a class schedule posted. When Dr. Cooper swung open his door, Henry could see wide windows that looked out onto the front lawn. A small but sturdy-looking desk sat at the opposite end, and bookshelves lined either wall. A couple of worn chairs sat in front of the desk.

"Please, sit down." Dr. Cooper gestured to the chairs before setting his briefcase on a pile of papers. He sat in a black leather office chair behind the desk. "How was your first week of classes?"

"Good." Henry nodded his head. "I'm, um, a little over my head in some classes."

"How so?"

"Oh, just thinking about all the projects and papers that are due soon. I feel like I just got here, and it's already time for midterms."

"That happens."

"But I'm making lots of friends." Henry paused. He wasn't sure that Dr. Cooper cared about whether or not he was making friends. "I mean, I'm sure they'll make good study partners for my classes."

Dr. Cooper laughed. "Making friends is a good thing. They don't have to be study partners, although that's always a plus." He tapped his fingers on the desk. "What about church? Did you visit any congregations on Sunday?"

"Yes. I walked to the University church with some friends. It was good. I didn't get a chance to go to the Bible classes beforehand." He rubbed his neck. "We got a bit of a late start."

"Do you have anywhere you're going on Wednesday nights?"

Henry shook his head. "I've been going to a devotional with some of the basketball players, but it's not really my thing."

"Well, I mentioned it in class last week, but I'd like to invite you to the Bible study at my house." He smiled warmly. "It's all current or former students, who took this very honors Bible class. I'm sure you'll find lots of like-minded people. Some really great kids come every week."

Henry nodded. "I'll try. If I don't have too much going on."

"Please come, Henry. My wife is making brownies and hot fudge sundaes this week. You don't want to miss it."

Henry shrugged. "All right. How can I say no?"

Dr. Cooper grinned. "Great. We'll be expecting you." He pulled the briefcase off the floor and took out a couple of legal pads and a textbook. "Now, about that research paper."

Henry took a deep breath. "Right."

"I have a few topics to choose from former semesters if you don't feel ready to pick out a topic on your own."

He handed Henry a piece of paper. Henry's gaze was drawn to one topic in particular.

"How about one on Paul? Maybe this one, Paul and Barnabas?" He remembered stories about Paul from Sunday School back in Shady Springs.

"Great choice. I have a couple of books reserved in the library, which should be very helpful. Once you've had a chance to read over them, let me know if you need help finding more information."

Henry stood. "Thank you, Dr. Cooper. I really appreciate your help. None of my high school teachers were this invested in me."

Dr. Cooper smiled. "I remember what it was like, being away from home for the first time. Struggling with a full course load. I want to see you succeed, Henry, and I am always here if you need help."

Henry swallowed past the lump in his throat. "Thank you." He nodded briefly, then headed out the door.

The library was only a few steps away, and Henry still had a while before his next class. Might as well check out the books he needed before lunch and read them that evening.

A blast of cool air hit him when he entered. As he walked up to the reference desk, a girl with a familiar mop of curly hair stood talking to the student worker.

Cate Hodges had not been unkind to him the past week, but she hadn't been friendly either. She would give a terse nod if they passed each other in the student center. Or she might say "Good morning," if they happened to be checking their shared mailbox at the same time. Otherwise, she didn't speak a word to him.

Henry wasn't eager to run into Cate right at that moment. He turned to his left and saw the line of pay phones against the wall. It had been a whole week, and he hadn't called home once. He felt around in his wallet and found some loose change. His mom should be at work right now. He would just call the house and leave a quick message letting them know he was doing well.

"Hello?"

Henry fumbled the phone. "Mom? Sorry, I thought you'd be at work."

"Well, your father thought I should take some time off."

"Oh." Henry cleared his throat. "Dad's home?"

"Yes. I was thinking about staying home anyway, since I've been a little sick."

"You doing okay, Mom?"

"Sure, Henry. What do you need?"

"Nothing. I just wanted to let you know I'm doing well."

Something rustled on the other end of the line. His father's voice rang through the phone. "Are you out of money?"

"Hi, Dad. No, I'm fine. I'm planning to get a job on campus."

"Good. I don't want you getting lazy just because you're in school all day. You need to learn to take care of yourself."

"I can take care of myself."

"You haven't flunked out of your classes yet?"

"No, Dad. I'm doing fine."

"Well, it's still early."

Disappointment settled in Henry like lead in his gut.

Henry's dad breathed heavily on the other end. "Is that all?"

"Yeah, Dad. I just wanted to say *hi*."

"All right then."

"Bye, Dad."

The line went dead. Henry hung up the phone and shook his head. Would they never change? Even after Henry got all *A*'s in high school and a scholarship to a four-year university, his parents still didn't believe he could succeed in life. They never imagined he could make something of himself and get out of that small town.

A glance at the reference desk told Henry that Cate was no

longer there. He expelled a breath and stood up straighter. He couldn't keep dwelling on his parents if he wanted to do well in school. Focusing on them would only bring him down.

"Hi, I'm looking for some books that Dr. Cooper put on hold. For Honors New Testament."

The blonde girl behind the desk peered up at him. She had a cute smile. "That's so funny, I just helped someone else from that class." She pulled a piece of paper out and handed it to him.

Henry scanned the list of titles. "How about these two? Life of Paul and The Pauline Letters?"

"I just pulled those same two books!" She giggled. "They're over on the table there."

He flashed a smile at her. "Thank you so much."

The girl's cheeks turned pink. "You're welcome. But you may have to share them."

Henry cocked his head. "What do you mean?"

"Well, I could be wrong, but I'm pretty sure someone just checked both of those books out. The ones you said you wanted."

Henry frowned. "But I thought Dr. Cooper reserved those books."

The girl shrugged. "I guess she's in the same class as you."

"Isn't there a rule about not checking out reference books?" He leaned against the desk. "Could you help me get them back?"

She shook her head. "They're not technically reference books, so you'll have to take it up with Dr. Cooper. I'm just a student worker. I don't make the rules."

Henry pushed himself off the desk. "Thanks anyway."

She called after him. "Let me know if you need anything else."

Henry walked to the table where the two books sat. He scanned the area for Cate. Her bag was in one of the chairs, but he didn't see her anywhere. He flipped open the top cover and read the table of contents. This one had an entire chapter on Paul and Barnabas. He pulled out the book underneath.

"Hey! What are you doing?" Cate was in his face, and she was not happy. "Those are mine."

"Technically, they belong to the university."

Cate rolled her eyes. "Yes, but they're on loan. To me. Right now."

"I need these books for my paper on Paul and Barnabas."

"And I need them for my paper on Paul in prison."

Henry sighed. "So, what are we supposed to do?"

"Um, *we*? I think you mean, what are *you* supposed to do? Because I'm doing just fine. I checked out these books first, and you can wait until I'm finished to read them."

"But I need them to write my paper. How do I know you won't use them the whole time and hang me out to dry?"

"I promise to write my paper quickly. You'll have plenty of time."

"Dr. Cooper assigned this topic to me knowing that you were also writing about Paul. Maybe he assumed we would be reasonable, mature people and share."

Cate huffed. "Maybe you should just go take it up with him then."

Henry picked up his backpack. "Fine. If that's what you'd like me to do."

Cate grabbed his arm. "No, wait." She sighed. "I don't want to give him the wrong impression. How would it look if we came whining to him about sharing books?"

"Not great. That's why I'd rather we come to an agreement."

Cate rubbed her forehead. "All right. How about I write up a schedule? I get the books until Saturday evening—"

"But!"

"—and then you can have the books until the next Saturday."

Henry blew out a breath. "Okay. What about the next week?"

"We'll see if we each need more time at that point." She shrugged. "I'll probably be finished, and you can use the books."

Henry shifted his weight.

Cate cocked her head, not quite so irritated. "Does that sound fair?"

He nodded. "Fair enough."

Cate clapped her hands once. "Good. Now get out of here so I can work."

Henry laughed. "Okay. But don't forget. Saturday evening."

Cate tapped her temple. "Got it." She sat at the table and straightened her pencils and paper.

"Meet you in the cafeteria?"

She looked up, confused. "Pardon?"

"To trade books. Want to meet for dinner on Saturday in the cafeteria?"

She shrugged. "Sounds good." She shooed him away. "Now leave. Please."

Henry saluted her and flashed his teeth. "Aye, aye. See you later."

Good thing he hadn't expected her to say goodbye, or else he might have been disappointed. Cate was already at work, furiously taking notes. Henry swiveled and walked back out the door. He sure hoped Cate could stick to her word and finish quickly. Otherwise, they might actually have to work together, and he was very sure that would end terribly.

8

PRESENT DAY

A sea of white greeted Catherine as she opened the door to the bridal shop in downtown Fayetteville. Every possible shade surrounded her—off-white, cream, ivory, true white. And every possible embellishment adorned the dresses—pearls, sequins, lace, beads. The bright afternoon sun was reflected a million times over in the shiny finishes in the store and shimmery details on the gowns.

Catherine took a deep breath.

Her own wedding had been a very simple affair. She and Henry hadn't had a lot of money to spend on a large celebration. Her parents had given her some funds with the agreement that Catherine could spend it however she chose. And Catherine chose to spend that money on a down payment for a small house in the heart of Shady Springs, a place that had since been sold and turned into a hair salon.

Catherine traced her fingers over a particularly bedazzled gown with a mermaid-cut skirt and a heart neckline. She never cared for extravagance. She'd worn a dress she found on sale through a newspaper ad. It had lace sleeves and a short train and, after a few alterations, looked beautiful in pictures. To top it off, she'd sold the dress for more than she bought it.

There was some money for a wedding. Catherine had known for over twenty years that this day would come eventually, and she'd set aside a small amount in a mutual fund a long time ago. What had accrued was enough for a modest celebration. But not quite enough for something like the over-the-top dress currently in front of her.

"Mom, look at this one." Maddy held up a dress with a full, tea-length skirt and three-quarter length sleeves. The top was simply cut with a lace overlay.

"That's beautiful, Maddy."

Smiling, she tilted her head and gazed at the dress. "Hmm, I think so too."

"I'd be happy to pull that for you."

Catherine turned around to see Julie Ortega, the manager of the bridal salon and a friend of Madeleine from church in Shady Springs.

Madeleine hugged Julie and gave her a big grin. "Thank you so much for squeezing us into your schedule."

"Of course. I am happy to help." Julie squeezed her back, then pulled away, glancing around the store. "Now, before we get started, are we expecting anyone else to join us today?"

"Yes. I asked Aunt Clara and my dad to come."

A gasp escaped Catherine's lips, but she attempted a cough to cover it up. "Oh, I didn't realize Henry would be here too."

Madeleine winced. "I know it's unusual."

"Not at all." Julie waved her hands. "I have dads in here all the time. Lots of women want to share this special day with their fathers."

Madeleine twisted the ring on her finger. "It's just that his studio is so close. And I know he wants to be included. I thought it would be nice for him to come and hang out." She looked at her mother, eyebrows raised in a pleading expression.

Placing a hand on Madeleine's shoulder, Catherine nodded. "Sure. It's fine with me. I'm glad he'll get to see you in your dress." It was her fault, after all. She'd been pushing Maddy to make amends with Henry. She just hadn't realized it would put them in proximity so often.

"Thanks, Mom." Madeleine's smile broke through. "And if it's really weird, we only have to spend an hour with him."

A bell jangled as the shop door opened. "Hey, there, Maddy-Maddy-Bo-Baddy!" Henry walked straight to Madeleine and gave her a big bear hug. "Is it cool that I'm here?"

"Of course, Mr. Mullins," Julie said. "I was just telling Madeleine we get a lot of dads in the store." She checked her smart watch. "I'm going to go ahead and get set up. If we wait on Clara, we could be here all day."

She showed Catherine and Henry to a couple of seats, then pulled Madeleine aside to take her measurements.

His brow furrowed, Henry turned to Catherine. "Is it really okay that I'm here?"

Despite the tangle of emotions inside her, a small part of her was glad to have Henry beside her. She patted his hands on the armrest of the chair. "Yes. If Maddy wants you here, then I do too."

Henry gave a small smile. "She's really trying to include me." He shook his head. "How did we get such a great girl?"

Catherine sighed. "I don't know, Henry. I really don't know."

The bell at the front of the store rang again, and Clara stepped through, a giant purse slung over her shoulder. "Sorry I'm late!"

Catherine patted the seat next to hers. "Come join us."

Clara plopped down and then looked past Catherine. "Henry!" She popped up again to give him a big hug. "I didn't know you'd be here too."

Before Henry could be forced to explain himself again, Catherine interjected. "Maddy asked him to come."

Clara raised her eyebrows. "She's really come a long way in the past year, huh?"

"We both have." Henry nodded.

Finished with the measurements, Julie and Madeleine returned. "I've asked my assistant manager to run the store this morning, so we have as long as you need."

Julie turned to Catherine and Henry. "We've already discussed your budget, and I think it will be possible to get a dress that Madeleine loves within that price range."

Henry shifted in his chair. "I'm happy to help make up the difference if there's something more expensive Maddy wants."

"That won't be necessary." Catherine didn't even try to keep the anger out of her voice. There would be no offers to buy Maddy's love. He'd have to earn his way back into her heart, proving his trustworthiness over time.

"All right." Henry cleared his throat. "Just, uh, keep my offer in mind."

"Thank you, Daddy. I'm sure we'll be fine." Madeleine smiled at him.

"So. Let's talk about the style of wedding you would like." Julie pulled her clipboard up. "How many people will be attending?"

Madeleine shrugged. "I'm thinking around a hundred."

Clara raised a finger. "Don't forget the church members."

"Of course," Madeleine said. "We'll invite some people from the church."

"Not the whole congregation?" Clara asked.

Catherine raised her eyebrows. "That would be a lot of people."

"But A.J. has been the youth minister for years now." Clara pressed on. "Everyone will want an invitation."

"I don't want to offend anyone." Madeline chewed her bottom lip.

Julie interrupted. "How about we say one to two hundred? Just for the sake of the survey."

Exhaling, Catherine massaged her forehead. *Just breathe. This is a happy occasion.*

"That sounds fine." Madeleine nodded, but she shot her mother a worried glance.

Julie moved on to the next item. "How about the venue? Are you planning to get married at the Shady Springs church building, or were you thinking of another place? A garden or a chapel?"

"Well," Madeleine said. "It will definitely need to be indoors and have heating because we'd like to have a Christmas wedding."

"Ooh!" Clara clapped her hands. "You'll have to have it at the church building then."

"Why?" Henry asked.

Clara turned to him. "We always have the most beautiful poinsettias and greenery at Christmastime. And we already have some candelabras and twinkle lights in storage."

"Plus, all those decorations from the seniors' banquet last year," Julie said.

"Yes!" Clara wagged her finger. "And we might be able to repurpose some of the decorations from last year's Vacation Bible School. Remember?" She pointed to Madeleine. "It was forest ranger themed. We have all those tree rings and faux evergreens."

"All right." Madeleine turned to Julie. "For the purposes of this questionnaire, let's assume we're having a winter wedding at the Shady Springs church."

"That sounds lovely." Julie's eyes crinkled as she smiled.

Madeleine squeezed her friend's shoulders. "Thanks, Julie. I think A.J. will be happy with it too."

"You're a lucky girl." Clara nodded. "That man's a keeper for sure."

"He's the lucky one." Catherine and Henry spoke simultaneously. They turned to each other and laughed. Madeleine had often been the only thing they could agree on. Even in their difficult patches, they could both say they were crazy about that girl.

Julie placed her clipboard under her arm. "You four sit tight. I'm going to pull some dresses to get us started."

Sighing, Madeleine sank down in one of the chairs. "It's all feeling more real now." She rubbed the ring on her finger.

"Just wait until you try on the dresses." Clara grinned and patted Madeleine's knee. "You're going to make the most beautiful bride."

"I'm actually *really* excited about our next stop." Madeleine rubbed her hands together.

"What's that?" Henry asked.

"Cake tasting," Catherine, Clara, and Madeleine all replied.

Henry rolled his eyes. "You Hodges girls and your sweets." He laughed.

Madeleine and Aunt Clara shrugged at each other.

"Hey." Catherine raised a finger. "I'll have you know, I haven't had any sugar all week."

"Making you even more excited to eat some cake today, I'm sure." Henry's lips lifted in a smirk.

Catherine pursed her lips, hating to admit he still knew her so well. "Yes. All right. I've been saving up my carb allowance for today."

Julie and another woman walked out. "We've got the fitting room all ready for you. Catherine, would you like to come back?"

"Sure." Catherine squeezed Madeleine's hand as they went to the back of the store.

"Right here." Julie showed them to Madeleine's stall.

After putting on the foundation garments, Madeleine opened the door for her mother. The room was larger than most store fitting rooms but became very cramped when Julie handed them a frothy gown made of tulle. Catherine unzipped the dress and did her best to slip the thing over Madeleine's head.

"Too poofy?" Madeleine turned around.

Catherine, smushed to the corner of the room, nodded. "Maybe a bit."

"Let me see." Madeleine stepped out, took one look in the mirror and shook her head. "Nope."

The next dress she tried on had a lot less tulle with a lace overlay and long lace sleeves. "This one might be a bit too formal." Madeleine twirled around.

Catherine waved her hands. "Go show Aunt Clara and your dad."

"What do you guys think?" Madeleine gave a catwalk strut for them.

"Very nice!" Clara clapped her hands.

Henry cleared his throat. "Love it, sweetie." He quickly wiped the corner of his eye.

Catherine caught Julie by the elbow. "How much is that one?"

Julie showed her the tag as Madeleine peeked around. Catherine whistled. Julie nodded. "It is a bit on the high end of your price range."

"It *is* the high end of our price range."

"Yes," Maddy said. "Let's look at some other dresses."

She tried on about five more. Each time, something was not quite right. Too short, too wide. The train was too long, the cut was too low.

"This is the last one I pulled, but we can try more. I've got some ideas based off the feedback you gave." Julie handed the dress to Catherine. "And if there isn't something in the store, we can look through a catalog. Of course, our seamstress is always happy to make adjustments."

For a small fee, I'm sure. Catherine sighed. She wished she could afford to buy Madeleine whichever dress she wanted. But there wasn't a lot of wiggle room in the budget, and she knew they were only at the beginning of the planning process. There would be a lot more places to spend money before this wedding finally happened.

"I don't want to take up too much of your time, Julie." Madeleine said. "We can come back another day if we need to."

"Don't worry. I told you, I want to be here. I'm having a blast!"

Catherine slid the dress over Madeleine's head. As she buttoned up the back, she could tell something about this dress was special. However, it didn't leave Madeleine with much room to breathe.

"Is it too tight?" Catherine tugged a bit to pull the two sides closer together.

"No, it fits perfectly."

Catherine patted her shoulders. "All done. Let's see it in the mirror."

She gasped as Maddy stepped out under the bright lights and into view of the tri-fold mirrors. This was the one. If the dress was too much money, she would just have to make it work.

"I love it, Mom. It's perfect."

"I don't think we're going to need to try on any more dresses." Catherine shook her head in wonder, her hand over her heart.

"Can we see it?" Clara called out from the outside.

"Here I come." Madeleine walked out slowly and turned so Clara and Henry could see the dress in all its glory.

"Oh, wow." Clara held her hands to her face. "You have got to get this one. You look amazing."

Madeleine smoothed the dress down. "What do you think, Daddy?"

Henry nodded, his eyes misty. "I love it." He cleared his throat. "What do you think, Maddy?"

"I love it too." She turned back to Catherine. "What do you say, Mom?"

"I say let's buy it! You look absolutely beautiful." Catherine hoped her grin contained all the excitement she felt. Seeing Maddy in the dress brought up a swell of sadness, but she only wanted her daughter to feel happy about today.

Grabbing Catherine's arm, Maddy frowned. "Are you sure I should buy it today? What if I change my mind later?"

"Why would you? You're not going to find anything better than this."

Madeleine's scowl slowly cleared as she smiled back at Catherine. "Okay. Let's get it."

While Catherine made payment arrangements with Julie at the front desk, Madeleine set up a time to meet with the seamstress about alterations.

"I'm not sure you're going to need any alterations, sweetheart." That dress fit like it was made for her.

"You're probably right, but I can always cancel later." She tucked the appointment card in her purse. "Was it too much money? I didn't even look at the price."

"That's okay. It was in our budget." She showed Madeleine the receipt. It was just barely in the budget. Madeleine might have to cut back in some areas. But Catherine wanted her daughter to be happy with her wedding dress. She didn't want Maddy to regret what she wore on the biggest day of her life.

"Thanks, Mom." Madeleine grabbed Catherine's hands. "Thanks for being here and for putting up with me."

"Oh, sweetie. I wouldn't miss this for the world."

As Catherine and Madeleine joined the others in the parking lot, Madeleine spoke up. "A.J. is going to meet us at the bakery in Springdale, and then we're going out to dinner together. You're all welcome to join us if you like."

Clara waved her hands. "No, thank you. I was thinking we

three grown-ups should get together to discuss engagement party plans."

Madeleine cocked her head. "Are you sure you don't want any help?"

"No." Catherine squeezed her shoulder. "As long as you are still free that weekend and can get us a guest list, we will take care of the rest."

"All right. If you're sure, then I will leave it all in your capable hands."

Clara rubbed her hands together. "Now, let us eat cake!"

9

PRESENT DAY

Catherine checked her phone again.

"Still nothing from Clara?" Henry gazed at her, raising his eyebrows.

"No." *Buzz, buzz.* She glanced down at the screen. "Here we go."

She frowned and showed it to Henry. "It just says. 'Sorry, can't make it. You two eat without me.'"

Henry shrugged. "Weird."

"Very weird." Catherine pursed her lips. "I hope she's okay."

"I'm sure she's fine." Henry waved her off.

She furrowed her brows. "What if Clara's been in a car accident or something?"

Henry took a drink of his sweet tea. "Wouldn't she tell you if that were the case?"

"You're probably right. I'll just text to make sure." The answer came back quickly. "She says she's fine. Just can't make it."

"Hmm. Should we go ahead and order then?"

Catherine sighed. "Sure." She waved the waiter over, a

young handsome man. "So sorry for the wait. Could we place our order now?"

After they'd both put in their requests, a burger for Henry and a salad for Catherine, silence fell over the table.

"So." Henry fiddled with the paper wrapper for his straw. "Cake tasting went well, I thought."

"Yep. Can't go wrong with a traditional white wedding cake." She tapped her nails on the table. *This is so awkward. Clara's going to pay dearly for ditching us.*

"And dark chocolate for the groom." Henry twirled the wrapper around his index finger. "It'll be delicious."

She rubbed her right thumb over her left. "Everything tasted amazing."

He looked up at her. "I saw the bakery has won a bunch of awards."

"Did you notice the picture from the TV show?"

"Yeah." He went back to playing with the wrapper, twisting it around on itself. "Pretty cool that they were on Spectacular Cakes."

Fidgeting in her seat, Catherine checked her phone again. "So."

Henry drummed his fingers on the table. "It's been a while since we've eaten dinner together."

Not wanting to admit she'd been thinking the same thing, Catherine gave a slight nod.

"Probably since before—"

"A long time." Catherine interrupted him. She couldn't remember the last time they'd been out for a meal together. Undoubtedly, they'd been on a date. Which meant it would have been before their marriage imploded. There hadn't been a lot of dates in the last years before Henry left.

Slapping her hands down on the table, Catherine pasted a smile on her face. "I guess we should go ahead and plan the party even though Clara isn't here."

"We should." Henry nodded. "I mean, how often will we even be in the same place?"

"Right, we need to take advantage of this chance." She pulled out a notepad and a pocket planner from her purse. "I'll probably be coming to town a little more to help with the wedding. But if that won't be until next December—"

"You won't need to come here too often."

Funny how he still finished her sentences.

"Right." She opened her planner. "Are you free the same weekend in October?"

"Yes, I double-checked with Leah, and I'm good to go."

Who was Leah? Oh, wait. "Leah the assistant?"

"Yeah." He smiled and looked off in the distance. "She's really great. I don't know what I ever did before she came along."

"Hmm." Catherine cleared her throat. "Well, I'm glad that relationship is working out nicely." Exactly how great *was* this Leah?

"Sure. We do have a good relationship."

Jealousy bubbled inside her, but Catherine pushed it down. Henry wasn't hers to be jealous over. "Anyway, if that weekend works for you, we'll plan on Saturday evening. I was thinking maybe we could get a caterer and have it at Clara's place. Her backyard would be really lovely on a cool October night."

Henry frowned. "Wouldn't catering be expensive? We'd have to pay for it to be delivered all the way to Shady Springs."

Catherine cocked her head. "Not if we find a place nearby."

Henry opened his hands on the table. "Unless things have changed a lot in the past few years, there aren't a lot of local options."

"There's a new place in Shady Springs, across from the park. Or we could ask Julie to help out."

"Julie? The bridal shop lady?"

"Yes." Catherine was happy to know something about Shady

Springs that Henry didn't, for once. "Apparently, she runs the food ministry at church."

"Okay," he dragged the word out. "But I would imagine that usually entails bringing food to sick people and new mothers. Not catering engagement parties."

"Fine." She admitted her defeat. "You're probably right. What did you have in mind?"

Henry paused, concern written across his face. "I don't want to upset you."

Catherine waved away his fears. "Don't worry about it." The party was all about Madeleine and A.J. She shouldn't let her own competitive spirit ruin the event.

He pulled out his phone. "I made a list of places in Fayetteville with large rooms we could reserve."

"Nothing too large, I hope. I'd like to keep things somewhat intimate." *Also, inexpensive, if at all possible.*

"No." He shook his head. "It would only be big enough for twenty to thirty people."

"How about ten to twenty people?"

"Sure. Anyway, I found a few restaurants. My favorite is this one." He tapped on his phone and handed it to her across the table.

"Looks cute." It was a website for an Italian place. The graphics were nicely designed and the pictures of the food made her mouth water. "Almost makes me wish we were eating dinner there."

"I've never been before, but they have great reviews."

Catherine scrolled through their photo gallery. "Is this a picture of their private room?"

"I think so, yes." He leaned across the table to look.

A whiff of Henry's cologne drifted over to Catherine. She took a deep breath. Another sniff and she was back in college thirty years ago. A young freshman was smiling at her. Butterflies fluttered in her stomach.

"What do you think?"

Blinking quickly, she cleared her throat. "Looks great. Let's consider a few more places but keep it on the short list."

Henry's phone buzzed. He took it back from Catherine. "It's just Leah checking in."

Jealousy flared in the pit of her stomach again. "You sure do talk about Leah a lot."

Not looking up, he shrugged. "We spend a lot of time together."

Catherine's face grew hot. She wasn't sure why she was acting this way. She hadn't been with Henry in more than a decade.

"Cheddar bacon burger?" Their waiter showed up with a plate for each of them. "And the grilled chicken salad for you."

"Thank you." Catherine beamed up at him. "Could I have some more water, please?"

"Of course." He grinned at her and then turned to Henry. "Anything else?"

"No, we're good." Henry gave a tight-lipped half smile.

"What was that?"

Henry feigned innocence. "What do you mean?"

"Why were you so rude to him?" She could still read him like a book, and something was up. Henry never looked at people like that.

"I was rude?" He raised an eyebrow.

"You gave him *this* face." Catherine mimicked Henry's look with a grimace.

"I smiled at him."

She shook a finger at him. "No, trust me. That was not the signature Henry Mullins smile. That was a get-out-of-here look."

Henry sighed. "Well, to be honest. I didn't like the way he was flirting with you."

Flirting?

"He's young enough to be our son, Henry. What are you

talking about?" Had Henry caught that she said *our* son? He seemed not to notice her slip of the tongue.

"The way he winked at you and then turned to me like I'm chopped liver."

Catherine raised an eyebrow. "And how does one address chopped liver, exactly?"

"The way he looked at me, I'm pretty sure."

The waiter walked back to their table. "Here's your water, miss. How does everything taste?"

Catherine smiled at him. "Oh, delicious. Thank you so much."

Henry coughed as the waiter walked away. "You haven't even touched your food!" He wagged a finger at her. "And you were flirting back!"

Opening her napkin, Catherine pulled out a fork. "I don't know what you're talking about. I was just being friendly."

Eyes wide and mouth open, Henry stared at her. "I'm positive he winked at you that time."

Catherine shrugged and took a big bite of her salad. "I wasn't lying. It *is* delicious."

"Um." Henry gestured awkwardly.

"What? Do I have something in my teeth?"

"No, I was just wondering if you mind if I say a prayer."

"Oh." Catherine hurried to put down her fork and finish chewing. "Of course."

"I'm going to pray that God forgives you for lying to the waiter."

Catherine kicked him under the table.

He winked at her.

Her stomach dropped.

When Henry offered her his hand, she pretended not to see and folded her own hands and bowed her head.

"Father, thank you for this meal and places that prepare food for us. Thank you for a successful day of wedding dress shopping. I ask that you bless Madeleine and A.J.'s upcoming marriage. In Jesus' name we pray, amen."

"Amen."

The table was quiet as they both chewed their food. It gave Catherine some time to think.

She didn't like that Henry was jealous of the waiter, even if it did flatter her. And she really didn't like that she was envious of Leah's relationship with him. Spending time with Henry but not actually being *with* him was driving her crazy.

Catherine asked the first question to pop into her head. "Is your burger good?"

"It is." He nodded.

They ate in relative quiet for a while. Catherine wanted to break the silence, but everything sounded stupid in her head. Why was she so nervous around Henry?

The waiter came back to refill drinks. "Everything all right?"

"Great," Catherine said. "Could we have two separate checks, please?"

Henry mumbled a protest through a mouthful of French fries.

"Of course. Would you care to try some dessert? We have a new autumn berry cobbler that's amazing."

"No, thanks." Catherine dabbed her lips with her napkin. "And could I have a box, please?"

"I was planning to pick up the check," Henry said as the waiter left the table.

"Why?" The only reason for him to pay for her would be if they were on a date. And this was definitely not a date.

Henry sighed. "To be nice, Cate. I was just trying to do a nice thing."

"Well, thanks for the sentiment."

"Are you done already?" Henry had only made it through about half of his burger.

"I'm getting full. Besides, I figured you were ready to see the end of our waiter."

"Hmm." With an acquiescent smirk, he ate another bite and then picked up his phone. He scrolled through a little while and began typing.

Catherine pushed the rest of her salad to the side of the plate. "I'm sure they won't mind if you stay and finish your food."

"What?" Henry looked up at her watching him. "Sorry. I just remembered something I needed to tell Leah." He tucked the phone back in his pocket.

"Here you go. Let me know if there's anything else I can do for you." The waiter handed them the checks and a box. Henry gave the man his credit card before he left.

Catherine transferred her remaining salad to the box and closed the lid. A phone number in black marker was written on the top.

Ugh. She hated it when Henry was right. She yanked her wallet out of her purse and pulled out some cash. She didn't want to miss out on credit card points, but she needed to get out of the restaurant before that young man got back. Her cheeks burned. She flipped over the box of salad to keep Henry from seeing, but she wasn't fast enough.

"Ha!" Henry's eyes lit up when he spotted the phone number. "I knew it! He *was* hitting on you!"

"Why do you care, anyway?" Catherine slapped the cash down on the table.

Henry's eyes flashed with hurt. "Why do you think I care, Cate?" His breathing quickened, and he grabbed her hands across the table. "The same reason you get angry every time I mention Leah."

Now it was her turn to pretend innocence. "I don't know what you mean."

"Yes, you do." Henry's eyes met hers. "Cate, can't you feel something?"

"It feels like you're yanking my fingers."

Henry let go of her hands, but his gaze held her captivated. "I can't shake it. Even after all these years."

Her eyes stung. Deep breath. "Henry, don't."

"Please, Cate. Would you ever consider giving me a chance again?"

Just as she was about to speak, the waiter returned. "Here you go, sir." He picked up Catherine's money and smiled at her. "Thank you."

Catherine's stomach turned. He was just a kid, probably around Madeleine's age. She averted her eyes just in case he planned to wink at her again. She waited until he'd turned a corner, then she picked up her things to leave.

"Wait." Henry followed, quick on her heels. "Can we talk?"

"There's nothing to talk about."

Henry grabbed her shoulder, but she shook him off. She took the side exit out of the restaurant and hurried to her car.

"So, you're just going to ignore me?" Henry side-stepped until he was standing in front of her.

Catherine took a deep breath and lifted her gaze. His blue eyes caught her own.

"Cate." He placed his hands on her shoulders. "I love you. I never stopped after all these years."

Her heart rose like a helium balloon but doubt immediately pulled it back down. His actions certainly didn't support his claims.

"That's hard to believe," Catherine scoffed. "After everything you put me through. If you really loved me, you wouldn't have left, you wouldn't have cheated on me."

Henry hung his head. "I know it sounds crazy, but all that wasn't about you. It was about *me*. I had so much to work through."

"But why did you have to leave? I could have helped you!" She waved her fist in the air. "We could have worked through it together."

"You're right, I shouldn't have left." His gaze lifted to hers again, his eyes full of regret. "And I know I can never convey how truly sorry I am." Slipping his hands down to her forearms, Henry squeezed gently. "But could you let me try?"

Fear coursed through her. Catherine stepped backward. "I-I don't know. I need to think about it."

"I understand." Henry nodded slowly but he didn't back away.

Without meaning to, Catherine stepped closer. Only inches away, she could feel the warmth radiating from his body. A longing for him took over her. She reached for him.

Henry closed the distance between them, capturing her mouth with his.

She could cry, the kiss felt so good. Not just the feeling of their lips together, but his arms around her waist, and his soft cheek beneath her fingers.

It was as if they'd never parted. As if the eleven years had never happened.

But they had.

Like a jolt, the realization of what she was doing struck her. "I'm sorry, I shouldn't have …" She took a step back, then two. "I can't—"

"Don't be sorry."

For once, she couldn't read his expression. Did he regret the kiss? Was the sadness in his eyes from the fact that she'd pulled away or the fact that they'd kissed at all? Or was it because he, too, couldn't erase the damage of their failed marriage from his heart?

A sudden and unwelcome urge to comfort him overwhelmed her. As much as she was still nursing her own wounds, her heart ached for Henry. But there was nothing she could do for him, nothing she could allow herself to give him. "Goodnight, Henry." She reached for her keys and clicked the unlock button.

"Goodnight, Cate."

Catherine allowed herself one more glance into his eyes. A flood of emotions washed over her. Hurt, sadness, anger, fear, and desire all mixed together.

After Henry walked to his car and drove away, Catherine sat in the quiet of her own vehicle.

God, I know I don't pray often enough. I'm sorry.

She rested her head on the steering wheel.

Please give me the strength to say no.

She wanted so badly to hold him in her arms again, to be held by him. One kiss would never be enough. But could she go down that road with Henry again?

Catherine groaned. What had she done?

10

AUGUST, FRESHMAN YEAR

Henry blew a big breath out from his cheeks. He placed his hand on the door handle. His hands slipped right off. He wiped his sweaty palm on his blue jeans. He took another deep breath.

What's the big deal, Henry? They're just a bunch of nerds from your honors classes.

By this point, Henry knew all of the other honors students pretty well. They'd had a week and a half of classes together plus a welcome barbecue at the Honors House. They were all nice enough. But smart. All of them were so smart. And they just assumed that Henry was too.

You are smart. At least, you were in the small pond of Shady Springs.

It was true he'd scored high on his SAT. Henry had always done well on tests. But succeeding in college as the very first person from the Mullins family to go on to higher education was a whole different story. Henry knew he was only one crashing wave of homework and midterms away from drowning.

Just go inside. You look like a dweeb standing out here.

Footsteps fell on the sidewalk behind him. Henry turned to see Catherine and another girl coming up to the Coopers' house.

Henry waved. He pretended to be waiting on the girls to open the door.

"Hi, Cate."

Cate looked surprised to see him but not necessarily unhappy. "Hello, Henry." She turned to the girl beside her. "This is Tracy, my roommate."

"Hi, Tracy." Henry stuck out his hand.

A faint pink blush crept over her cheeks. "Hi, Henry."

He was pleased to see that his smile had the usual effect on her ... unlike her roommate.

"Tracy is shy, so don't try any of your tricks on her. I won't allow it." Cate linked her arm around Tracy's.

Tracy raised a single eyebrow and scowled at Cate, but she remained silent.

Henry held up his hand. "I promise, no tricks. I will behave like a perfect gentleman." He held open the door. "Nice to meet you, Tracy."

The benefit of arriving with Cate and Tracy was that no one paid much notice to Henry when he walked in. He was able to observe for a minute before joining the crowd.

The front door opened to a short entryway and a large living room. Small clusters of students gathered at the couches or stood by the bookshelves. He could hear more around the corner. Several people held mugs or cups. Most of them had Bibles. Good thing he'd remembered to bring his.

Right away, Henry recognized almost everyone there. He let out a breath. Maybe he wouldn't be too out of place tonight. He could just keep quiet.

"Hiyah, Henry!" A large hand slapped Henry on his back.

"Kevin. Hey." Henry gave a small smile to his classmate. "How's it going?"

"Good, good." Kevin turned to the other young man standing beside him. "Have you met Artie? He's a couple of years ahead of us. Art and I were just talking about the reading assignment for Intro to Honors."

Henry nodded. "That was a doozy." It had taken him the better part of an afternoon to work through it. Time he'd really needed to study for a political science test.

"And, as I was saying to Kevin, was a complete waste of your time." Artie landed a hand on Kevin's shoulder. "Kevin thinks that every assignment a professor gives him must have been handed down from Mt. Sinai."

Henry vaguely recognized the reference to Moses and the Ten Commandments.

Artie rolled his eyes. "I don't know why they have you reading all these modernist philosophers when we should be focusing on postmodernism. That's the new wave."

Kevin shrugged at Henry as if to say, *Sorry I got him started.*

Henry smiled back at Kevin before replying to Artie. "So, who do you think we should be reading?"

Artie rattled off a long list of people Henry had never heard of before.

"Don't even get him started on politics." Kevin stage whispered to Henry.

"Oh, man!" Artie moaned. "I mean, have you read the stuff they published in the school newspaper? It's ridiculous! Where do they find these people?"

Henry cleared his throat. He was way out of his element and wouldn't be able to feign interest for much longer. Besides, he thought Anna had done a great job with that newspaper piece on Bob Dole. "Do you fellas know where I might be able to find a glass of water? I heard there might be brownies."

Artie frowned. "I can't have anything with nuts. I'm allergic."

Kevin gestured to an entryway in the back of the room. "Kitchen's back that way."

Giving a finger salute, Henry left as Artie continued to bend Kevin's ear about his foreign policy opinions.

Behind the couches and past a wall of bookshelves was a cheery kitchen with a long island through the middle. Several girls gathered at a dining table in the next room.

Cate and Tracy leaned against the kitchen counter with a middle-aged woman. She had full, shoulder-length hair, bright blue eyes, and a warm smile.

"Henry," Tracy asked. "Have you met Mrs. Cooper?"

"Hi, Henry." Mrs. Cooper stuck out a hand. It wrapped around Henry's with a gentle warmth. "Glad to have you. Call me Sheila."

She pointed to the counter behind her. "Would you like something to drink? We have coffee and tea."

"Water would be great, thanks."

"Henry's a freshman honors student," Cate chimed in.

"That's great. Most of the students here come because they're in Nathan's—I mean Dr. Cooper's—honors Bible class." She waved around the kitchen. "But others we've personally invited, or they came with friends."

"Like me," Tracy said. "I needed a place to go, and Cate invited me to come with her."

"And we're so happy you did." Sheila smiled and squeezed Tracy's shoulder.

"Hello, Henry. Glad you could make it." Dr. Cooper walked through the kitchen. "Let's all gather up and get started." He gestured toward the living room.

After singing a few songs and saying a prayer, all the students opened their Bibles to Ephesians.

"We've only just started with the introduction last week, so those of you who are joining us for the first time haven't missed out on anything." He clapped his hands together once. "All right, let's begin with an overview of the book of Ephesians."

Henry stayed quiet most of the evening while he absorbed everything he could from the young men and women around him. Just like in class, they all seemed to be ten steps ahead of him.

Henry had gotten a good enough education in Shady Springs. And the church members—especially Jason—had taught him an incredible amount in such a short time. But these kids had been going to church since they were in diapers. And they all took their spiritual wisdom for granted, it seemed. In class, they spoke to each other and to him like they assumed he had the same advantages they all did, making references to church leaders or books he'd never heard of.

"In chapters five and six, Paul writes about what it looks like to live a Christian life. He talks a lot about submission, which is not too popular nowadays."

Artie snorted. "That's putting it mildly."

Henry thought about his own parents. "I think some people take it too far, though. I mean, what if your husband is abusive? Or what if your boss is immoral?"

"Government officials and slave owners were certainly immoral in Biblical times, and Paul still asked people to submit to them." Artie raised his eyebrows, ready for Henry's response.

Henry knew Artie was smarter and better educated than he was, but he just couldn't let this go. "I think Christians are sometimes seen as empowering abusers and promoting unhealthy relationships. And the model of marriage in the Bible is not like that."

"Yes," Cate chimed in. "Like in verses twenty-eight and twenty-nine, 'husbands should love their wives as their own bodies' and 'just as Christ does the church.'"

Kevin and a couple of other students nodded their heads.

"There's this stereotype of women in college. That we're only here to get our 'M-R-S' degree." She emphasized her point with air quotes. "And that is not *at all* why I'm here. I came to get an education, not a husband. I deserve a degree and a career just as much as my male counterparts."

"Great." Dr. Cooper cut in. "We're going to dive into all of that more deeply later, but let's keep these points in mind."

A bubble of hope rose up in Henry's chest. Cate stood up for him. And she'd been nice to him all evening, introducing him to people, teasing him in a good-natured way. He didn't expect her to become his best friend anytime soon, but he was glad she didn't seem to hate him anymore.

After the Bible study had wrapped up, and Mrs. Cooper had served her delicious brownie sundaes with hot fudge, Cate and Tracy moved to leave.

"I think I'm about to head out. Would you like me to walk you girls home?"

Cate turned to Tracy, questioning, then back to Henry. "Sure." She shrugged her shoulders.

Henry said his goodbyes to Kevin and Dr. Cooper.

"Thank you for the dessert, Mrs. Cooper. It was delicious," Henry said on the way out.

"Please call me Sheila. Especially if you'll be coming back every week." She raised her eyebrows, encouraging him to say that, *yes*, he would be back again.

"I think I will. Thank you for having me ... Sheila." Overall, the experience had been less painful than he had anticipated.

She smiled with approval as they walked out the front door.

There was only really enough room for two people at a time on the sidewalk, so Henry lagged behind the girls at first. He finally gave up and walked in the grass beside them. "So, Tracy, where are you from?"

"Fort Smith."

"Not too far from me!" He nudged her in the arm. "I'm from Shady Springs. Ever heard of it?"

Tracy pursed her lips in thought. "I'm pretty sure I have. Don't you guys have a craft fair in the fall?"

"Yes! And we've got a big park in the middle of town with cool springs."

She nodded slowly. "That's sounding familiar."

"You should come down sometime."

"I'd like that."

"Cool." Henry nodded, thinking. "Got any favorite restaurants downtown? I'm always looking for a new good place to go."

Tracy's eyes lit up. She must have been dying to talk about her favorite burger and barbecue joints.

They walked and talked for a while, passing the business building and the student center before turning on to the front lawn. The girls slowed when they reached a large red brick building with white columns.

As he and Tracy talked, Henry noticed that Cate grew more and more subdued. When she finally spoke, her voice cracked a little. "Here we are."

Tracy waved and headed inside. Before Cate could follow, Henry tugged at her arm. "Hey, thanks for having my back tonight."

Cate cocked her head, a puzzled look on her face.

"You know, when Artie was going on about submission." Henry waved his hands.

"Oh." Cate frowned a little. Henry couldn't help but think how cute her lips looked bunched up like that. "I honestly believed what I said. I thought you had a good point."

"Well, thanks anyway."

Cate wrinkled her nose. "I'm not going to be one of those girls who spends all her time flirting and dating around. I'm not here to get an engagement ring. I'm here to get a diploma."

Henry involuntarily took a step back. Her voice was so passionate. "Good for you. Me too." He rubbed the back of his neck. "Actually, I haven't told a lot of people this, but I'm the first one in my family to go to college. So, it's really important for me to stay focused."

She nodded. "Maybe we can keep each other accountable. No distractions."

"Yeah, no distractions." Henry dipped his chin.

"Okay. Guess I'll see you in class tomorrow." Cate gave a small wave and then let the door close behind her.

"What are you so happy about?"

Henry looked up to see Jason and Raymond a few feet away on the sidewalk. Henry hadn't realized he'd been smiling to himself.

"Nothing, just having a nice night." He quickened his pace to catch up with them.

"Did you finally get out of your room and meet some people?" Jason raised an eyebrow.

"Why would I need to meet people when I have *you* as a friend?"

Raymond guffawed and shook his head.

Jason jostled Raymond's shoulders before continuing. "You're always welcome to come with us on Wednesday nights, but it looks like you found a Bible study to go to. One with girls." He waggled his eyebrows at that.

Thank goodness it's dark out. He was sure his face was turning red. "Yeah, just a bunch of people from my Bible class at Dr. Cooper's house. Mostly freshmen."

As much as Henry felt out of place at the Coopers' house, he felt even more uncomfortable around a bunch of seven-foot-tall collegiate athletes at Jason's devo. They all had a bond that Henry didn't share. And, for better or worse, the honors students seemed to claim him as one of their own now. Plus, the presence of females certainly didn't hurt the experience.

"Tell him about what happened at practice the other day." Raymond nudged Jason.

"Oh, man." Jason groaned. He proceeded to go into great detail about an amazing three-point shot from behind the paint.

Henry nodded and voiced his appreciation in all the right places, but his mind was still back at the girls' dorm with a certain curly-haired brunette from Kansas.

11

PRESENT DAY

"Mom, do you know Mrs. Smith's phone number?"

Catherine had just returned from work when Madeleine called out of the blue. "Not off the top of my head, but I can look it up for you."

"Thank you."

Pause.

"Oh, right now? Okay." Catherine stepped out of her work shoes and washed her hands at the kitchen sink. "Give me just a minute." She'd been hoping for a shower, but that would have to wait.

After drying her hands, Catherine wandered down the hallway to the desk in her bedroom where she kept her address book. "Here it is."

Catherine read off the phone number.

"Great. Thanks, Mom."

When Madeleine didn't offer any more information, Catherine pressed. "So, are you going to tell me why you need Mrs. Smith's number? Are you planning a reunion or something?" Mrs. Smith had been Madeleine's high school art teacher and supervisor while teaching summer art camps, but she couldn't think why Madeleine would need to call her.

Madeleine cleared her throat. "I'm not sure if anything will come of it, but I'm applying for a job."

"Oh, really?"

"I need to ask if she'll be a reference for a teaching job. In Shady Springs."

With all the time Madeleine was spending in Arkansas, it made sense she'd be looking for employment there. Especially now that she was planning a wedding with A.J.

"Well, I think that's a great idea. But don't you need a teaching certificate?"

"Eventually, yes. But right now, they just need a long-term substitute teacher. As long as my references check out and my background check comes back clean, I'll be good to go."

"So, you already have the job?"

"Not exactly, but almost. It's so late in the year that most teachers already have jobs."

"Well, that works out nicely for you."

"It does."

"What would you be teaching?"

"Oh, that's the best part. Their art teacher got unexpectedly pregnant. I mean, she's married, and they wanted kids, but they weren't really planning to start just yet ... Anyway, I'd be teaching art once she takes maternity leave."

"And when will that be?"

"After Christmas break."

"That's a few months away. What are you going to do until then?"

"I've been thinking about that. I'd like to go ahead and get my teaching license and start subbing parttime. And there's an artist who runs painting parties in the back of one of the antique stores downtown. She usually works with adults. They serve coffee and everything. But I've asked if she'd like me to run some workshops for kids on Saturday mornings once a month."

"Wow, that sounds perfect. Is all that going to give you enough money? What about your job waiting tables here in Kansas City?"

"Oh, I haven't been on the schedule for a long time. I've been too inconsistent to be worth keeping around. Besides, they've got a fresh crop of college students in town. They don't need me there anymore." Madeleine sighed. "Actually, Mom. I'm thinking it would make sense for me to start moving my things out."

"Oh." She knew Madeleine had been wanting to move out. That was her goal eventually. And now that Madeleine was engaged, her leaving was inevitable. But Catherine hadn't realized it would happen so fast.

"I mean, not tomorrow, but soon. I asked Aunt Clara, and she said I could stay with her as long as I needed to. I'm planning to pay rent, but we haven't hammered out a price yet. She'd like me to stay for free, of course, and I'd like to contribute *something* at least." Madeleine paused to take a breath. "Mom? Are you still there?"

"Y-yes. I'm here. That sounds like a good plan, sweetie."

"I've been talking forever about getting my own place. Now, it looks like I'm never actually going to be on my own. I'll just move in with Aunt Clara and then A.J." She said it like a joke, but she didn't laugh at the end. Was Madeleine depressed or was it just a bad connection?

Catherine paced the hallway as they talked, but she paused when she got to Madeleine's room. Most of the things from her childhood were long gone—stuffed animals and dolls, boy band posters, prom corsages. But a few mementos stuck around. Catherine picked up a picture on Madeleine's dresser. It was the two of them in front of the art museum. They were pretending to play badminton with one of the giant shuttlecocks outside. Maddy had loved visiting the art museum, especially in the early days after their move to Kansas City. They would take a picnic lunch and scour the area for free parking. It was a cheap way to spend the day doing something fun together.

Catherine hadn't been at all surprised when Madeleine wanted to study art in college. She took after her father in her creative drive. Catherine suspected Maddy and Henry were more alike than either of them realized.

"Maddy, I'm really proud of you. I think—I know—you're going to make an excellent teacher."

"Thanks, Mom."

She could almost see the smile on Maddy's face on the other end of the phone call.

After Henry left, Catherine wasn't sure Madeleine would ever have a relationship with her dad. As year after year went by with no contact, a wide chasm had formed between father and daughter. Then one day, Henry phoned Catherine to say he'd graduated from a rehabilitation program and was back in Northwest Arkansas, ready to start over. Catherine had kept Henry's sobriety a secret, but after several months of keeping in touch with Henry, it was obvious he was ready for a second chance at a relationship with his daughter.

Madeleine had resisted at first. In fact, things were pretty dicey for a while. Eventually, Maddy was ready to forge a new relationship with her father and begin the process of forgiveness. Catherine was proud of the bridge Madeleine and Henry had built together.

Rubbing her thumb over Maddy's face in the picture, Catherine cleaned a smudge from the glass. Now, Maddy was about to get married and move out. She was getting a steady job, something Catherine had prayed about for many years, and she was making plans for the rest of her life.

God, what am I going to do all alone in this house? For just a moment, she allowed herself to imagine what life would be like if she wasn't alone anymore. If Henry were back.

"Would you like me to start packing things for you?" Catherine mentally shook herself awake from her daydreams.

"Oh, no, please don't worry about that," Maddy said. "Although I wouldn't mind if you would help me find some empty boxes."

Catherine smiled. "I can do that."

When Maddy paused again, Catherine wondered if she was twisting her hair or biting her lip. "Could you help me with something else?"

"Of course. What do you need?"

Maddy sighed. "Ever since A.J. proposed, I've been feeling worried and nervous."

"Why?"

The other end was silent. Catherine waited.

"What if I mess up? What if one of us dies young like Uncle George? Or what if we get a divorce like you and Dad?"

Catherine hadn't expected those questions. Maddy and A.J. had always seemed like such a great couple. She figured Maddy would be overjoyed to be getting married. But the puzzle pieces started to click into place. Maddy's anxiety at the dress fitting. Her lack of enthusiasm anytime someone mentioned the wedding. Even her questions the night of the proposal. "So, you've got cold feet?"

"Can you call it that when we've only just gotten engaged?"

"I don't know, but I think it's perfectly normal."

"What do I do?"

"Do you love him?"

Maddy answered without hesitation. "With all my heart."

"Then you'll be fine."

"But didn't you and Dad love each other?"

Catherine sat on Maddy's bed. "We did, but we were different."

"How?"

"Your dad had a lot of underlying problems. Issues with his parents and depression. You two won't be anything like us."

"But how do I know?"

Catherine thought for a minute. "Are you going to set up some premarital counseling?"

"A.J. and I are planning to ask Sam Sullivan to counsel us. We're also hoping he'll marry us."

"I'm sure he'll say yes." The preacher at the Shady Springs church had been working with A.J. as a mentor and fellow minister for a while and would likely be honored to officiate the wedding. "I'm glad you're getting counseling. That's an excellent plan."

"Did you and Dad get premarital counseling?"

"Sort of, yes. We just didn't delve into everything we should have. And there were some issues that didn't surface until later. It's complicated." Dr. Cooper had tried his best, but even he couldn't prevent their eventual breakup.

"Can you uncomplicate it for me?"

"What do you mean?"

Madeleine let out a breath into the phone. "Could you tell me about you and Dad? I hardly know anything about your relationship. And I think if I knew what went wrong for you, then maybe I could keep myself from going down that same path."

"Okay." Catherine wasn't sure this exercise would be helpful, but she was willing to try. "Where would you like me to start?"

"Start at the beginning. How did you meet?"

"Well, that's a funny story." Catherine smiled as she settled back into the pillows on Maddy's bed. "Did I ever tell you that your dad and I shared a mailbox in college?"

12

AUGUST, FRESHMAN YEAR

The smell of meatloaf greeted Henry as he walked into the cafeteria Saturday night. He checked in with the cashier in the front before loading up his tray with the hot meal and a chocolate milk. He never would get over the convenience of a college cafeteria. A warm meal and any soda he could wish for, plus a bowl of cereal or a slice of pizza if he wanted. He could grab a cookie or ice cream for dessert, and on his way out, he deposited his tray with the dishwashers and walked away—no dirty dishes to clean. Never in his life had he eaten so well.

"Hey, Henry!"

Henry turned around to see a friend from his English class. "Jeff, how's it going?"

"Great, just working tonight." He gestured to his black uniform that Henry hadn't noticed earlier.

"You like working here?"

Jeff shrugged. "It's fine. I can get a lot of hours if I want, and the pay is pretty good."

"Hmm."

"You thinking about applying?"

"Maybe." Henry still hadn't had any luck finding a good job

on campus. He'd hate to lose the magical convenience of the school cafeteria, but he wanted a paycheck even more.

"You should do it. Then we'd get to work together."

Henry nodded. "Yeah. I'll put in an application."

The young men said goodbye to each other, and Henry spotted his usual table. It wasn't difficult to find, since half the guys there were giants.

Jason waved him over to an empty seat. "Got the meatloaf?"

"Looked good enough." He scanned Jason's tray. "Got the ... everything?"

"Yup." Jason shoved half a slice of pizza into his mouth.

After sitting, Henry glanced around the busy cafeteria.

"You expecting someone?"

"Yeah." He continued to scan the crowd. "A girl from my Bible class."

"One of those girls from the other night?" Jason gave him a significant look.

"Actually, yes, but it's not like that. She's just bringing me a library book."

Jason grinned knowingly. "That's how it always starts."

"Oh." Henry stood. "There she is."

Cate and Tracy had just made it through the line and were headed to the drink station. Henry waved his arms over his head, and Cate eventually spotted him. She thumped the two books down on the table but continued to stand as she held her tray. "Here you go. Enjoy."

"Thanks. Uh, Cate and Tracy, this is Jason. Jason, Cate and her roommate, Tracy." Henry gestured to each party as he made the introductions.

Jason leaned over the back of his chair. "Why don't you ladies join us?"

"We were supposed to meet ..." Cate trailed off as she looked over her shoulder.

"I don't think they're here." Tracy looked at Henry before

leaning toward Cate. "I'm sure they won't mind if we go ahead and sit down."

Cate sighed. "Sure." To Jason, she said, "Thank you. I think we will join you."

Jason jumped up and grabbed an empty chair from another table. Henry scooted so Cate and Tracy could sit next to each other.

"So, Tracy ..." Jason pulled out the chair and swept his hands out like a host at a restaurant. Henry almost expected him to pop out a clean napkin over Tracy's lap when she sat down. "Tell me about yourself."

While the two of them talked, Henry and Cate ate in silence.

Henry cleared his throat. "Thanks for the books."

"Of course." Cate dabbed her lips with a napkin and took a sip of water. "I've got a good outline and all of the important quotes I need written down."

"Good." Henry chewed on a bite of meatloaf before tearing off a piece of his roll. He glanced over at Tracy and Jason. "Looks like those two are hitting it off."

Cate looked over her shoulder for a long time before responding. "Have you known Jason a long time?"

"Very. We didn't start hanging out until junior high, but I've known him since I was five." He noted Cate's concerned look as she watched Tracy. "He's a great guy. He got me to start coming to church with him and taught me everything I know about the Bible."

Pausing, Henry thought for a minute. "Well, everything I knew before I met Dr. Cooper. I feel like I've learned another lifetime's worth of information in his class."

Cate nodded as she chewed. "He's a really good teacher." She waved her fork. "He actually went to school with my parents."

Henry's gaze shot up. "Really? You've known him a long time?"

Cate shrugged. "Not very well. My parents have a lot of friends from college who we would see at homecoming or wherever."

"So, you came here with a lot of connections." It wasn't a question as much as an observation. Cate probably didn't even realize how much of an advantage she had.

"I guess, yeah."

"That's really cool. Jason's the only one I knew here at first."

"You came to Halloway because of him?"

Henry nodded. "He was the first real Christian influence I had in my life. I didn't want to lose that. Plus, I knew if Jason thought it was a good school, it must be." He took a drink. "You're a nursing major from Kansas, right?"

Cate nodded. "I'm impressed you remembered that."

"It's come up in class a few times." He shrugged off her comment but feared he sounded like a stalker.

"I don't actually remember what your major is or where you're from." She blushed and bit her lower lip.

Henry waved her concern away. He was just glad she wasn't acting like she hated him anymore. "I'm from Shady Springs. It's about three hours away in Northwest Arkansas. And I'm a business major."

Predictably, Cate's eyes glassed over a little. Majoring in business meant a reliable paycheck down the road, but it didn't exactly excite the ladies.

"I thought about majoring in art. But I wanted a little more job security."

"That's one of the nice things about a nursing degree. I know I'll always have a job if I need one." She sighed. "That is, as long as I make it into the nursing program."

Henry shook his head, confused. "Why would you not make it in?"

"It's not guaranteed that everyone will get in. There's an application process and everything."

Henry whistled. "I had no idea." He looked at Cate carefully, the way her eyes pierced him through. The way her nose wrinkled a little when she concentrated back on him. The way her curls fell over her face when she cocked her head in confusion.

"What?"

"You'll make it in."

She gave him a little smile. "You think so?"

"I know so."

Now a grin cracked her face. Henry had never seen her really smile before.

"You have a dimple. Right there." He touched her cheek, just barely.

Cate brushed him away and looked down at her plate. "I know, it makes me look like a child."

"Not at all." Henry added, quieter, "I think it's very cute."

Before Cate could respond, Jason thumped the table. "Hey, Mullins."

"What's up?"

"Do you wanna take a trip home next weekend?"

Henry shook his head firmly over Cate's head, but Jason didn't seem to notice.

"Tracy wants to see the park and the craft fair. I think it could be fun."

Tracy grabbed Cate's arm. "The way Jason describes Shady Springs, it sounds so adorable. We have to go."

Clearly, there was more than one thing from Shady Springs that Tracy thought was adorable. She looked up at Jason with doe eyes.

"I've got a big paper coming up." Henry patted the books on the table.

Jason booed loudly.

"We could work together on the trip." With a hopeful expression on her face, Cate swiveled to face Henry.

Henry's stomach roiled. Shady Springs was the last place on earth he wanted to be at that moment. He was finally finding a groove on the college campus, balancing coursework and meeting new friends. The thought of going back home, even for just a weekend, was too much.

But the look in Cate's eyes. And Jason's pleading face. More than anything, Henry wanted to make them both happy. He shrugged. "I guess so."

Jason clapped his hands once, loudly. "Awesome." His eyes glinted. "I'll need to coordinate the details with Tracy here." The two of them huddled together, ignoring Henry and Cate again.

"Well, I suppose if I'm going to be heading out of town next weekend, I'd better get started on my paper." He stood to go. It was rude to leave Cate alone with Jason and Tracy, but he didn't have any more energy left now that he'd agreed to go back home. He wanted to drown himself in textbooks and papers.

Wiping her mouth, Cate finished chewing her bite of food. "See you around?"

Henry nodded. "See you later."

13

PRESENT DAY

"I found this while packing." Catherine looked up as Madelene set a box on the coffee table. "What is it?" She marked a spot in her book with a finger, then slid a bookmark into place. Sitting up, she examined the cardboard box. Her brows knit as she read the outside.

Ever since their last conversation about Catherine and Henry's early days, she couldn't get him out of her head. Had her constant thoughts of Henry summoned these mementos?

"I know I shouldn't have opened it, but the address on the outside reminded me of your story about how you and Dad met. It looks like your care package from college."

Wow, so many memories. Catherine nodded to her daughter, but her mind was lost in the past. "It's not the same one, but yes, this box is from Halloway."

"I thought maybe we could go through the box together," Madeleine added, a hopeful expression on her face. "And you could tell me more about you and Dad."

"I already told you about your father and me." She'd spent at least an hour reliving the story of how they first met and became friends.

"We barely scratched the surface, Mom." Madeleine fought to keep her voice level. "Please. I really think it will help."

Catherine rubbed her forehead. "Fine." She lifted the first items out of the box. There was a rock shaped like a heart, a movie ticket, a stack of letters, several photographs, her old club T-shirt. Mementos of a young college student.

"What about this one?" Maddy held up a bracelet. "Did Dad buy this for you? It looks like the one I bought at the Shady Springs Harvest Festival when I was a kid."

"Dad didn't buy it for me, but it's from the first time we went to the festival together." The corners of her mouth lifted in the smallest smile. "I think that's when I first saw him as more than just a friend."

"Can you tell me about it?"

Catherine patted the couch cushion beside her, and Madeleine snuggled in.

"My friend Tracy had a thing for your dad's friend, and we all drove to Shady Springs one weekend ..."

* * *

September, Freshman Year

Henry shifted in his seat in Jason's van. The hands on his watch ticked down. The miles on the interstate flew by. And with each minute and each mile, Henry drew closer and closer to home. He marveled at how quickly Halloway had become more like home to him than Shady Springs had ever been.

Henry turned to the seats behind him to distract himself. Tracy was chatting away. Who knew that girl could talk so much? Cate caught him staring and winked. His cheeks grew warm.

The drive had gone by quickly—too quickly. With only one stop for gas, the towns whizzed by—Vilonia, Conway, Alma. Then they came to Highway 71—one of the most dangerous roads in the country. It twisted and turned Henry's gut in knots.

The girls oohed and aahed over the green mountain vistas. The foothills and plateaus of the Ozarks stretched out before them. Just a few dots of brown and orange broke up the dark emerald blanket of trees. The weather was cooler up north but autumn hadn't truly arrived yet.

Henry pressed his eyes shut as Jason whipped through a particularly tight curve. Even before becoming a Christian, Henry would say a prayer anytime he drove through these mountains on the way to a basketball game or field trip. Something in him cried out to God in times of distress. *Please keep us alive.* And when he made the trip to Halloway only a few weeks ago. *Please help me make it through this semester.* Now his heart begged for something different. *Please help me survive this trip home. Please let Dad not be there. Please let it just be Mom.*

Jason had offered to let Henry stay at his place. But that would have meant sleeping on the pullout couch so the girls could get the guest room. And Henry didn't know how he felt about Cate seeing him first thing in the morning. Would he wake up extra early and brush his teeth? Would she see him in his pajamas before he showered? What if she asked why he wasn't staying at his own place?

Better to just suck it up and face his fears.

Jason made it to Fayetteville before he needed to stop for gas again. They pulled into a station on 12th Street. Henry got out to stretch his legs while Jason pumped the gas. The smell of gasoline always made him a little sick. The combination of the stench and his own anxiety had his stomach turning.

"I'm gonna walk a bit." He nodded to Jason.

"Okay, but don't take too long."

Walking to a patch of grass not far away, Henry could breathe a little easier. He rolled his shoulders and stretched his neck. *God, please help me to survive this weekend.*

Shoes crunched in the gravel beside him.

"How's it going?" Cate tilted her head and pursed her lips.

Henry licked his own lips and faced the traffic. "Great. How are you?"

"Fine." She paused. "You just seem off today."

Henry tried smiling, hoping to cover up his anxiety, but the expression felt empty. "Off how?"

"You're always so confident and smooth. You seem shaken."

"Just a little carsick, that's all." Henry attempted a smile again. He wasn't sure if it worked or not because Cate rubbed his arm and gave it a squeeze before walking back to the car.

They loaded back into the van, and soon enough, a large wooden sign greeted them. "Welcome to Shady Springs." Engraved on the sign was a spring flanked by tall oak trees. As much as Henry dreaded facing his parents, the familiar sights of downtown Shady Springs bolstered his nerves.

Passing by Spring Park, they saw vendors setting up their booths. "Ooh, is that the Harvest Festival?" Tracy pressed her fingers up against the window.

"It will be." Jason turned and smiled back at her.

When they pulled into Henry's driveway, Jason hopped out to help with luggage. It was only a small duffel bag, and Henry felt silly walking beside Jason with nothing in his hands but a couple textbooks.

"We'll see you tomorrow morning at the fair, okay?" He set the duffel down and gripped Jason's shoulder. "Call me if you need anything."

Henry nodded. "Thanks, man."

Jason smiled and hopped back in the van. He gave a quick salute before zooming down the street.

Henry took a deep breath. He was all alone now. He pulled the key out of his pocket. Opened the door.

Another breath and dread filled his stomach. It smelled like pot roast, and that could only mean one thing. Henry's dad was home. His stomach dropped. *My prayers didn't work.*

He slipped off his shoes and dropped his bags by the front door. "Mom? I'm home."

"Henry?" His mom poked her head around the corner. She wiped her hands on a dish towel and came to give him a hug. Her voice was barely above a whisper. "I didn't know you would be home. Did you call?"

"I left a message."

They both glanced over to the answering machine on the end table. Sure enough, a red light blinked.

"Sorry about that."

"It's okay, Mom." Henry put his arm around her. He cleared his throat. "Is, uh, is Dad home?"

"He's taking a nap right now. I've got supper in the oven." She stepped back and looked him over. "You look real good, Henry. Are you doing okay? Are you just home for a visit?"

Henry nodded. "I caught a ride with Jason and some friends. They wanted to go to the Harvest Festival and see Shady Springs."

Mom barked a quick laugh. "Not much to see." She turned to walk back into the kitchen. "Go set down your bags and wash up for supper. But be quiet." As if he needed to be told.

Henry picked up his shoes and his bag from the front hall and carried both to his bedroom. He glanced around. It seemed like ages since he'd moved out, but it had only been a few weeks. The room already smelled stale and musty. Like dirt and moth balls and cigarette smoke. Had he forgotten to empty out his dirty clothes, or was his room just returning to its natural state? Maybe that's what his room always smelled like, and he'd never noticed.

He ran his finger over the top of his bookshelf and came back with a thin layer of dust. Except for a stack of mail on the chest of drawers, it didn't look like anyone had touched the place since he'd left. He rifled through it before throwing all of it in the trash can.

Henry sat and bounced a couple of times on the bed. He hadn't bothered to turn the light on, and he could see a faint glitter of dust in the fading light from the window. There was something changed about the room that he couldn't quite put a finger on. Almost as if it was haunted. Perhaps by the ghosts of Henry's past. He gave a small shiver, then hopped up to help his mom in the kitchen.

"Need me to do anything?"

"It's almost ready. Could you get some drinks?"

"Sure." Henry grabbed a couple of beers from the fridge for his dad and filled two glasses of water for his mom and himself. The ice bucket needed refilling, and he pulled out the trays from the freezer to do the job. He tried his hardest to make his motions smooth and keep his volume down, but the ice cubes still made a small thud as Henry twisted them out of the trays and into the bucket. "How have you been?"

"Oh, fine. Your dad's been gone a lot, but that keeps him happy. The money's been good."

Henry nodded. "How about *your* work?"

His mom turned to him with a sparkle in her eyes. She loved her job as a secretary at Shady Springs Elementary. She was about to say something, maybe tell a funny story about a student or teacher. Or maybe let him know about an accomplishment of hers. Then the bedroom door slammed. The light drained out of her eyes, and the color left her face.

"What's all that racket, Barb?"

Henry squared his shoulders. "Hey, Dad."

Only fazed for a moment, Henry's father continued into the

kitchen. "Didn't know you'd be home." He cocked his head a bit. "You flunk out already? Only been gone a few days."

"No, Dad. I'm doing fine."

Dad's gaze drifted over the kitchen, taking in the green beans on the stove and the drinks on the table. He grabbed a can before heading to the living room. "Let me know when it's ready."

Henry stared after him until he'd left the room. "Were you going to say something about work?"

"I don't remember." Mom flapped her hands, brushing away the sour mood left in the room by Dad. "Tell me about school."

"I got a job on campus, in the cafeteria. I start on Monday." Henry talked about his new boss and Dr. Cooper and all of Jason's teammates and taking photos for the school newspaper. "It's hard. Harder than I thought it would be." He paused in setting plates on the table. "But I think I'm going to be okay, Mom."

She reached up and pushed his bangs back with her thumb. Then she patted him on the cheek. "I'm glad to hear that, Henry. Now help me get this roast out."

Henry checked the clock. "Seven o'clock. Right on time."

"Listen, Henry." His mom took both his hands in hers. "I'm glad to see you, I really am. But next time, you need to call."

"I tried—"

"We both know you always intentionally call while I'm at work. Next time you need to make sure. I just don't know what he's going to be like now."

Henry scanned her eyes for more clues. "What do you mean? What's he done?"

"Nothing." She waved away his concerns. "You know how touchy he's always been about college. You'd better not talk too much about school. And next time, call."

"Mom—"

"That food ready, yet?" The recliner groaned as Henry's dad stood and made his way to the eat-in kitchen.

"Sure is, Bobby." Henry's mom gave him a warning look. *No talk of school.*

Henry got through almost the whole meal.

"You learning everything you need to know at that college of yours?"

How should he answer his father's question? If he said yes, then his dad would call him out on smarting off and being too good for his britches. If he said no, then he'd wonder why anyone would pay so much money to go to a no-good school anyhow.

"Not yet, sir."

His dad grunted. "What are you studying again?"

"Business."

"You know, my brother owns a business. You could've worked for him."

Henry pushed down his frustration. "Uncle Jimmy is an electrician. I want to go into accounting or finance or maybe start my own business."

"You should've worked for him, and maybe he'd let you run the company someday."

He shook his head, impatient. "Dad, we've already talked about this. Jimmy is planning to leave his company to his sons. And I don't want to be an electrician."

"What? You too good for that?"

"No, Dad—"

"It's honest work, Son. You too good to get your hands dirty?"

Henry chuckled. He couldn't help himself. "Electricians don't get their hands *that* dirty. And I'd have to go to a different school."

"You smarting off to me?"

His stomach dropped out. "No, sir."

Henry's dad stood quickly, reminding him that he still wasn't as tall or as strong.

Without thinking, Henry rose as well. He backed up against the wall, cringing unconsciously. Too many years of living under the thumb of Bobby Mullins had taught him to shrink in fear. But a bubble of anger grew inside of him. Why should he be afraid? He didn't need his father anymore. He certainly wasn't getting a penny of his money. Only a roof over his head if he ever came back to Shady Springs. And why should he come back when he was treated like this?

Raising his head, Henry stared his father in the eye. No way was he going to back down again.

Dad lifted his hand. Henry's breath caught in his throat. His father almost never resorted to violence.

"Listen, I didn't mean to—"

"Yeah, you never do."

A light flashed the moment before he felt anything. His head slammed against the wall and his teeth clicked together. Knees buckling, his hands reached out for something to grab onto. He steadied himself on a chair.

"Don't you dare come into my house and talk down to me."

Henry darted a quick look to his mother.

"Don't look at her. She's not going to help you."

Mom glanced up for a moment, then back down to her plate. She shook her head.

Shame bloomed in his chest. Henry slumped over. "Yes, sir," he choked out. He started to leave the table.

"You sit down and eat."

Henry jerked to a stop. He sat, his head still hung.

"You can leave when I say."

They finished their meal in silence. Only the sounds of chewing and clinking silverware permeated the thick quiet. Henry swallowed his food, but it all tasted like cardboard now.

"Delicious meal, Barbie." Henry's father shoved back from the table. He gave his wife a peck on the cheek, then grabbed another drink from the fridge and returned to the living room.

"You shouldn't have said anything." Mom's whisper slit through the silence. She began to clear the table of its dishes. "I told you not to talk about school. You know how he gets."

"I tried, Mom." Henry stood.

She shook her head, not hearing. "He's a proud man, you know. He doesn't like to feel small. He doesn't like you moving out and talking like you know everything."

"Mom, it's not like that."

Holding up her hand, she cut him off. "Just leave. I can clean up myself."

Henry slipped away to the bathroom to check his reflection in the mirror. His face where it had hit the wall was red and puffy. He turned on the faucet and splashed his raw skin with cold water.

Back in his bedroom, Henry did what he always had when he needed to escape. He pulled out his textbooks and got to work. For hours, he lost himself in the life of Paul and his missionary journeys with Barnabas. When he could only write in gibberish as his head bobbed and his eyes drifted shut, Henry switched off his desk lamp and crawled under the covers.

In the dark, his mind replayed images of dinner. His dad's hand, the dining room wall, the linoleum floor as he slumped back to the table. A montage of all the times his dad had beaten down his spirit ran in a loop in his mind, faster and faster until they blended together.

He'd tried to stand up to his father tonight, but what good had it done? In the end, he'd cowered just like he always did.

Henry rolled over and clamped his eyes tight. He searched his memory for something—anything—to take his mind off his father.

Cate.

He sighed.

Cate's curls and her smile. The way she pursed her lips when she concentrated. The way she wrinkled her nose when she laughed.

God, let her never learn the truth about me.

14

SEPTEMBER, FRESHMAN YEAR

Henry checked his watch again. He probably shouldn't have left his house two hours early, but it sure was nice to slip out while his parents were still sleeping. Plus, it had given him time to walk to the park instead of asking for a ride.

He'd made a couple laps around the festival area while vendors set up tents and concession trailers. He watched a country singer perform a sound check with his guitar. And he admired each and every quilt and tractor on display.

At fifteen minutes past the hour, Henry spotted a familiar lanky man walking toward him. "Jason! There you are!"

"Hey, Henry!" Jason beamed and waved. "You been here long?"

Henry shrugged. "Not too long."

"This is so cute." Tracy gazed at the park, her eyes huge.

Cate stared at Henry. "Did you hurt your face?"

Reaching up, Henry touched the place where his head had hit the wall the night before. "Oh, um, yeah. I guess I forgot where all the doorways in my house were while I was gone to college." He laughed. "Ran right into the wall last night."

Tracy laughed along. "That sounds just like something I would do."

Cate scrunched up her lips, but she didn't say any more.

"Did you guys have a good night last night?" Henry fell into step with the group as they walked toward the first tent, a woman selling paintings.

Cate nodded. "We played games. And we tried to make brownies." She and Tracy giggled. "It did not go well."

"Ah, sorry to hear that." It stung a little to think of the three of them having fun and making memories without him.

Jason gave him a sympathetic look. "You should come over for dinner tonight. I know Mom wouldn't mind one more."

"Sure." Henry smiled. "I'd like that." He didn't care if Jason was extending an invitation out of sympathy. He'd take whatever he could get. Anything would be better than another dinner at home with his father.

They walked through the park at an ambling pace, admiring the arts and crafts in each tent.

Cate sniffed the air. "Do I smell funnel cakes?"

Patting his pocket, Henry jingled a little spare change. "I'll get a couple for us to share."

"Thanks, Henry." Cate grinned up at him, and he felt more like a million bucks than the five he had in his pocket.

"Henry Mullins, is that you?"

Henry turned around to a female voice behind him.

"Beth, hi!" He gave the blonde girl a big hug. And to her boyfriend, he slapped a high five. "Hey, George!"

Already that day, Henry had seen about a dozen people from high school. Beth and George were some who were still there, finishing up their last year before heading off to college. Word around town was that Beth and George started dating after prom last spring and had become pretty serious over the summer.

"Are you home for the fair?" George asked.

"Yeah. I rode back with Jason Jones. And some friends."

Henry waved to Cate and Tracy. Cate waved back but frowned as soon as Beth turned around.

"They're cute." Beth pinched his arm, teasing. "Are they both here for you?"

"Oh, I don't know about that." Henry rubbed the back of his neck. "For all I know, they both have a crush on Jason."

George guffawed. "Knowing him, that's probably true."

Jason walked over from the booth he'd been admiring, dragging Cate and Tracy along with him. "Beth Rinehart and George Lewis, right? How's high school treating you?"

"Oh, you know." Beth shrugged. "How are you? How's college?"

"Great. We've about got Henry set up with a date every night."

"Very funny, J." Henry rolled his eyes.

"Cate and Tracy are two of the lucky ladies." Jason draped an arm over the shoulders of both girls.

"Stop it, Jason." Tracy laughed, slapping Jason's hand.

Cate looked annoyed, but she didn't move out from under Jason's arm. "It's not like that. We're all just friends."

"Well, don't have too much fun." Beth squeezed Henry in a hug and gave him a peck on the cheek. To the girls, she said, "Take care of our Henry."

With a final wave, she and George sauntered off.

Henry stepped up to the counter and ordered two funnel cakes.

"Some friends from high school, I assume?" Cate was no longer next to Jason and stood with her hands crossed over her chest.

"Yeah. They're a year younger than we are."

She nodded. "That Beth seemed to like you."

"No," Jason responded. "Beth and George are dating. At least they were during the summer."

Cate raised an eyebrow. "She seemed awfully flirty."

"That's just Beth."

"That's just *Henry*." Jason corrected him. "All the girls loved him in high school."

"Oh, yeah?" Cate looked him up and down.

His cheeks warmed. Henry shrugged. "I did okay, I guess."

"Henry had a pretty girl on his arm all through school. Since junior high, probably."

"The same girl?" Cate's tone of voice had a hint of surprise. He couldn't tell if she was impressed or disturbed by Jason's account.

"No." Henry shook his head. Jason was not painting a very attractive picture.

"That's the kicker, it was a different girl every few months."

Henry frowned. *What's his aim here?* Jason was making him sound like a jerk. "I didn't want anything too serious. I've never planned to stick around Shady Springs."

"Hey, Henry!" Jessie Reeves popped her head out of the funnel cake trailer. "Are these yours?" She held two plates of hot, fried dough in her hands.

"Yeah. Thanks, Jessie."

"Good to see you, Mullins!" She waved and ducked back inside.

He turned to see Jason doubled over laughing.

Henry elbowed him, jabbing a little sharper than necessary. "I'm not a player. I just had lots of friends in school."

With an expression of unbelief, Cate nodded slowly, her lips pursed. "I can see that."

"Here you go." Henry shoved a hot plate in Jason's hands, none too gently.

"Thanks, man." Jason's lips twitched with glee. He was clearly enjoying giving Henry a hard time.

They walked in contented silence, Tracy and Jason sharing one cake and Cate sharing the other with Henry.

Henry tried to give Cate most of the cake, only taking some when she offered the plate to him.

"How about we sit down?" Tracy asked. She wiggled her fingers, white dust flying everywhere. "I'm getting powdered sugar all over my shorts."

Jason nodded, his mouth full, and pointed them over to the nearby picnic tables. He plopped down in the middle. Tracy sat on one side of Jason, and Cate sat on the other. Henry slid in across from Cate, the plate between them.

In the pavilion behind Henry, a bluegrass band played. A toddler in a stroller held a red balloon as her mother wheeled her past them. An elderly couple carrying kettle corn and a giant wreath laughed about something together.

"This is nice." Tracy smiled up at Jason.

"Hmm." Cate nodded.

"I'm glad you talked us into going," Jason said. "It's great to get away from campus and homework for a bit."

Cate groaned. "Don't talk about homework. I have so much to do."

Wincing, Tracy shrugged. "I'm just going to cram everything into a Sunday night study session."

"How about you, Henry?" Cate asked. "Did you get much done on the paper last night?"

Henry licked the powdered sugar off his fingers before answering. "I finished a rough draft."

"I'd be happy to look it over for you later. Maybe on the drive home?"

"I'd like that. Thanks."

Tracy winked at Jason. He nudged her with his knee. What were those two up to?

"How was dinner with your parents?" Cate asked. "Was it good to see them?"

Jason almost choked on his bite of funnel cake.

"Are you okay?" Tracy patted his back.

Still coughing, he waved her off. "I'm good. Thanks."

Although he'd give anything to move on to another topic, Cate still watched Henry, expecting an answer.

"It was fine. My mom made a big dinner since my dad was home."

Jason winced apologetically, but the girls didn't seem to notice.

"That's nice," Cate said. "I bet they miss you."

What could he say? "Want to go look at some tractors?"

"Why not?" Tracy brushed the rest of the powdered sugar off her fingers. "Let's go."

Picking up their plates, Jason headed to the nearest trashcan.

Cate walked ahead with Jason and Tracy while Henry fell behind a bit. Asking someone about their parents was normal. He knew Cate hadn't meant to stir up anything. But Henry felt as though he were skating on thin ice. If he thought about his dad too much, he'd have to punch something. And if he punched something, he'd be just like his dad.

They walked slowly through a line of tractors, all of them older than he was. Henry wished he had a camera with him to capture the way the girls laughed as Jason climbed on top of one. But he winced when his grin reminded him of the sensitive spot on his face.

Dad hadn't hit him much. Only a handful of times. And, honestly, it wasn't the violence that gave him the emotional scars he wore. It was the way his dad looked at him.

At first, Henry hadn't known any better. He assumed all fathers treated their kids with cool indifference. But when he went to school and saw other children with their parents, he suspected something was wrong with his family.

His best friend in elementary school, Curtis Evans, had a big dad. Taller even than Henry's dad, and broader too. He seemed to block out the sun when he stood up. But when Curtis broke his arm at recess one day, Henry had watched Mr. Evans race onto the playground from the parking lot and cradle Curtis in his arms. Henry stared in awe, his fear and worry for his friend forgotten, as he watched the grown man shush and coo over his child like a mother hen.

Bringing his attention back to the present, Henry watched as his friends walked past the tractors to a large canvas tent full of tables. Cate and Tracy stopped at the very first stall to look at earrings and bracelets. They chatted with the shop owner as they held different items up to show each other. Sticking close enough to see the girls, Henry pretended to be interested in a booth full of bottles of spices and canned jellies. The scents coming from the table reminded him of the dinner his mom had cooked the night before, something she only ever did when Dad was home.

Henry was thankful his dad hadn't been around more often growing up. When it was just his mom and him, things were great. Barb Mullins wasn't the poster child for motherhood, but she wasn't a bad mom, either. She fed him enough and made sure his clothes were clean. She went to parent-teacher conferences and sometimes read to him. Henry was relieved that at least one of his parents had been normal. And as long as his dad was out of town driving his truck, Henry's childhood had been happy.

Things hadn't started getting tense at home until middle school, when Henry joined the quiz bowl team and tested into advanced classes. He'd had a particularly attentive English teacher, who insisted he should be challenged academically. Henry started needing things like signed permission slips and rides to school on the weekends.

When Dad was gone, Henry's mom gave him a lift anytime he asked. But when Dad was home, he wanted Mom home, too, and Henry had to call Curtis to ask if he could bum a ride with them. Mr. Evans started picking Henry up every time they had a tournament and giving him a ride home every time they had a late practice at school. Sometimes, Henry liked to pretend Mr.

Evans was his dad too. It would've been a lot easier if they'd looked alike. But Curtis was black, and Henry didn't even remotely resemble their family. And then Curtis moved away in the eighth grade. He sent about three or four letters, and then Henry never heard from him again.

The girls finished browsing the jewelry and moved on to a table with quilts, potholders, and other home decor items. For all Cate's talk of not wanting to date or settle down with anyone, she got pretty animated looking at quilted table runners. He could easily imagine her happy at home with a family of her own.

When Henry first started hanging out with Jason, he'd had a gaping hole in his life. He knew his father didn't love him. And his mother was only really there for him when his father wasn't around.

But Jason loved Henry like a brother. From the first time they hung out after school, he was kind to Henry like no one else. It started with invitations to dinner, and then Jason asked him to come to church. At first, Henry walked the half mile to the church building in downtown Shady Springs. When Jason found out, he started showing up at Henry's house to give him a ride every Sunday morning, Wednesday night, and anytime the teens were getting together for an activity. Jason had given him a place to belong and the hope of a Heavenly Father who loved him, no matter what. Even when his earthly father didn't love him.

Thinking of his friend, Henry searched for him in the crowd. Jason had run into someone from high school. Henry waved and smiled, but stayed put.

Henry found another table with stacks of books. The man who appeared to be the author stood talking to a woman, pointing to the back of the novel she held in her hands. Currently, Henry didn't have time for reading anything that wasn't assigned by a professor. Looking up, he saw that the girls had returned to the jewelry booth they had started at. Cate was handing over cash and holding two bracelets in her other hand. Jason joined them and beckoned for Henry to come over.

It was just like Jason to make sure everyone was included. When Henry started attending church with Jason, he felt like a normal kid with a normal family. People there welcomed him, and no one asked about his parents. Most of them knew anyway since there was no such thing as privacy in a small town. They welcomed him and made him feel loved.

Now that he was in college, Henry felt normal almost all the time. He was still terrified sometimes that he would flunk out, and his new life would all be taken away. But when he was in class or eating in the cafeteria with his new friends or at Dr. Cooper's Bible study, he felt like maybe he fit in with all the other students.

Henry caught up to the other three. He pushed all thoughts of his dad aside, chatting happily about Shady Springs and college classes and the country music band coming to campus soon. He pasted on his trademark charming smile and laughed along with everyone else.

He couldn't let Cate start asking questions about his family. He couldn't let her find out the truth that he was just a nobody. That he would never amount to anything. That his own parents didn't even love him.

Someone like Cate, who was pretty and innocent and smart, would never understand his struggles. There was no way she'd want to hang out with him if she knew what his life was really like.

15

SEPTEMBER, FRESHMAN YEAR

*A*fter a full day at the Harvest Festival and a delicious dinner of lasagna, Henry returned to his parents' house happy and full. He snuck past the living room quietly, gave his mother a peck on the cheek in the kitchen, and then returned to his room to read until he fell asleep.

The next morning, Henry waited in his desk chair, watching through the window for Jason. He arrived to pick up Henry for church just like he had since high school. Jason pulled into the driveway, a song playing so loud the deep bass bee-bopped hard enough to rattle the panes.

Jason and Cate both stepped out of the vehicle, Cate looking extra nice in her Sunday dress, and made their way toward the front door. Hopping up, Henry grabbed his duffel bag and Bible off the bed and raced to intercept them. But it was too late. He'd just made it to the living room when Jason's loud knock reverberated through the house.

Jason knew better, but he must have forgotten—if you're going to be loud in the morning when Bobby Mullins is home, you'd better be prepared for some wrath.

Footsteps pounded down the hall. Henry rushed out the door,

hoping to be out the driveway before his father got to him. He shot Jason a glare for his carelessness, then caught Cate's gaze. She stared at him like he'd lost his mind.

"Henry, is that you makin' all that racket?" His father, dressed in his bathrobe, burst through the front door. "What is all this?"

"I'm just headed out, Dad. I'm going back to school today." He walked toward the van, tugging Cate's arm as he went. She resisted a bit at first, her feet firmly in place and her gaze frozen toward his father. But after a moment, Cate and Jason woke from their daze and followed Henry's lead.

His dad waved his hands around, stepping off the porch. "Who's this? This your girlfriend?"

Henry stopped in his tracks. "No, Dad. This is my friend, Cate."

Her hand trembled, but she stuck it in Dad's direction, taking a step toward him. "Hi, sir. I'm Cate Hodges. I'm in the honors program with Henry." Was she trying to make a good impression? Or was she just crazy?

Ignoring her, Bobby turned toward him, eyebrows raised. "The honors program. So, she's a big shot like you, Henry." His gaze shifted to Cate now. "Well, you better stay away from this one. Don't let him knock you up."

Cate's cheeks burned a bright red. Her mouth hung open. "I'm not like that, sir. I'm focusing on my education."

Mirth danced in Dad's eyes. "Sure you are, sweetie."

A spark lit in Henry's belly.

"Stop, Dad. That's enough." Henry couldn't help it. The spark grew to a burning fire. He could listen to his dad tell him he was good for nothing all day long. But there was no way he was going to let him talk to Cate like that.

Dad rounded on him.

With all the strength Henry could muster, he moved one step

closer, putting himself in front of Cate and only a couple feet away from his father.

For a moment, Henry didn't know if his dad would have the audacity to slap him then and there in front of his friends. Dad appeared to have the same thought cross his mind. His eyes flashed for a moment, and then he blinked.

"I'm leaving now." Henry spoke with more conviction toward his father than he ever had before.

Without looking back, Henry pushed Cate inside the van and climbed in after her. Jason rushed into the driver's seat, turning his key in the ignition. They drove away, and no one spoke for a long time.

"I'm sorry, Henry." Jason broke the silence first. "I should've—"

"No, J. It's not your fault."

Henry didn't dare sneak a look at Cate's face until they were seated in the church auditorium. She had a sweet, beautiful voice as she sang the hymns from the songbook, but she was so quiet, Henry could barely make out the words.

He stole glances here and there during the sermon. Her face was ghost white at first. As the lesson went on, she grew more and more like herself. Henry didn't hear most of the sermon, his mind still back in the driveway.

What will happen now? Now that she knows the truth about me?

Henry asked himself those same questions all the way back to school. Tracy seemed to be blissfully ignorant of the whole situation and chatted happily most of the trip. Jason made jokes and sang loudly to the radio.

After they'd been on the road for about an hour, Cate leaned forward and tapped him on the shoulder. "I could read your paper and let you know what I think."

"Thanks, Cate. I'd appreciate that." He pulled the paper from his bag and handed it over without meeting her eyes.

Cate held a pen in her hand. "Do you mind if I make some corrections?"

"Not at all."

Right away, she began marking up the page.

Wow, it must be worse than I thought. Henry was glad someone with a critical eye was taking a look at what he'd written before he handed it in to Dr. Cooper.

The journey back seemed to drag on and on. Henry listened to the light scratch of Cate's pen on paper. He smiled and nodded in all the right places while Tracy talked.

After two hours that felt like twenty-four, Jason pulled over at a gas station. They all piled out to visit the restroom and stretch their legs.

"Here you go." Cate handed Henry's paper back to him. "It's pretty good. I changed some words around to strengthen your thesis. And you should switch your second and third points. Otherwise, I just made some adjustments to your grammar here and there."

"Thanks, Cate. Listen—"

Cate stopped him. "If this is about earlier this morning, you don't have to say anything."

Henry wasn't sure what that meant. Did she not want to talk about what happened in order to spare Henry's feelings? Or was she ready to throw in the towel on their friendship?

"Okay."

Cate furrowed her brows. She started to say something but stopped herself. "I need to use the restroom."

Henry stepped aside so she could pass. He looked over the blue markings on his paper, but the lines blurred.

From the moment he stepped foot on campus at Halloway University, he knew he needed to keep his two lives separate. Shady Springs and his parents were his past. College and beyond, his future. He should never have let Jason talk him into this trip.

When they climbed back into the car, Henry vowed to himself that he would never speak about his father to anyone again.

Maybe some girl, someday, would give him a chance. But it was too late for Cate Hodges. She'd never want to be with him after today.

* * *

Present Day

"Do you feel any better about getting married to A.J.?" Catherine found her daughter brushing her teeth and in her pajamas. Boxes full of Madeleine's possessions sat in stacks along the hallway.

Catherine had made a big show of deciding to redecorate Madeleine's bedroom and turn it into a home office and guest room, which was ridiculous. She'd give anything to freeze time and keep her daughter home forever. But she was being a good mom and letting her baby bird fly away.

She just wished Maddy seemed more confident about leaving. After hours of stories and chats about her ancient romance with Henry, Catherine wasn't sure she'd helped one bit. She'd only served to stir up her own confused feelings.

Spitting out her toothpaste, Madeleine wiped her mouth before answering. "It's not A.J. that's the problem."

"Well, I'm glad for that. I don't think I could've hand-selected a better man for you."

"I agree with you there." Madeleine chewed her lip and leaned against the doorframe of the bathroom. "It's me. I need to decide for myself if marriage is worth the risks and if I have what's required to make it work."

"I don't know if anyone is truly ready for a commitment like that." She and Henry had thought they were, but they couldn't have been more wrong. "You have to rely on God's strength and not your own." If only she'd listened to her own advice as a young woman.

Madeleine nodded. Both had only recently come back to faith and the Church. Catherine wondered if her daughter felt strange about taking spiritual advice from her.

"You think I should move forward with the wedding? Should we celebrate the engagement?"

"Only you can decide that." Catherine brushed a strand of hair from Maddy's cheek. "I can tell you that I think you should talk to A.J. about how you feel. Sooner, rather than later." A small voice inside her wondered if Maddy might be retreating into a corner like her father had always done, rather than confronting the problem head on.

"I know." Madeleine's gaze lowered to the floor. "I just can't bear to break his heart like that."

"Better now than down the road. It will double the heartbreak if he learns you didn't confide in him." She spoke from experience. Henry's silence had multiplied their problems. "It'll be good practice for marriage."

Madeleine nodded. "I'll see how I feel after the engagement party. I don't want to ruin the big night for him if it all turns out to be nothing. After his family leaves, I'll tell him everything."

"Okay, sweetheart."

"Thanks, Mom. And thanks for agreeing to tell me about you and Dad. I know it can be painful to relive the past."

Catherine's mouth twisted in a smile. "Actually, it's been kind of fun. I'd forgotten so many of the good times. It's nice to remember why I love your father so much."

She patted her daughter's arm and made a quick exit.

Did I just say love? *As in, present day, still in love with Henry? I hope Maddy didn't catch my mistake.*

Because it had been just a slip of the tongue. As much as she wanted to rekindle something with Henry, she couldn't let

Maddy get her hopes up. Then they'd both be broken-hearted over that man. Again.

16

PRESENT DAY

The weather had just turned cool enough for a sweater, and Catherine gave a delicious shiver as a breeze swept through the air around her. It was four in the afternoon on a Saturday, and she was getting ready to celebrate the impending —no, upcoming—marriage of her only child. Her beautiful Maddy was getting married.

She shut her car door and gazed up at the restaurant, Gustosa. It was even cuter in person than the pictures. She had wanted to try out their food before hosting the engagement party, but driving four hours south just to taste some lasagna seemed a little ridiculous. She decided to trust Henry and their online reviews. *Hope that doesn't turn out to be a mistake.*

Her sister stepped out on the other side of the car. "Mm. It smells like garlic and basil. I bet they use fresh tomatoes."

Clara was the gardener in the family. Catherine never saw the point in wasting her hard-earned money, not to mention precious little free time, purchasing and planting and nursing vegetables she could just buy at the grocery store. But Clara loved that kind of thing.

"If their spaghetti is half as good as yours, I will be satisfied."

"Oh, I'm sure it's much better. I've heard lots of good things."

"You haven't eaten here either?"

Clara shook her head. "No, but don't worry. It's just a small engagement party among friends and family. What could go wrong?"

Side by side, they marched up to the restaurant, bearing some decorations and gifts for the bride and groom. Inside, they saw a dining room of wood tables polished to a shiny gleam, bright white walls with large photographs, pendant lights, and a marble bar with black metal stools. A few diners sat here and there, but the evening rush had not begun. Behind the bar, a young man polished glasses while talking to a young lady. The woman turned at the sound of the door opening and walked over to Catherine and Clara.

"Just the two of you?" She grabbed a couple of menus from a stand.

"Actually, we're here for the Mullins party. We reserved your private room."

"Of course." The woman set down the menus and checked a smartwatch on her wrist. "I'm afraid we weren't expecting you quite so early."

"Our reservation is for four o'clock to eight o'clock, correct?" Catherine asked.

"I'll check, but I had you written down for six."

"That's when our dinner is scheduled, but we were supposed to be on the books starting at four. We're serving appetizers and beverages at five." Already, Catherine could feel her blood pressure rising and the evening had only just begun.

"I can go ahead and let you in the room to get ready." She beckoned for Catherine and Clara to follow her. "But we haven't had time to clean up from the last reservation." She opened the double doors to the room.

"Oh." Clara let her bag of decorations fall with a thud on the floor. "This won't do."

Strung from the ceiling was a large banner that read. "It's a Girl!" Pink and yellow balloons, plastic baby bottles, and toy pacifiers were strewn all over the room. The chairs were covered in pink wrapping paper with baby hand- and footprints. The table was adorned with confetti made to look like little tiny baby feet.

"No, this won't do at all." Catherine sighed. "We'd better get to work right away."

The hostess checked her watch again. "I need to be available to seat guests, but I can help a little here and there." She propped the doors open to a mostly empty dining room. "I'm very sorry about the mix-up."

Catherine opened her mouth to say something not-too-nice, but Clara interrupted her. "That's all right, hon. These things happen."

Swallowing her remarks and her frustration, Catherine nodded once. No sense in wasting time complaining. Better get to work and get the job done.

They stripped the long tables of their tablecloths and the chairs of their covers. The hostess took the linens to the back before she was called away. A few moments later, she returned with Henry.

Thoughts of their shared kiss threatened to overtake her. But this was not the right time to rehash that night. She cleared her throat and gave herself a mental shake.

"What happened here?" Henry's gaze roamed over the baby decorations. "I think Maddy won't be too pleased if we announce a baby at her engagement party."

Catherine rolled her eyes. "Hence the quick cleanup. No more sarcastic comments from you. Let's get to work."

"Right." Henry rubbed his hands together. "What would you like me to do?"

With a huff, Catherine gestured broadly with her hands. "Pick something. Do it."

Clara gave Catherine a pointed look. To Henry, she said, "How about you get rid of the balloons?"

Henry snapped. "I'm on it."

Flashbacks of their marriage scrolled through Catherine's brain. It was the same thing every time she needed Henry's help. She blew out a breath. Perhaps she'd been too harsh, but she really did not have time to micromanage him right now.

Together, they finished clearing up the leftover decorations and opened their own bags. A couple of staff members from the restaurant came to sweep and take away the trash.

Catherine checked her phone. "Only fifteen minutes until Maddy shows up."

"Maybe she'll be late." Clara bit her lip as she surveyed the room.

"She gets that from me, I'm afraid." Henry shrugged.

"All right, Clara and I can set up our decorations. Henry, you get a table ready for gifts." Catherine handed Henry a small bag with cards and gifts.

"Got it." Henry took the bag and got to work clearing off one of the side tables.

The hostess came in with new linens, which she spread out on the tables in the center of the room. Catherine and Clara filled vases and galvanized metal buckets with fresh flowers and set them up on top of the clean white tablecloths. They flicked on tiny battery-operated tea lights.

When Henry was finished with the gift table, he helped Clara and Catherine hang a banner that said "Congratulations!" in the back of the room. They stepped back to survey the decor just as the hostess and a waiter came in with plates, glasses, and silverware.

"I think we just made it in time." Catherine checked an app on her phone. "Maddy is a few minutes away."

"Good idea booking this restaurant, Henry!" Clara rubbed his shoulder. "I think Maddy is going to be tickled pink."

Henry beamed. "I hope so. I've let her down in so many other ways. I just want her to know how much I care about her."

"I think she's starting to see." Clara gave his arm a gentle squeeze.

Shaking her hands, Catherine let out a slow breath. The fizzy anxiety in her gut hadn't gone away even though the room was ready before any of the guests arrived.

"You okay, Cate?" Henry lifted an eyebrow.

"Yes. Just nervous, I guess." She turned to him. "I haven't actually met A.J.'s parents before. We've never been in Shady Springs at the same time, and he doesn't talk much about them. All I know is they live in Little Rock, they have two other children, and Mr. Young is pretty stern. I think they might be a bit more formal than we are, Henry."

Henry raised an eyebrow and pointed to his chest, mocking. "*Moi*? You think someone is fancier than Henry Mullins?"

Some of Catherine's tension subsided as she laughed. "Hard to believe, I know. It doesn't really matter, I guess, but I want to make a good impression." She shook her head. "It's silly. I don't know what I'm so worried about."

Henry started to say something but was interrupted by Maddy and A.J. bursting through the double doors.

"Oh, my, Mom! This is beautiful!" Maddy ran over to give her mother a hug. "Thank you, guys!" She squeezed her aunt and dad in turn.

"Yeah, you really didn't have to go to all this trouble." A.J. gave Catherine a side hug.

"Oh, it was no trouble at all." Catherine waved her hands, barely catching an incredulous stare from her sister.

"You're worth every bit of trouble and more." Henry smiled at his daughter.

The waiter and the hostess came back with pitchers of water and tea and trays of appetizers.

A.J. stepped aside to allow them to pass. He gestured out to the parking lot. "I think my parents were right behind us driving in. I'm going to go see if they're outside." He gave Madeleine a quick kiss on the forehead before leaving.

Seeing the two of them together, it was obvious how much her daughter loved A.J. Unfortunately, loving feelings were not always enough to keep a marriage together. Catherine had learned that from experience. Still, she hoped Maddy could work through her doubts to make their relationship work.

"Who else are we expecting?" Clara asked.

"Sam Sullivan, Julie Ortega," Catherine ticked off each person on her fingers. "A couple of A.J.'s friends I don't know, and Maddy's friend Staci."

"Staci couldn't make it, but she sends her love," Maddy said.

Hearing more people enter the room, Catherine turned to face them.

A.J. had always said he resembled his father, and now Catherine could see it. Arthur Young was A.J. with about fifteen more pounds and a mustache. He was a little shorter, his hair was graying, and his face was marked with a few wrinkles, but it was almost like looking into A.J.'s future, seeing the two of them together. Except where A.J. was exuberance and youthful energy, Arthur was cold and uptight. His mouth seemed stuck in a permanent scowl, the corners turned down under his mustache. The hair of his eyebrows grew wild and bushy in such a way as to make his expression both intimidating and angry. No hair grew on top of his head, making his mustache and eyebrows even more impressive.

Ginger Young had more sweetness about her countenance. She was visibly thrilled to be with her son, her arm around his waist. Her blonde hair curled and glowed around her face. Her smile stretched from ear to ear. And the Young sisters bounced around with the same electricity that A.J. possessed.

Catherine decided to face the most intimidating challenge head-on and introduce herself to Arthur Young. "Arthur, it's so good to finally meet you." She gave him a big smile and stuck out her hand.

Arthur didn't take her hand. He tilted his head and narrowed his eyes. "Cate Hodges? Don't you remember me?"

17

PRESENT DAY

*C*atherine froze, her smile plastered on her face, her hand hanging midair.

"Artie Young? Is that you?" Henry stepped in front of Catherine and held Arthur at arm's length. "Man, you've changed."

"You, too, Henry." Arthur laughed, and the transformation in his face was almost shocking. Turns out the man had teeth and eyes. All that scowling had made her wonder.

How could Catherine not have seen it before in A.J.'s face? Of course, he was Artie's son.

"Cate, you remember Artie from college? He went to Dr. Cooper's Bible study."

"Sure, yes, of course." Catherine regained her composure and smoothed out her dress. "So nice to see you again. I don't know how I never put two and two together."

"Young is such a common name." Ginger added from the side.

Artie went on. "I wasn't sure myself until I heard Madeleine talk about you two. When she said you both went to Halloway, I just knew it had to be Cate Hodges and Henry Mullins."

"You didn't say anything about that, Dad." A.J. chimed in.

Artie waved him away. "I wanted to see for myself."

Catherine figured she would have suspected who Arthur Young really was if A.J. ever actually talked about his family. And she wasn't sure if she had ever known Artie's last name. It wasn't something she'd ever asked about. "A.J. never mentioned that you went to Halloway."

A.J. shrugged. "I didn't know you two went there. I had no idea you knew each other."

Ginger smiled sweetly. "How nice to discover this connection."

Clara waved. "Hey, there. I'm Clara Lewis, Maddy's aunt."

"This is Ginger." Arthur put his arm around his wife's shoulders. "And our daughters, Felicity and Olivia."

While Felicity's hair was blonde like her mother's, Olivia's was a rich auburn that matched her brother's and father's locks. They both looked to be in their late teens.

"Felicity is at Halloway right now. Olivia is about to start at the University of Arkansas Medical School. We couldn't convince her to go to a Christian college." Arthur's tone was chagrined, but Catherine could tell he held a soft spot for his youngest daughter.

"I want to study medicine, and I got a great scholarship. Besides, I'm saving everyone a ton of money by staying at home." Olivia poked her father's side.

Clara smiled at Olivia. "Well, my husband went to the University of Arkansas, and he turned out pretty great."

"Is your husband here?" Ginger asked, looking around.

"Oh, no, He died a few years ago." Clara stated it in such a matter-of-fact way that only Catherine could detect the sadness in her eyes.

"I'm so sorry." Ginger looked horrified.

Clara grabbed her hands. "Thank you, but please don't worry. I'm not easily offended."

Madeleine laughed loudly. "That's the understatement of a lifetime."

The front doors of the restaurant opened again, and A.J. left to greet his friends.

"Please, everyone, let's all get something to eat and drink." She pointed to the table against the wall. "And gifts and cards go over there."

The Young family mingled with the Mullins family. A.J.'s friends joined the happy chaos. Julie Ortega also showed up with a box in her hands.

"Sam texted to say he's running late. We should go ahead and get started without him." Clara linked her arm with her sister's. "Seems like everyone is getting along."

Catherine nodded. "I guess I was worried for no reason."

"Was Arthur a good friend of yours in school?"

"Not really, no. He was a little older, and we didn't hang out much." She lowered her voice. "He was always a little combative. And very sure of himself, if you know what I mean."

"Well, people change. Maybe he's softened a bit over the years."

"Hmm."

Artie did seem as though he'd mellowed a bit, but not much. She'd never much cared for him in school and was relieved to know how different everyone said he was from his son. Madeleine would not have fallen in love with someone like Artie Young. What had Ginger Young seen in the man?

Catherine attempted to mingle and meet some of A.J.'s friends. She spoke a bit with Julie and Sam when he showed up. Everyone seemed to be having a good time. Seeing Maddy's glowing face made all the money and effort worthwhile.

She made her way over to Ginger Young to try and become friends with the woman who would be her daughter's new mother-in-law.

"Hi, Ginger. Thank you so much for coming."

"Thank you for inviting us. I wondered if I'd ever get to meet you."

"Well, I can't get down to Arkansas very often with work."

"Maddy said you're a nurse. I'm sure that's very demanding."

"It is, but I love keeping busy." Catherine smiled. "And it gives me a way to feel useful, now that Maddy is grown." She took a sip of her water. "And what do you do?"

"Oh, I stay at home."

Oh, great. Catherine plastered a smile on her face. She hoped she hadn't offended Ginger by basically saying that she was useless now that her children were gone.

Ginger went on. "I studied business management in college but wanted to be around for my kids when they were young."

"Oh. Henry studied business in college too."

"Hmm. And he takes pictures?"

"He owns his own photography business. He's quite successful."

"Well, perhaps that will be one way to save money on the wedding."

"Yes."

Catherine hoped she seemed calm on the outside because on the inside, she was scrambling. *How can I make nice with this woman?* She'd already stuck her foot in her mouth. But she couldn't apologize without offending Ginger even more. She decided to launch into the subject that every mother could get behind. Talking about her own children.

"Tell me what A.J. was like growing up. Was he always so energetic?"

Ginger's eyes sparkled. *Bingo.*

"Yes. Once when he was a boy, we put him on a soccer team to try to run off some of his energy. All the other little kids were picking daisies or hanging off of the goal net, but A.J. ran circles around them all."

"So, he's always loved to run?"

Nodding, Ginger swallowed a drink.

"Has he always wanted to teach?"

Ginger's eyes narrowed. "No. He struggled a bit in college trying to find a major." She frowned a bit. "Arthur wanted him to study something more practical."

"Like business?"

"Yes, but A.J. just loves school so much, he wanted to learn everything."

"I hear he's a great teacher."

Ginger nodded politely as she looked over to where Artie and Henry stood.

Catherine followed her gaze. She leaned in to hear what Artie was saying but now that she wasn't talking to Ginger anymore, she could hear loud and clear.

"What happened to you two after college? I thought you were perfect for each other."

Henry shrugged. "I made some bad decisions and had to face the consequences."

"You cheated on her?"

"Yes, among other things."

"Didn't you try to work it out?"

"We did, for a while."

"What happened?"

In hopes of diffusing the situation, Catherine inched her way closer.

Henry answered. "I was trying to fix myself, and I just couldn't. I needed God's help."

Swallowing a gulp of iced tea, Artie continued. "Don't you think you've set a bad example for Madeleine?"

"What do you mean?" Catherine noticed that Henry couldn't quite keep the ice from his voice.

"I mean, how do I know she's not going to follow in your footsteps?"

Henry's face clouded with anger. "Cheat on A.J. and get a divorce?"

Glancing around the room, Catherine noticed a platter of pesto meatballs sitting on the appetizer table.

"A.J. said there were years when Madeleine didn't hear from you, and she and Cate weren't even going to church. He said Madeleine left the faith altogether."

Henry nodded. "That's true. But Maddy got baptized and has made a huge transformation."

"But that was only a year ago. How do I know—"

"Meatball?" Catherine picked up the platter and practically pushed it into Artie's chest.

"What?" Artie blinked and looked at the tray in front of him. "Uh, sure. Thanks."

"Sweetie, are those—" Ginger stepped in to intercept, but Artie had already swallowed one and reached for another.

"Aren't they delicious?" Catherine asked. "Henry did such a great job of finding this place."

"Honey, did those meatballs—" Ginger turned to look at the food labels on the table.

Artie tried to pop another in his mouth, but Ginger swatted it out of his hands. "Look, Arthur! It says they're pesto meatballs."

"Yes." Catherine didn't understand why Ginger was acting so upset.

Now Artie's eyes widened. "Oh, no."

"Did you bring your EpiPen?"

"EpiPen?" Did Artie have an allergy?

"What is he allergic to?" Catherine reached for her purse on a chair nearby.

"Tree nuts. And most pesto has pine nuts in it."

Catherine found what she was looking for. She handed an antihistamine to Artie. "Here. Take this."

Artie blinked but otherwise didn't move. Taking the pink pill from his hand, Ginger placed it on his tongue. She gave him a glass of water.

"I'd like to take Artie's pulse, if that's okay." Catherine stepped in without waiting for permission and placed her fingers on Artie's wrist. She counted heartbeats, watching the time. One-fourteen. His heart rate was elevated, and he definitely needed to see a doctor, but she didn't think he was in immediate danger.

Turning to Ginger, she asked, "What normally happens when Artie has an allergic reaction?"

"It's been so long." Ginger shook her head. "His tongue swells sometimes. And one time it got really bad."

"Did he go into anaphylactic shock?"

Ginger nodded. "I think so. We went to the hospital, but he had his EpiPen that time." She wrung her hands. "We should've brought it with us. It's just been so long ..."

"It's okay." Clara stepped in now and rubbed Ginger's back.

Catherine looked around. The spectacle had drawn quite a crowd. Everyone in the room watched them, whispering to each other or staring wide-eyed.

"I don't think that Artie ate enough to have a severe reaction, but I would feel more comfortable if he went to the hospital."

Artie perked up now. "I'm fine. I don't need to go to the hospital."

"Please. We want to make sure you're okay."

"I'm telling you right now, I'm fine."

"I'll drive you, Dad. Come here." A.J. stepped in and supported his father on one side, while Henry helped on the other. Artie tried to shake them off but clearly needed the assistance standing.

"Where are your car keys, Mom?"

Ginger froze for a moment, then launched into action. "Keys. They're in your father's pocket. Arthur, dear, can you give A.J. your keys?"

"I don't need to go to the hospital, and I can drive myself."

A.J. rolled his eyes. "Let's just go for a walk then."

Behind his dad's back, A.J. beckoned for his sisters to join him. He silently pantomimed turning a key and pointing to his mom's purse, and Ginger got the picture. She rummaged around in her bag and pulled out what must have been an extra key fob. She handed it to Olivia, who passed it on to her brother. The Young family all made for the door.

"Mom, I'd better follow them." Maddy came up beside her mother. "Just in case."

"Of course. I understand you want to be with A.J. right now."

"Everything was really nice."

Catherine nodded. She couldn't think of anything to say.

"Thanks, Mom."

"I'm so sorry it ended this way."

"It's not your fault."

"Well, it kind of is."

Madeleine cocked her head to one side. "What do you mean?"

"I gave him that meatball. I was just trying to get him to stop talking."

Madeleine gave a mirthless laugh. "Well, it worked."

"I am so sorry."

Madeleine squeezed her mother's arm. "You didn't know." She turned toward the door. "I've gotta go. I'll call you later."

After Madeleine rushed out, Catherine turned to face the rest of the people in the room. She looked at Henry. "What do we do now? We can't have a party without them."

Henry shrugged. "We already paid for the food."

"I don't know if I can eat now."

"I sure can." Sam Sullivan stepped forward. "I vote we enjoy the dinner. Arthur is going to be just fine, and we wouldn't want a delicious meal to go to waste."

"Wise words," Clara added. "I vote we eat too."

Henry looked at Catherine, a question in his eyes. She nodded slowly. "Sure, let's eat." She gave a weak smile.

The tables had been set with salads and glasses at each place setting. A few minutes later, a pair of waiters came in with chafing dishes and trays of hot pasta. They placed baskets of bread and a large tiramisu dish on the tables. Henry spoke briefly to one of the servers, presumably about payment or tips, as Catherine ushered everyone into the buffet line. Henry asked the guests to bow their heads as Sam led a prayer for the food.

Catherine tried her hardest to enjoy the evening. She put her phone on vibrate but placed it in her lap. She caught herself checking every few minutes to make sure she hadn't missed a call from Madeleine. Finally, as everyone was finishing their dinner, Madeleine reported that Arthur had made it to a clinic and had been cleared by a doctor. He was going to be fine, but the family was too tired for any more festivities. A.J. needed to stay with his parents and let them into his house.

Do you want to drop by and pick up your presents? Catherine typed a quick reply.

Sure. And I'd like to say hi to everyone before they leave.

I'll try to keep them around for a while. Catherine showed her phone to Clara beside her. Clara nodded and passed the phone down to Henry. He caught her eye and then stood.

"Hey, everyone. Thank you so much for coming to celebrate Maddy and A.J. I know it meant a lot to them that you were here. I want to let you all know that Artie, uh, Mr. Young is doing just fine. He's headed back to A.J.'s place with the rest of the Young family. Maddy is on her way back to say hi to everyone. If you're able, please stick around."

He nodded his head, gave a small smile, and sat down again. Catherine's heart sank. *Henry must be so disappointed. This was going to be his way to show support for Maddy, and I completely ruined it.*

18

PRESENT DAY

By the time Maddy showed up at Gustosa, A.J.'s friends had left, and only family members, Julie, and Sam remained. Felicity and Olivia Young had decided to tag along. "We're starving, and now that Dad's fine, we'd just be twiddling our thumbs at A.J.'s place." Olivia grimaced.

"I saved some boxes of food before they cleared everything away." Clara pulled the girls over to a table and set them up with a couple of to-go boxes full of bread and pasta. Madeleine grabbed a breadstick from the table.

Catherine greeted her daughter with a hug. "It's only seven, and we have the place until eight o'clock. We could take the time to open some of your presents if you like." She gestured to the small table covered with cards and a couple gift boxes.

"Oh, would you? I'd love to see you open mine." Julie smiled encouragingly.

"Uh, sure." Madeleine nodded her head and wiped her fingers on a napkin.

Grabbing a chair, Catherine pulled it over to the gift table.

The first gift Maddy reached for was a beautifully wrapped box with a large silver bow tied around turquoise wrapping paper. "Oh, Julie." She pulled out a pair of gorgeous white heels. They looked just low enough to be comfortable.

"I got them to match your dress. If they don't fit, you can always return them."

Madeleine jumped up to hug her friend. "Thank you so much, Julie."

Julie beamed. "I'm happy you like them."

Clara gave a cookbook. It had been ordered from one of those online photo printing companies and was filled with personal recipes and family photos. "Those are all my best recipes. Well, most of them." She hugged her niece.

The next present was a marriage book from Sam. "It's by one of my favorite preachers, out of New York City. I knew A.J. liked his sermons, so I thought he'd appreciate it."

Madeleine gave a sad smile. "I'm sure he'll be thrilled."

A pang of guilt squeezed Catherine's heart. It was her fault A.J. wasn't here to receive the gift himself. Maddy was having enough trouble as it was, and now Catherine had made everything worse by ruining the celebration and causing A.J. to leave.

"How about this card?" Clara thrust a blank envelope into Madeleine's hands. Some guests had given the couple gift cards or notes of congratulations and advice. Madeleine slid her finger under the flap and pulled out a card.

Catherine groaned. "Oh, dear."

It was a pink card with tiny footprints all over the cover. The outside read "Congratulations on your bundle of joy!"

A snicker or two broke out from where A.J's sisters sat.

Maddy's cheeks turned from pink to bright red. "Um, anyone want to claim this one?"

"I can explain." Catherine spoke up.

"Mom?" Madeleine's mouth hung open, her expression was hurt and betrayed.

"It's my fault," Henry interjected. "I was supposed to clean up the gift table."

"We all missed it," Clara said.

"Could someone please explain this to me?" Madeleine was clearly losing her patience.

Catherine, Henry, and Clara all began talking at once.

"The party before ours was a baby shower—"

"And they were supposed to clean it up—"

"But there was a mix-up with the reservation time."

"And we thought we got everything—"

"But we must have missed that card." Catherine snatched it from Madeleine's hands. She took a look at it briefly before she started to crumple it in her fist.

"You can't just read someone's mail and then throw it away." Henry gave her a pointed look.

Catherine furrowed her brows. A pang of guilt pricked her heart, but she ignored it. She examined the ball of paper in her hands. "There wasn't a check or anything. They'll never miss it. What are we supposed to do, track them down?"

"Just give it to me, please." Henry attempted to straighten out the creases and set it on the table.

"Well, if there aren't any more gifts, I'm sure you're all ready to go home. And I promised to pick up some groceries for A.J." Maddy stood. She seemed to be avoiding eye contact with Catherine.

"All right." Catherine clapped her hands. "Thank you, everyone, for coming and for bearing with us. I hope the rest of your evening is much less exciting."

Waving, Sam and Julie left the restaurant, escorted by Clara.

Catherine joined Felicity and Olivia as they helped Maddy pack up her gifts. "I'm so sorry about how everything happened tonight."

Madeleine shook her head slowly. "I know, Mom. It's not

your fault. You did everything you could." She gave a weak smile. "It's been a long day. I just need to go home and rest." Catherine pulled her daughter in for a hug. "I didn't mean for it to go so poorly."

"It's okay." Madeleine shrugged, her shoulders barely raising under Catherine's arms. She stepped back.

Despite her reassurances, Catherine couldn't shake the feeling that her daughter was still upset with her. Maybe Maddy just needed some time to recover from the disastrous engagement party. "I'll see you at Aunt Clara's house later?"

"Of course. See you later." Madeleine beckoned to Felicity and Olivia. She gave her dad a quick hug and a smile on the way out. Maybe Catherine was imagining things, but it seemed like Henry's hug and smile were much more genuine.

Catherine surveyed the damage. There were still a few boxes full of leftovers, even after the girls had demolished a couple. The waitstaff would clean up the trash and dirty linens, but Catherine needed to pack the centerpieces in her car. She placed the flowers and tea lights inside the bags she'd brought. She looked around again and realized she'd need Henry to pull down the banner.

He'd stepped out of the room, so she poked her head out the door to find him. Scanning the dining area, her mouth dropped when she found him at the long marble bar in the center of the restaurant. He handed the bartender a wad of money.

Catherine's blood turned cold inside of her. How could he possibly be drinking again? After everything they'd been through?

She closed the door a little too hard and turned with her back against it. Deep breath.

I'll just get the banner myself.

In a blind rage, Catherine dragged a chair beneath the banner. She stood to reach it but realized she was still a few inches short.

She pulled a table over. She had just climbed on top when she heard the door open.

"What in the world are you doing, Cate?" It was Clara.

Catherine shot Clara an angry look over her shoulder. "What does it look like I'm doing? I'm taking down the banner."

"Why didn't you ask Henry to get it?" Clara moved closer as if to catch Catherine when she inevitably fell.

Catherine pulled one side of the banner down. But as she reached for the other side, she realized that it was too far away from the edge of the table. She hopped up on her toes.

"Because." Hop. "Henry is at the bar." Hop.

"What?" Clara dropped her hands. "Was he—?"

"Yep." Success. Catherine grabbed the banner and crawled off the table. "He was handing cash to a bartender. What else could that mean?"

Clara shook her head. "I don't know what to say. I thought—"

"Yeah, I did too." Catherine sat down, finally allowing herself to process what she'd seen. After almost five years sober, Henry had decided to throw it all away. Honestly, it didn't add up. Tonight had been stressful, but was it worth all that?

"Maybe there's an explanation." Clara bit her lip.

"I can't think of anything. I mean ..." She trailed off and shook her head. "No, I can't think of any good reason for him to be talking to a bartender." She stuffed the banner into a bag with the other decorations and hoisted it up on her shoulder.

"Well, you're about to get your chance to ask him."

Catherine turned as Henry walked into the room, a grin on his face. "You should've waited for me to help you with that."

Catherine waved his comment away impatiently. "That doesn't matter. What matters right now is that you were at the bar buying a drink when you've promised to never do that again. How could you?" She blinked away the sting of tears. "I just can't—I can't look at you right now." She walked as quickly as she could to the parking lot.

The pounding of Henry's footsteps chased after her. "Wait up, Cate. It's not what you think."

She didn't stop until she'd reached her car. She had to press the key fob three times as her fingers just wouldn't work right. She lifted the bag into the car and slammed the trunk shut before facing Henry.

"Then what is it?"

"I was just tipping the waitstaff and handing over the baby card. I couldn't find the hostess, and he promised to get the money to the right people. That's all it was, I promise."

Catherine nodded her head slowly. The angry red fog inside of her cleared. His explanation made sense.

"See? No reason to be upset."

"Maybe not, but ..." She leaned on the car for support.

"But what?"

"I'm just so tired, Henry. I'm exhausted. All the times that I trusted you, and you let me down have caught up with me."

Henry's lips turned down. "I'm so sorry."

"I keep thinking that I can move on. That I've finally forgiven you and let everything go. And after you told me you still loved me ..." She shook her head. "I honestly thought."

She looked at Henry. His thick brown hair had always been a little rumpled but now had some grey sprinkled in. His brown eyes were still kind, albeit with a few more wrinkles around them.

"I thought maybe we could try again. Because the truth is, I never stopped loving you, either. And I've tried so hard." She took a shaking breath.

Henry made to reach for her, but she pushed him away.

"No, I can't. I need to let you go and move on."

"But it was nothing. I didn't drink again. I won't ever drink again."

"I know. But I don't think I can ever trust you again. It's over. Forever. It's really over." She stared straight into his eyes. "We will never be together again."

Henry looked as though he'd been slapped. He stepped back slowly. His lips moved as if to speak, but no sound came out. He dipped his chin and turned around, then got into his car and left.

Catherine watched him go and then sank into the seat of her car. She tried to catch her breath, but every time she took in a gulp of air, she needed more. *I'm hyperventilating. I need to slow down my breathing.* Her brain kicked in before her body would cooperate. She counted her breaths. Then she checked her pulse. *Slow, steady.*

Steps sounded outside the car. She looked up to see her sister.

"Get out. I'm driving us home."

Catherine stepped out and walked around to the passenger side without protest. She leaned her head against the window as Clara started the car.

"Did you hear all that?"

"No, but I watched it happen. It looked bad."

Clara didn't break her gaze from the stores and restaurants out the window as they passed by. "I told him we can never be together. I told him that I still love him, but I can't ever trust him again."

"You still love him?"

Catherine wiped a tear from her cheek. "I guess I never stopped. But you knew that, didn't you?" She turned to look at her sister.

Clara nodded. "I suspected as much, yes."

"It's over now. It's really over."

And, maybe, if she repeated it to herself enough times, she'd convince her heart to finally let go.

19

OCTOBER, FRESHMAN YEAR

*E*ver since their trip to Shady Springs, Tracy and Cate had been spending more and more time hanging out with Jason. Just about anytime Henry saw him—in the cafeteria, on the front lawn, at the bowling alley, or in the student center—Tracy and Cate were nearby. And today was no exception.

Henry slid into the seat next to Jason at lunch. Raymond and some other guys from the basketball team were sitting across from them. Tracy was on the other side of Jason, and Cate sat next to her.

"Ask him." Tracy prodded Jason's side.

"Ask me what?" Henry barely looked up as he moved his plate and drink off his tray.

"He's going to say no." Jason nudged Tracy back.

"Not if you ask nicely." Henry could hear the pout in her voice as he set his tray at the end of the table.

"Why don't *you* ask him? That's the whole point of Sadie Hawkins, anyway."

Henry looked up in time to catch the puppy dog eyes Tracy gave Jason.

Jason turned to him. "The girls want to go on a scavenger hunt."

"Okay." Henry wasn't sure how that could possibly involve *him* in any way.

"And we need a fourth person for our team."

"We're supposed to have two couples per team."

"A scavenger hunt?" Henry had never been a competitive person, and he barely knew his way around the campus. But time spent with Cate would be well worth any humiliation he might suffer.

"You know, for Sadie Hawkins week. The Student Association is having all those activities leading up to Homecoming."

"So, it's like a date?" Henry was more surprised than hopeful, given Cate's firm stance on dating in college.

"No." Cate leaned back and looked him square in the eye. "No distractions, remember?"

"I remember." Henry gave a knowing wink to Cate. She hadn't been rude or standoffish since their fateful trip to Shady Springs, but he hadn't received any positive signals either. He hoped they could at least salvage their friendship.

Cate gave a satisfied nod and returned to eating her salad.

"Please, Henry? Cate is too stuck on her no-dating policy to ask anyone herself. We need you." Tracy turned her big blue eyes toward Henry. If she wasn't so obviously into Jason, he'd find her pretty cute. As it was, he felt himself soften and smile at her.

"Sure. I'm supposed to be taking pictures for the paper anyway."

"Yay." Tracy gave Jason a peck on the cheek and stood to squeeze Henry in a hug before bouncing off with her empty tray. "I'm going to go sign us up. Cate, come on."

Cate saluted the guys before she walked off after her roommate.

"I thought that Tracy was supposed to be the shy one."

"Says who?" Jason spoke around a mouthful of pizza.

"That's how Cate introduced her to me. She said Tracy was shy and told me not to flirt with her."

Jason laughed. "That's 'cuz Cate wants you all to herself."

"What? No. Cate doesn't want to date. She has made that *very* clear." Henry speared another bite of green beans. "What about you and Tracy? What's going on there?"

Jason shrugged, but his cheeks turned a bit pink. "I don't know. I asked her out last weekend."

"What? How did I not know about this?"

"You've been pretty busy with homework."

It was true. Henry's nose had been in a book right up until his last midterm that morning.

"How'd it go?"

"He didn't get in until curfew." Raymond raised his brows across the table.

"Thanks, Ray." Jason took another massive bite of pizza. Guy sure could put away the carbs.

"That well, huh?"

Obviously trying to act nonchalant, Jason lifted his shoulders. "We just went to dinner. It was nice."

The guys across the table whistled and cheered.

"Jones has got a girlfriend." Raymond chanted in a sing-song voice.

"Real mature, fellas." Jason stood up and swallowed the last of his soda. He pointed some finger guns at Henry. "You better be practicing for that scavenger hunt. I don't wanna let down my new girlfriend."

"And how in the world am I supposed to do that?"

Jason gave a happy smirk as he practically skipped away.

Henry chatted a little with Raymond and the guys, but most of their talk centered around people he didn't know and classes he'd never taken. He finished his meal in a few minutes and waved to them on his way out.

The sky had darkened while he was in the cafeteria, and a cool breeze blew across the front lawn. The leaves on the tall oak trees were beginning to turn from green to orange and brown. Several students sat in the white wooden swings or on picnic blankets on the ground. Someone was playing a country song on a guitar.

Henry still hadn't switched from short- to long-sleeved shirts, but it was about time. He at least needed to bust out his jacket.

Looking around, a lonesome feeling settled in his heart. Henry always had tons of friends around in Shady Springs. He'd grown up knowing everyone and hadn't really met anyone new until coming here. College was a lot to adjust to.

Henry sat in one of the empty swings and kicked his legs out from underneath. Now that midterms were behind him, his mind had the freedom to slow down a little.

I might actually pass all my classes. The thought made him smile. *I might actually graduate with a college degree.* That made him grin even more.

So what if he hadn't made a huge effort to make new friends and meet new people? Jason was the best friend anyone could have. And Henry was getting to know the other honors students.

And I'm going on a scavenger hunt on Monday. He chuckled, then checked to make sure no one heard him. Cate walked down the path from the direction of the library.

"Hey, Hodges."

"Hey, yourself."

He patted the empty spot next to him on the swing. Cate balked for a moment, then she shook her head and sat down.

"What's wrong? I don't bite, I promise."

"Nothing. It's just a silly superstition."

Henry had no idea what she was talking about, and it must have shown on his face.

"Three swings and a ring? You've never heard of it?"

He laughed and shook his head. "So, if you swing three times—"

"With the same person."

"Then you'll get a ring?"

"An engagement ring, specifically." Cate ducked her head, but he detected a slight blush on her cheeks.

Henry nodded. "I'm starting to see what you were talking about the other night."

It was Cate's turn to look confused. "What night?"

"At Dr. Cooper's house a few weeks ago, you were saying some people expect girls in college to just find a husband and not focus on academics."

"Yeah." She waved her hand over the swing. "Welcome to the Marriage Factory."

"Is that why you don't want to date anyone?"

"I mean, I don't want to *never* date anyone." Cate looked down at her lap again.

"Just not in college."

She shrugged. "I don't want people thinking that's why I'm here." She twisted her fingers in her lap. "I do want to get married *someday*."

He nodded slowly and started to push the swing. "But don't you want to marry a Christian man?"

"Of course."

"And aren't there a lot of Christian men here?"

"Listen, I get your point. It's the same one my parents, and Tracy, have made many times. But I don't want to be like my mom. I don't want to be in the background of someone else's story." She looked him in the eye. "I'm smart, just like you. I know I am."

Henry was baffled. "Smart like me?"

"Yeah, I can keep up with everyone in class too. But because I'm a girl I have to work twice as hard to be taken seriously."

"Cate, what are you talking about?" He tapped his sneakers on the ground, stopping the swing. "First of all, everyone takes you seriously. You are *very* serious." Maybe too serious. "Second of all, *I'm* not that smart."

"Yes you are. I read that research paper for Bible. It was excellent. And you always have great comments in Intro to Honors."

"Hmm. Thanks." *Cate Hodges thinks I'm smart.* He kicked his feet out again. "Well, if I'm smart, then you're a genius. Besides, we all know that nursing is a much harder major than business."

Cate smirked, but she didn't disagree.

They sat and swung for a while. Eventually, Cate reached out with the toes of her tennis shoes. She stood up, giving him a smile, and squeezed his hand.

"Thanks, Henry, you're a good friend." She walked backward and called out. "See you around."

"See you around." Henry pushed himself in the swing a few more times. He did have a friend. His hand warmed where she'd touched him.

It felt good to have a friend, until he realized something. It hit him like a sudden punch to the chest. He didn't want to just be friends with Cate Hodges. He wanted much more.

20

OCTOBER, FRESHMAN YEAR

Click. Click. Henry snapped photos as a group of students stood in a circle on the front lawn. After a few good shots, he stowed the camera away in its bag.

The student association vice president called over the crowd from his spot on the fountain steps. "Okay, you have one hour to find everything on this list and meet back here at the reflection pool." The students buzzed with excitement. "Everyone got it?"

Henry nodded quickly, looking to his left and right at his teammates.

"Ready, set, go!"

Henry resisted the urge to bolt as Jason grabbed his forearm and pulled him into a huddle.

"Listen, Mullins. We've got a plan. We're going to split the list."

Henry scanned the items typed on the piece of paper. Rock shaped like a heart, business card from a faculty member, a pair of rubber gloves.

"How about we split it by location. Tracy and I can head south and get the painted grass from the football field and a songbook from the auditorium. You and Cate can go north for the cafeteria tray and the brick rubbing. On the way we'll look for a rock shaped like a heart. I'll get the club T-shirt and roll of toilet paper from my room. You find a business card from a faculty member and gloves."

Cate stabbed her finger at the list. "Who has a penny? Anyone got a penny from before 1950?"

They all emptied out their pockets and purses. Only six pennies between them and all after 1950.

"Let's just keep moving. Meet back here at six-fifty. That'll give us time to pick up whatever we missed."

Henry checked his watch. It was just past six o'clock. "All right, good luck."

As Henry raced after Cate across the front lawn, he cradled his camera bag to his chest. He'd be in huge trouble if anything happened to the equipment.

"Have you had supper yet?"

"Why?" Cate raised an eyebrow.

"Because." He panted. "We're going to have to use a meal to get into the cafeteria. I just didn't want you to have to waste a meal."

Cate waved him away. "Don't worry about it. I've got meals to spare."

"How about I get the rubbing of a name from the sidewalk and you sneak out the tray?"

Cate nodded. "Do you have some paper?"

Henry held up the scavenger hunt list.

"What about a pencil?"

Henry patted his pockets but came up empty.

"Here." She stopped a minute to look through her purse. "Take mine."

"Thanks. See you in a few minutes."

They parted ways. Henry looked down at his feet as he walked until he came to a spot where someone had engraved a name into a brick in the walkway. "In memory of P.L. Maynard."

He whipped out Cate's pencil and began to rub the lead against the white paper. It was a little, nubby thing, and the wood had been chewed on. *Cate chews her pencils. Interesting.* Near the eraser end, the metal was bent too. The whole thing would have been disgusting if he didn't find it so endearing. Cate Hodges always seemed to have it all together. But it would appear she had bad habits just like everyone else.

"Quick, let's go." Cate rushed out of the cafeteria, a rectangular bulge under her jacket. She gave a nervous glance behind her before pulling out a brown plastic tray. "I don't think anyone saw me. I'm going to bring it back, anyway, so it's not really stealing."

"No. And we did take it as part of a sanctioned school activity."

"What do you want to bet they didn't run this list past a faculty member?"

Henry scanned the items on the paper again. She was probably right.

"Speaking of faculty, do you know anyone who would give us a business card?"

"I don't know anyone near here." She looked around at the buildings nearby. The student center, the art building, and past that, the nursing building.

"What about your nursing professors?"

She shuddered. "No. They scare me."

"I'm not scared. Let's just walk this way until we find someone."

The art building was closest, so they ran through the front door. There weren't any open doors down the first hallway. They passed glass windows where clay pots sat out. Henry poked his head around another hallway and noticed the gallery had a new exhibit. No longer photography, but watercolors and oil paintings. "Those are beautiful."

"Stay focused, Mullins." Cate slapped his arm.

"Why are you like this?"

"Like what?" Cate burst ahead and toward the back door.

Henry gulped in a breath of air. "Like you're hyper and panicked?"

When she stared him in the eye, he saw a crazed look he hadn't noticed earlier. "I want to win!"

"Oh, okay." Henry nodded, hoping his facial expression wasn't as nervous as he felt on the inside. He had no idea Cate was so competitive. It made sense, of course. All those honors kids had a crazy competitive side. And they took everything so seriously.

A middle-aged man with brown hair walked down the hallway close to them.

"Excuse me." Henry waved him down. "Are you a faculty member?"

"Sure." He gave a warm smile.

"Would you mind giving us a business card? It's for a scavenger hunt."

The man shrugged good-naturedly. "No problem. It's in my office." He turned around in the opposite direction and beckoned for them to follow.

When they came to his office, the man pushed open the doors, and Henry gasped. On every wall were photographs. Some in color, some black and white. One sepia-toned. "Wow."

The man looked around him as if noticing the art for the first time. "Oh, thanks."

Among the photos were prints and a few paintings.

"Do you teach photography?"

He chuckled. "How can you tell?" The man handed a card each to Henry and Cate. "Take as many as you want. I had way too many printed for the last conference I went to."

Henry read the card before he slid it into his back pocket. Professor Darren Skinner. "Your pictures are amazing. Did you have some up in the gallery earlier this semester?"

He smiled. "That was from a trip we took last summer."

"It looked like a really great trip."

Professor Skinner nodded, staring into the distance. "It was."

Cate tapped her foot impatiently. Henry knew he should hurry things along, but he was enjoying talking to Professor Skinner too much.

"I take photos for *The Talon* sometimes."

Mr. Skinner's eyes lit up. "Ah, a fellow photographer."

Henry shrugged. "I enjoy it. I used to do the same thing in high school, take pictures for the yearbook and the school paper."

"That's how I started too. I couldn't afford a camera of my own so I'd steal the school's camera."

"Me too!" Henry laughed, gesturing to the bag hanging from his shoulder.

Cate cleared her throat.

"Oh, sorry." Henry grimaced. "We've got to go. Thanks for the cards."

"Sure thing." Professor Skinner waved. "You should take my class next semester."

"I'd like that, but I'm not sure if it would fit in my schedule."

"Think about it. You could use it as an elective."

"Henry, please." Cate practically pulled him out the door.

"I'll think about it," Henry called out. "Thanks!"

Cate groaned. "Henry Mullins, you are ridiculous. We're on a deadline." She tapped her watch. "You can't just stop and chat with everyone you meet. We're competing in a scavenger hunt, remember?"

Henry slapped his forehead. "I should have asked if he had any rubber gloves!"

"No way. I am not letting you go back in there." She twisted her lips to one side. "I have rubber gloves in my room."

Henry raised an eyebrow at her.

"For cleaning my dorm room."

He stopped in his tracks. "You clean your dorm room so well you need rubber gloves?"

"No more talking. If we get my gloves, we need to run across campus. And I mean actually run, Mullins." She looked him up and down. "You are huffing and puffing like the big bad wolf. Think you can handle it?"

His cheeks grew warm. It had been a little while since his basketball-playing days. But there was no way he was going to let a girl outrun him, heavy camera bag or not. He gave a curt nod.

They sprinted across the front lawn, almost knocking into a guy on roller skates. Henry caught up with Cate in between the English building and another dormitory. He beat her to the front doors of her dorm by half a second.

"Wait here." Cate shoved the cafeteria tray into Henry's hands and zipped inside.

Leaning against the brick wall of her dorm building, he took several gulps of air. *Don't know why she wanted me to come with her when I can't even go up to her room.* He could wait in the lobby, but he figured he'd be ready to go faster if he just stayed where he was. How long would he have to wait alone, outside a girls' dorm? Another guy paced the sidewalk nearby, his arms crossed. He gave a polite nod.

"Waiting for your date?" He wore a collared shirt and appeared to be freshly shaved and showered.

"Yeah, no, I mean, it's complicated." Henry shrugged.

"I hear you." The other guy chuckled. He glanced up to see a pretty girl wearing a denim dress and lots of lipstick. "Have a nice night. Good luck." He waved to Henry and took the girl's arm in his.

Henry wished he had a date tonight, a real one. Someone to take to the movies or dinner who didn't want to keep him at arm's length. Grimacing, he remembered his lack of funds. He'd need cash before he could take anyone on a nice date.

The door clicked open, and Cate rushed out. She flashed him a smile, and Henry's heart skipped a beat. He changed his mind. There was no one he would rather spend time with than Cate Hodges. Even if she just wanted him as a friend.

"Let's go back to the reflection pool. I think it's time to meet up."

Henry checked his watch. "We still have ten minutes. Let's walk by the flower beds over there and check for a heart-shaped rock."

They walked, a little slower this time, and watched their feet. Cate picked up a pebble that was really more of a triangle. "This could work in a pinch."

"Maybe."

"Look, I see Jason and Tracy. Let's go."

Pocketing the rock, Cate pulled Henry's hand as they raced to meet their teammates.

Jason ran toward them with Tracy riding piggyback. He carried a T-shirt like a sack, stuffed with assorted objects. Jason beamed at his friend.

"This was the only way I could keep up with him." Tracy hopped down to the sidewalk. "Did you two find a penny?"

"No." Henry shook his head. "I should've asked Professor Skinner about that too."

Jason spread out an armload of stuff, and they piled it on the cafeteria tray. A songbook from the auditorium, Jason's club jersey, a roll of toilet paper, the business card, a white blade of grass from the football field, the rubber gloves, Henry's pencil rubbing from the walkway.

"Did you find a rock shaped like a heart?" Tracy asked.

"Sort of." Cate pulled the stone out of her pocket. "Did you?"

"No."

"Okay, you go look for a better rock. We'll get the penny." Jason checked the paper. "And a drinking straw." He took off down the sidewalk, turned back to see Tracy lagging behind, and stopped to pull her up on his back again.

Henry chuckled. At least Jason was enjoying himself.

"Let's check the rocks behind the art building. I think there are some by the intramural field too." Cate took off jogging.

"Sure, okay."

They scanned the ground in silence, concentrating.

"Do you always talk to strangers?"

Frowning, Henry looked up in surprise. "What are you talking about?"

"Like how you just struck up a conversation with that art professor?"

Henry shrugged. "I mean, yeah, I guess."

"Hmm."

"Do you not?"

"No, never. I have a hard time talking to my professors."

"You seem fine in class."

"I hate it, though. I mean, something about Dr. Cooper makes me comfortable talking to him. Maybe it helps that I see him every week for Bible study."

There was undoubtedly something special about Dr. Cooper. "Yeah, he's cooler than the average professor."

"Right. But my nursing professors. And my math professor." She shuddered. "I couldn't just hang out in their offices and chat about art on the wall."

"Why not?"

She shrugged. "I guess I'm afraid of sounding stupid. Or asking the wrong questions."

"First of all, you couldn't possibly sound stupid—you're way too smart. Second of all, they're just people, and their job is to teach you."

"I guess so." She stopped at the same time Henry saw it.

They both reached out for a perfectly smooth, heart-shaped

stone. It even had a pink tinge. Henry's fingers touched Cate's. She looked up at him and dropped the rock. "Oh."

"Here." It took a moment, but Henry found the rock again and placed it in her palm. "Our heart." He closed her fingers over the stone. When she looked up into his eyes, there was a warmth he'd never seen before. Her lips parted.

"Come on, let's go!" Another couple raced by them on the way to the front lawn.

Cate shook her head quickly. The moment, whatever it was, had passed.

"We'd better go before someone beats us." Cate stuck the stone in her pocket and ran away.

* * *

"Looks like you've got everything here." A volunteer for the Sadie Hawkins scavenger hunt looked over their items with his clipboard. "What's this?" He held up the triangle rock they'd found earlier.

"Oh, no. I forgot to put out the good rock." Cate patted her pockets quickly and pulled out the heart-shaped one. She started for the judges, but Tracy pulled her back.

"No, if you go now, they won't count it. Right now, we've only got one team to beat. They might put us at the back of the line if we change things up."

Jason nodded. "Let's just see how we do without it."

Cate furrowed her brow, but she stepped backward.

"All right, it looks like we have our winners." A judge pointed to the team that beat them to the meeting spot. He handed them an envelope. The grand prize was a gift certificate to the food court on campus, the College Inn.

"And in second place is The Four Musketeers, Tracy Van Horn's team!"

A judge handed them each a bar of chocolate. Jason whooped and twirled Tracy around.

"Cheers." Henry tapped Cate's candy bar with his own. "Sorry we didn't win. I know it meant a lot to you."

She shrugged and smiled at him. "We got second, which is pretty good."

"See you guys tomorrow night?" Tracy raised her eyebrows. "They're showing a movie, I think."

"Sure thing." Jason smiled down at her.

"I'll go if you go." Cate turned to him.

His breath caught a moment before he could answer. "If it's as fun as tonight was, I'm in."

21

PRESENT DAY

Checking her phone again, Catherine jiggled her knees. Willing the minutes to fly by faster wasn't doing the trick. Still ten minutes until her lunch meeting. To distract herself, she glanced around at the artwork on the walls of the restaurant. It reminded her of some of the paintings Madeleine had done when she was younger.

The furniture was painted as well. Catherine examined the table under her fingertips, a mountain scene with an emerald castle. Her chair was covered with the deep grays and blues of a rainstorm. Two more chairs had a bright yellow sunny sky and a rainbow bursting through clouds.

A bell jingled as the front door of The Sandwich Shop opened.

"Ginger, hi!" Catherine rushed to give the woman a hug. Relief washed over her. "You're here. I thought you might not show up."

"Of course, I'm here." Ginger smiled, though she stiffened under Catherine's embrace.

Catherine steered her to the restaurant's counter. "Let's order something. My treat."

"Oh, you don't have to." Ginger's tone belied her words. Her expression told Catherine this was only the beginning of her long apology to the Young family.

"It's the least I can do. I feel so awful about what happened with the meatballs."

Ginger's face softened. "Arthur will be fine. He's still tired, but I'm a little glad for the peace and quiet." She grasped Catherine's arm. "I'm grateful we had a nurse there."

Firm in her regret, Catherine shook her head. "If I hadn't given him the meatball, you wouldn't have needed a nurse."

Ginger pursed her lips and tilted her head, acknowledging the truth of Catherine's statement. She turned to the menu. "What's good here?"

"I don't really know. Clara and Maddy recommended it." She scanned the list of sandwiches. "I think I'll get their harvest salad."

Ginger nodded. "Sounds good." She gestured to the girl behind the counter. "Two harvest salads, please. Hold the walnuts on mine."

The women returned to Catherine's table in the corner. Ginger sat in the chair painted like a rainbow.

Catherine took a deep breath and looked at the woman opposite her. If they hadn't gotten off to such a rocky start the night before, they might have become friends. Catherine hoped there was still a chance of that.

"I didn't have the opportunity to tell you last night how much I've loved getting to know A.J. He's been such a Godsend." She thought about the path her daughter might be on without her time in Shady Springs last summer. "He helped Maddy find her faith again, and I will be forever grateful to him for that."

"I'm glad they met, too, if just for that reason." Ginger gave a smile, but it seemed wistful and sad.

"You know, after Henry left, she was all I had. I'm afraid I didn't give her the spiritual upbringing she deserved."

"Why is that?"

"I had a rough patch with church for a while. A long while. But I've found my way back now." Watching Maddy forgive the church in Shady Springs and forgive her father had driven Catherine to examine her old life. She was making a real effort to follow her daughter's good example by spending each morning in prayer. She'd even started visiting different worship services in town.

"It's so important for new converts to have someone to go to for spiritual guidance."

"She has my sister and me and the church here. I've encouraged her to read her Bible and find out for herself what she believes." Catherine knew she wasn't strong enough to guide Maddy by herself. But Maddy had Clara, and now Henry. "And her father has made some great strides recently."

A young woman came by with their salads, bowls brimming with leafy greens, apples, raisins, nuts, and a tangy vinaigrette.

Ginger offered to say a prayer, so Catherine bowed her head. "Father, thank you for Madeleine and A.J. And thank you for new friendships." She squeezed Catherine's hand across the table.

Catherine echoed Ginger's "amen" and smoothed out a napkin over her lap.

Ginger blotted her mouth after chewing a bite. "I overheard Arthur talking to Henry last night."

"Me too." Here it came. Catherine just *knew* that Ginger was going to reveal her fears and concerns over the upcoming marriage.

"Arthur is ... very headstrong." She sighed. "I know you were friends in college."

"Sort of." Acquaintances, more like.

"Well, you may not have known he was on the forensics team all through high school and college. He did very well, actually."

"I believe that." As she speared a forkful of lettuce, Catherine remembered Artie back in college. Surely, his personality had mellowed over the years.

"Arthur loves a good debate and usually acts before thinking. He will take the strongest opinion possible just to have an enjoyable argument."

"He was like that in college too. I had forgotten." Catherine herself had been on the receiving end of Arthur's arguments more than once.

"Well, he hasn't changed a bit." She rested her chin on her hands. "He and A.J. butted heads a lot over the years. They have a hard time understanding each other."

"A.J. is so easygoing. I can imagine they must have their differences." Catherine smiled to herself as she pictured the effervescent redhead she'd come to love like a son. His ability to roll with the punches and keep his sunny disposition had earned her respect.

"Arthur didn't mean to offend you last night. I'm sorry." Ginger gave a small smile. "And I'm sorry for everything you've been through with Henry. I know it was hard for you and Madeleine."

Fighting the urge to stick up for Henry, Catherine bit her lip. Ginger and Arthur were right to have some concerns. She had plenty of her own. She and Henry hadn't provided the stable foundation for Maddy they'd planned. Their relationship had gone awry, and Maddy had been a casualty of their mistakes—Henry's alcoholism and adultery, Catherine's backsliding and forsaking of the church.

"She's almost a new person now, Ginger. She used to be so sensitive and almost bitter about the past. Now that she's found her faith, she's so much freer. I think she will be a wonderful wife to A.J."

Ginger's already light skin paled even further. "Really?"

"Sure. I know she has concerns and fears, but that's normal."

Ginger stared at her for a long time before speaking. "You don't know, do you?"

"Know what?" Catherine dropped her fork to the table.

"Madeleine and A.J. broke up last night."

22

PRESENT DAY

Maddy and A.J. broke up? Catherine's mouth gaped open. Why hadn't Maddy said something last night? She'd just gone straight to bed after she got home. "I had no idea."

"I wondered as much when you asked me to lunch. I thought perhaps it was to check on A.J." She dabbed her lips with a napkin. "Or to share information."

"So, Maddy broke up with *him*?"

"That's what I gather. He was too devastated and surprised last night to talk about it much."

"Maddy didn't say anything." She hadn't come down for breakfast this morning. Catherine had thought she wasn't hungry, but now she realized her daughter had been too grieved to eat.

"Did she say anything to you beforehand? Did she seem strange to you last night?"

"Last night was strange for everyone." Catherine wondered how much she should share about Maddy's misgivings regarding marriage. "Maddy has been struggling with cold feet. I knew she was nervous about the wedding, but I had no idea she would actually break things off with A.J."

Ginger twisted her mouth in a frown before taking a bite of her salad.

"It's not A.J.'s fault." Catherine rushed to clarify her statement. "Maddy is head-over-heels in love with him. She's just struggling with the whole concept of marriage." Catherine lowered her gaze to the table. "Her father and I didn't set the best example in that department."

"I don't know what to do about A.J. He's talking about leaving town soon and applying for grad school earlier than he'd planned." Ginger still held her fork, but she only toyed with the rest of her lunch.

"Let me speak to Maddy. Try to keep A.J. from making any rash decisions if you can."

Ginger sighed. "I'll do my best, but he's a grown man."

"I'm sure this is all a misunderstanding. Maddy just needs some time and perspective."

Catherine had thought her only mistakes the night before had been a disaster of an engagement party and a fight with Henry. Now she realized she'd let those things distract her from the real problem: Maddy was hurting. And Catherine would do anything in the world to prevent that from happening. If she was going to help fix this mess, she would need some wisdom. More than she had herself.

God, You know I can't do this on my own. Please help me.

* * *

Catherine knocked gently on Maddy's door. One of the two small guest rooms on the second floor of Clara's home had been converted into Maddy's temporary residence. The boxes they'd just packed a couple weeks ago sat against the far wall. A stack of books and art supplies crowded the small wooden desk. Maddy's pink pillow and favorite white chenille blanket adorned Clara's antique bed.

An easel was positioned facing away from the large windows to take advantage of the late afternoon light. Maddy sat on a stool behind a large pad of paper resting on the easel, a pencil in her hand.

"Hi, Mom." Maddy's hand moved down to her lap. Her lips twitched as though she'd attempted a smile, and really given her best effort, but she just couldn't bring herself to actually lift her lips.

Might as well cut to the chase. "I had lunch with Ginger Young today. She told me you broke up with A.J."

Maddy hung her head. She nodded slowly.

Catherine perched on the bed and scooted close enough to take her daughter's hands. "I'm so sorry, sweetheart."

Maddy's gaze met hers, and Catherine's heart broke in two.

"I didn't mean for any of it to happen the way it did, but now I guess breaking up is for the best." She scowled. "Better to do it now than after we're already married."

"Do you want to tell me what happened?"

Maddy raised one shoulder. "It started out as me sharing my feelings with him." She waved her hands to her mother. "Like you told me I should."

Catherine bit her lip to keep from interjecting. Did Maddy harbor resentment for her advice? She stood by her earlier statement that Maddy should communicate how she felt with A.J., though she hadn't expected it to end this way.

"A.J. was confused about why I was having second thoughts and why I waited so long to tell him. I tried to explain, but I did a terrible job." Maddy rubbed her temples with the fingers of her left hand. "He finally point-blank asked me if I wanted to get married.

"I tried to explain that it's not that I don't want to marry *him*." She turned to Catherine, the expression on her face begging Catherine to understand her. "It's that I don't think I can get married *at all*."

Catherine rubbed her daughter's back. She was at a loss for words. Through all the reminiscing, had Catherine skipped over all the ways in which her marriage had been wonderful? Had she been so focused on the hard parts that she'd forgotten why she married Henry in the first place?

"Hey there, would anyone like some tea?" Clara walked in the room with two mugs.

"Is that chamomile?" Her sister almost had a sixth sense when it came to heartfelt conversations. She always knew when to put on a kettle to boil.

"Sure is." Clara handed a mug to Maddy and then to Catherine. She sat on the bed next to her sister. "What's going on, Maddy? I've hardly seen you all day and you look far too sad for any young, engaged person."

Maddy looked into the cup in her hands. "That's because I'm not engaged anymore."

Clara furrowed her brows and shot an intense glance Catherine's way. Although they hadn't lived in the same house in ages, Catherine could still read her sister like a book. Clara hadn't seen this coming, she wanted to know if Catherine had known about it, and she was about to interrogate Maddy.

"What happened? I don't understand."

Maddy took a sip of the tea and blew out a breath. "The truth is, I don't think I can get married."

"What? Why not?" Clara, matchmaker extraordinaire, wouldn't be able to understand anyone not wanting to get married.

"I've always thought it's what I wanted. I dreamed about what dress I would wear and what the decorations would look like. And picking out all those things has been a lot of fun. It's almost been enough to distract me from the bigger problem."

"Which is what, exactly?"

Maddy lowered her mug and leveled her gaze on her aunt. "Why would I want to put A.J. through that? Or myself? Look at what happened to my parents." She swept her arm out. "Look at what happened to *you*."

"What happened to me?"

"You found the love of your life, had a few marvelous years, and then had him snatched away from you." She flicked her fingers with an air of frivolity, but her expression was deadly serious. "I love A.J. too much to let that happen to him."

"So, what? You'd rather he live a lonely, celibate life than have a few happy years with you?"

"No. Maybe I don't die. Maybe we get a divorce."

Catherine interjected. "Divorce doesn't just *happen*, Maddy."

"It happens to a lot of people."

"No, it takes two people to make that decision. And my marriage imploding doesn't mean that yours automatically would."

Maddy drank another mouthful. "But doesn't it? I know I'm a lot like Dad, everybody's always told me that. What if I ruin my marriage too? I couldn't risk that." She rose to set the mug down on the desk. "A.J.'s better off without me."

"I doubt he sees it that way," Clara said.

"Not yet, but he will." Maddy frowned. "He's pretty angry with me right now, I'm sure."

"Maybe," Catherine said. "But he's crazy about you. And I know you love him too."

Maddy nodded and lowered herself back on the stool. "You and Dad loved each other, and that didn't keep you together."

No, .it didn't. But maybe it should have. Maybe if Henry hadn't run away and Catherine hadn't always demanded perfection out of him, they'd still be together. "I love your father very much. I think I always will. And I don't regret our marriage. It gave me *you*."

"You don't wish things had been different?"

"I wish a lot of things had been different, but that doesn't mean I wish it had never happened."

Catherine stroked her daughter's cheek with one finger and lifted her chin. Madeleine's gaze met hers. "Maddy, I don't know how else to tell you this. You are *not* your father. You are your own person, and you have something your dad never had."

"What's that?"

Catherine took her daughter's hands in hers. "A family that loves you and supports you."

Clara added her hands to theirs. "And prays for you."

Maddy squeezed her eyes shut and bowed her head. As Clara prayed over Maddy and A.J., Catherine leaned her head on her sister's shoulder.

She hoped she hadn't completely ruined Maddy's future. What if her own failed marriage caused her daughter to never experience true love? How could she show Maddy that love was worth the risk?

Catherine's heart squeezed as she realized maybe she needed to hear that message as much as her daughter. She'd been too harsh with Henry and with herself. Why *couldn't* they have another chance?

They'd both admitted they loved each other. Catherine knew that after many years of trying to give up on Henry, she'd never be able to erase his name from her heart.

Maybe it's time to stop trying to cut Henry out of my life. Maybe it's time to bring him back in.

OCTOBER, FRESHMAN YEAR

Henry held a plastic scoop in one hand and a plastic bag in the other. Chocolate pretzels or gummy bears? Which ones would Cate like more? Waving the scoop in the air, he vacillated between the two. Running out of time. He shoveled chocolate-covered pretzels into the bag. Then he added a heaping scoop of gummy bears, just to be sure.

He tapped his foot as the cashier rang him up.

"Using your credit balance?"

Henry nodded and handed over his student ID card.

The cashier handed him a receipt and the bag. Henry practically sprinted for the door. He did not want to be late for what might be his only chance to woo Cate.

It wasn't a date, strictly speaking. Cate still hadn't budged on her no-boyfriend policy. But it was Sadie Hawkins week. And she'd asked him out to the movies. Heart singing, Henry raced to her dorm. If he didn't hurry, he might not catch her in time to walk her over. He poked his head in the lobby. Jason was waiting on a pink couch, so Henry walked in and sat beside him.

"Girls still not down yet?"

"Nope." Jason scanned Henry, a slow grin spreading across his face. "You dressed up."

"A little." Henry had changed into a collared shirt, although he still wore jeans.

"And you brought candy."

Henry gave a small shrug. "Thought it might help."

Jason laughed. "Don't worry. You'll be great."

They looked up as the sound of laughter echoed down the hallway. A cluster of four girls walked past.

"Did you and Tracy decide to meet up here?"

Jason nodded. "I thought so. Let's give them a few minutes and then we can see if they're already in the auditorium." He checked the clock on the wall. "We've still got a little time before the movie starts."

Henry's cheeks puffed as he blew out a breath of air. He jiggled his knees and looked around the dormitory lobby. He'd heard it had been renovated recently. The walls and furniture were a light pink and blue. A bored-looking girl sat at the front desk chewing bubble gum. She had a textbook in front of her but didn't seem to actually be studying, just scanning the pages.

He startled as footsteps approached. It was her. Cate. She and Tracy walked toward them. She had on a fuzzy purple sweater and some white pants. Something about her lipstick or the way she did her hair made Henry think she'd put some extra effort into tonight as well.

"You look really nice." He wasn't sure if he should hug her or give her a high five, so he just shoved his hand in his pocket.

"You too." She looked down at the bag of candy. "What's that?"

"Oh." He held it out to her. "I wasn't sure if you were a chocolate or fruit candy type of person, so I got both."

She grinned. "Definitely chocolate. Thank you. That was really sweet of you."

"Sure." He looked over to see Jason and Tracy headed outside. He stepped forward quickly to hold open the door. Everything inside of him hummed as he and Cate fell into an easy rhythm, walking together down the sidewalk.

After a quick stroll across the front lawn, they settled into the dark auditorium just as the music began. It was an older film, and Henry had seen it so many times, he didn't mind the distraction of having Cate right next to him.

Every time she shifted in her seat, every time she reached for a handful of candy, his eyes flitted to her. The warmth from her leg only an inch from his seeped in through his jeans.

This was torture. How could he endure a whole two hours beside Cate like this? A breath away from him, but not touching. He could grab her hand when the flying monkeys came on screen. He could fake a yawn and stretch his arm across her shoulders.

He settled for something a little less obvious. "Did I do okay on the candy?" He moved his head next to hers. The smell of her vanilla shampoo had him itching to bend a bit closer.

"You did great. Thanks." She tilted her head so close that wisps of her curly hair tickled his cheek.

He nudged her shoulder with his then settled in close so their arms touched. Her scent and her nearness were intoxicating. If he wasn't absolutely positive she would recoil, he would reach out for her fingers.

As time passed, Henry was drawn more and more into the movie. He'd almost forgotten where he was when he felt Cate shift beside him. Likely, she was uncomfortable and would move away from him. His heart constricted at that thought, but he was grateful for the time he'd gotten to be close. Then she leaned her head against his shoulder, and his chest reinflated with unexpected joy.

He could've stayed like that all night, but the film drew to a close, just like it always had. Someone flicked on the lights, and Cate straightened, almost as if she'd been caught doing something illicit. The magic was gone.

"You guys up for some ice cream? My treat." Jason stretched his arms above his head and rested them over Tracy's shoulders. "I just got some money from Mom and Dad."

Henry raised his eyebrows at Cate.

"Sure."

They piled into Jason's van and drove ten minutes to the diner on the outskirts of town. Tracy had called shotgun, although she didn't need to. Henry was happy to join Cate in the back.

"Did you like the movie?"

Cate beamed. "Yes! Ever since I was little, I've loved that story."

"It's one of my mom's favorites too." Henry smiled at a memory. "We used to watch it every time it came on television."

It was one of the rare occasions that the Mullins family would all come together in peace and quiet. Even if his dad was home, he'd join them in the living room for some popcorn. He'd take his place in his recliner, and Henry would join his mother on the couch or sometimes on the floor right below. It was all the sweeter for its rarity.

"Why do you love it?" Henry asked.

Cate looked out the window for a beat before answering. "For a while, I just liked the colors and the music." She grinned mischievously. "When I was going through my rebellious stage, I said it was because I wanted to watch a movie about someone getting out of Kansas."

Henry laughed. "I get that."

She sighed and thought a moment. "I think it's because I want to be like the main character."

"How so?"

"You know, at the beginning of the story she thinks she's all alone and the world is out to get her. But then she finds all her friends, and all they want to do is help her and work together. And then she realizes that she does have a family and a home."

"I always wondered about her parents."

Cate nodded. "Me too."

"Do you think that's why she tries to run away? Because she's going to find her parents?"

"No, I think she was scared. She couldn't bear to face the problems at home, so she left."

Henry could certainly relate to that sentiment.

At the ice cream shop, they all picked out milkshakes and settled into a booth, laughing about the scavenger hunt and Jason's impersonation of his economics teacher. Tracy and Cate shared about their desire to join a social club. Club week was coming soon, and they were both anxious about whether or not they'd get in the ones they wanted.

"I'll be nervous after I get in too." Tracy bit her lip.

"Why's that?"

"Because of rough week. I've heard the older girls do all kinds of terrible things to the pledges." She shuddered

"Pshh." Jason waved her off. "Pledges have it so easy now. My dad told me about all the stuff they used to do back in the old days. Now, they can't do anything mean or scary. Takes all the fun out of it."

"You're crazy." Tracy wagged her spoon at him.

"My parents have said the same thing," Cate said. "I guess it used to be much worse."

"Small mercies, I guess."

At the end of the night, Jason and Henry walked the girls back to their dorm. They still had a few minutes until curfew, and Henry wasn't ready for the night to end. He slowed his pace and tugged at Cate's arm.

"Hey, Cate. Can I ask you something?"

"Sure, what is it?"

"I know you don't want to date anyone right now, but ... if you did ..." He wasn't sure how to ask what was on his mind. He wasn't even sure what he wanted to say.

"Yes?"

"Cate, I want to go out with you. On a real date. Not a Sadie Hawkins pity date."

"It's not—"

He waved her off. "No, I know this didn't really count. You just wanted me to fill out the group so you weren't a third wheel. And that's okay. But ..." He rubbed the back of his neck. "I want to date you, Cate. I like you."

He couldn't tell for sure in the strange glow of the parking lot lights, but it looked like Cate might be blushing. "I like you, too, Henry."

"Then will you say yes? Will you go on a date with me?"

She shifted from one foot to another. "Let me think about it."

He grabbed her hands. "Don't think. Just say yes."

She started to talk again, but he placed his fingers over her lips.

"Cate. I promise I won't get in your way. Remember the movie? I don't want to walk alone anymore—I want to walk together, and I think you feel the same."

Her shoulders relaxed, and she gave a tiny, almost imperceptible nod.

"Yes?" Henry bit his lip to keep from crying out in elation. "Will you go on a date with me?"

"One date, Henry Mullins. I'll agree to one date."

"Dinner tomorrow?" He grabbed her hands. He'd get down on his knees and beg if he had to.

She shook her head. "I can't go out every night. Don't you people have homework?" She squeezed his hands back. "Friday night. I'll go out with you on Friday. And let me have the rest of the week to study."

"Deal." His grin had to be the size of a Kansas prairie. He

wanted to kiss her on the lips right then and there, but he made himself wait. He couldn't risk scaring her off before he'd even had a real chance.

"I'll see you around, Henry."

"See you around, Cate."

24

OCTOBER, FRESHMAN YEAR

Once Henry had some time to think about it, he was glad Cate hadn't agreed to a date right away. That gave him three days to plan, and he needed all the time he could get.

"Just take her to the movies." Frank, his roommate, was happy to help out at first but was growing impatient with Henry's worrying the closer they got to the date.

Henry groaned. "We just went on Tuesday. Besides, I want it to be something different."

"Take her out for dinner." Jason lounged on Henry's bed behind him, tossing a rubber band ball in the air.

"You know I don't have that kind of money."

"You've gotta eat sometime."

Henry tapped his pen on his desk and looked out the window. A couple of guys passed a football back and forth on their way to the front lawn.

"A picnic."

Jason sat up. "That's not bad. Where will you get the food? Or the basket?"

"I'll get to-go boxes from the cafeteria."

Frank nodded appreciatively. "I've got an old blanket you can borrow."

"You can grab stuff for sandwiches, some cookies, and some fruit. And bring a water bottle for yourself."

"Do you need someone to serenade you? My a cappella group could use the practice." Frank shot him a hopeful look.

Henry grimaced. Frank's group really did need the practice, but he wasn't about to offer himself up as their test audience. "I don't want to scare her away. That might be a bit much for a first date." He glanced around the room. "But I do need something else to send it over the top."

"How about a hike? You could take her to River Park and trek up to that rock."

"Not a bad idea," said Henry.

"Just as long as she doesn't get the wrong impression." Jason wiggled his eyebrows, and Henry snatched the ball away from him. Some of the parks around town were known for being secluded make-out spots. Cate would be less than appreciative of Henry appearing to push things too far right off the bat.

"I'll make sure we go when it's still light out." He snapped his fingers. "And I'll borrow a camera. We can get some photos of the view and develop them together."

"Ooh!" Frank clasped his hands against his cheek and fluttered his eyelashes, mocking. "So romantic!"

Henry threw the rubber band ball at his roommate.

"Seriously, man." Jason caught the ball after it ricocheted off Frank's head and the cinder block wall. "She's gonna love it. You'll get a second date for sure."

"Thanks, J. I hope you're right."

* * *

By Friday afternoon, Henry had purchased a roll of film and bummed a camera off the newspaper's photography editor. His excuse of needing it for practice was not entirely dishonest. He loaded up a box in the cafeteria with slices of bread, lunchmeat, fruits and veggies, and cookies. Only three cookies would fit inside, so he planned to give Cate the extra one. Cate always seemed to drink water when they ate lunch together, but he filled a cup with lemonade since it was a special occasion. He loaded everything into Jason's van and parked as close to Cate's dorm as he could manage.

His watch showed he was running a few minutes late, and Cate was perched on a sofa in the lobby when he arrived. Right away, he realized he'd made a mistake. He hadn't told Cate what to wear.

"You look amazing." It was true. She wore a long, floral dress and a hat with a bright flower made from buttons. She even smelled wonderful.

She beamed back at him. "Thanks."

"The only problem is ... I forgot to tell you—because I wanted it to be a surprise." The words rushed from his mouth in a jumble, probably as unclear to her as they sounded to him.

Her face fell. "What's wrong?"

"Nothing's wrong. But I thought we could go on a hike. I packed a picnic for us."

Cate lifted her dress to show some clunky brown boots. "I should be all right. As long as it's not too far. Or too muddy."

Relief washed over him. "Okay. Sorry I didn't dress up more."

"That's all right." She smiled back at him.

They walked out to the van and drove to the park in near silence. Henry needed to concentrate to not get lost. And Cate seemed to be inside her head more than usual. She stared out the window and fidgeted with her dress.

"It was nice of Jason to lend you his car."

"Mm-hmm." Henry checked for traffic as he turned. He hadn't driven since their trip to Shady Springs, and he'd never driven in this town before. At least he was driving a familiar car. He'd been behind the wheel of that van more times than he could count.

Henry drove farther and farther from campus, through residential areas and country roads. After about twenty minutes, they arrived at the park, and the tension left Henry's shoulders. He grinned. Even if he never found his way back to campus, he could die happy.

He raced around to the other side of the car, but Cate opened her own door before he could. No matter. He pulled the boxes of food out from the back and held out his elbow for her to take. By some miracle, she slipped her hand into the crook of his arm. His chest swelled.

They found a relatively flat space beneath a tree and spread out Frank's old blanket. The cookies had mostly survived the trip. Henry placed the unbroken ones closer to Cate. They put together sandwiches of turkey and ham and cheese. He'd even remembered to bring mustard and mayo. Henry held out a mayonnaise packet to Cate. "Want some?"

"Ugh, no." She shook her head vehemently.

"Not a fan?"

"Mayonnaise looks like the textbook pictures of clogged arteries. Or like fatty deposits. That stuff is nasty."

Henry chuckled. "Isn't it just eggs and vinegar?"

She shuddered. "Don't care."

He held up his hands in defeat. "Okay, okay. No mayo for you." He tilted his head and stared at her. The new discovery made him want to know everything about her. "What else don't you like?"

Cate chewed thoughtfully. "I don't like Swiss cheese or sweet pickles." She licked some mustard off her finger. "What about you?"

"I pretty much eat everything. However, I haven't had a wide variety of foods. I basically grew up on TV dinners." Henry hadn't meant to bring up his childhood or his family. He waited to see if Cate was thrown off.

"Really? My mom cooked every night growing up. It was basically a rule at our house that you had to be home for dinner."

Henry pressed a little further. He would reveal a little about his parents, but not too much. "If my dad's home, then Mom will make something nice. But when it's just the two of us, she makes whatever is as easy as possible."

"Does your dad work a lot?"

"Yes. He's a truck driver, so he's gone for long stretches."

Cate nodded. Henry figured she understood, to some degree, how relieved he must be when his dad was away. "So, it was just you and your mom a lot."

"Mm-hmm." How much should he tell her? Would she brush him off again? Or would she run away? He had a burning desire to learn everything about Cate, and he wondered if she felt the same way.

"Did you bring any napkins?" Cate swiped at the corner of her mouth with her thumb.

He groaned. "I'm sorry. I knew I was going to forget something."

"That's okay. I'll just ..." She brushed off her hands over the grass and winked at him.

"What about your family? What are your parents like?"

She smiled before answering. "My parents are very nice. My mom stays at home, and my dad is a dentist. He's also an elder at our church."

"Do you have any siblings?"

"One sister. She's a couple years younger than me." She twisted her mouth to the side and appeared to be assessing him. "They'll be coming to visit in a few weeks if you want to meet them."

"Are you afraid of introducing me to your parents?" He was only half-teasing. She seemed genuinely apprehensive.

"No, not at all." She rolled her eyes. "They can be a little embarrassing at times. I never know what they'll say."

Henry snorted. "Yeah, I'm sure I've got you beat."

Her cheeks turned red. "Sorry. I wasn't thinking." She took a bite of a cookie and looked away toward the trees.

"It's fine, Cate." He added the rest quietly. "I know you don't want to talk about it."

She looked up at him again. "It's not that I don't want to talk about it. I just don't want you to feel like you have to." She fiddled with a weed on the ground, wrapping it around her finger. "I don't care about all that, Henry."

"Really?"

"Yeah. I just like you for who you are. How your parents are doesn't matter to me."

Relief washed over Henry. He grinned at Cate, happy she still wanted to be with him after seeing his dad. That day, he'd been certain his chances with Cate were over. He'd more or less resigned himself to the fact he could never be with her. But now? There was hope.

They packed away the blanket in the van and searched for the trailhead. Henry pulled the camera out of its case. He'd already loaded the film inside and fiddled with the settings. Accounting for the evening light, he adjusted the aperture and shutter speed. They still had another hour or so until sunset, which Henry hoped would be plenty of time for their hike.

Cate was a trooper. She trudged along beside Henry, holding her dress high enough to stay out of the mud as their hike stretched on and on.

"You all right?"

She huffed a little. "Sure."

He couldn't help but notice the difference between their scavenger hunt and this trek through the woods. On Monday, Cate's competitive spirit had propelled her forward. Today,

Henry's eagerness to capture a stunning vista on film was what pushed them along.

"Sorry. I didn't realize how long the trail was. I'm sure we're almost there."

Cate gave a grimace that she must have meant to be a smile.

At last, they broke through the trees and came upon a small canyon. Henry grinned. It had been well worth the wait. Cate gave an appreciative nod and then plopped down on a large rock.

Henry crouched down. He steadied his elbows with his knees and clicked away happily. He didn't have much film, but he planned to use it all tonight. After snapping half a dozen shots, Henry turned to Cate.

"No, don't pose. Keep looking into the distance like that." Henry adjusted the focus until it was perfect. *Click.* He circled around to get a better angle.

"What are you doing?"

"I need more practice with portraits." *Click.*

She turned on him, a smirk on her face. *Click.*

Cate laughed and swatted at the camera. Henry almost missed the shot, but he captured her smile just in time. *Click.*

He sat down next to her on the rock. "Thanks for humoring me."

A cool breeze blew through the trees. Cate shivered.

"Here." Henry shrugged out of his denim jacket and offered it to her.

"Thanks." She pulled it over her shoulders and gave a little sigh as the shivers ceased. Henry swelled a little with pride at the sight of her wearing his jacket. It was like a scene from a movie.

"I don't know why you're taking pictures of me when you have this gorgeous view." Cate swept her arms out over the cliffscape, the rainbow of leaves, the far-off river.

Henry turned to her and waited until she met his gaze. "Catherine Hodges, you are more beautiful than any landscape."

Her mouth hung open, and she stared at him for one

heartbeat. Then she snapped her lips shut and quickly stood. "We'd better head out before it gets dark."

"Of course." Henry brushed the dirt off his pants.

The tension was thick as they walked together. Henry regretted embarrassing Cate, but he wouldn't take back what he said for the world. He meant every word.

Henry knew just how to get Cate talking again. "Tell me about your science classes. Didn't you have a test last week?"

Groaning, she launched into a monologue about her grades and her classes, upcoming exams, and papers to write. The walk back to the car took half as long as the hike out. Before he knew it, the van was within sight. Henry made a point to walk fast enough to open Cate's door for her.

She twisted her lips in an amused expression. "Thanks, Henry."

Praying he could find his way back to campus without incident, Henry started the car and backed out of his parking spot.

"I had a great time today."

Henry risked a glance over to Cate. "Me, too, but the night's not quite over yet."

"Oh?"

He smiled to himself. "Just wait."

25

OCTOBER, FRESHMAN YEAR

*O*n the way back, Cate only had to help him out once or twice with directions. Somehow, they ended up at Halloway without getting completely turned around. Henry parked behind the business building and turned off the car. This time, Cate waited so he could get to her door first.

"Thank you." She stepped out lightly, still wearing his jacket.

"It's just this way." Henry directed her to the Student Center. "Patrick assured me no one else would be here since the paper just went out this morning."

The side door was unlocked, and Henry showed Cate up the stairs and across a dim hallway.

"Who's Patrick?"

"My photography editor." He rubbed the back of his neck. "Technically, you're supposed to only use the darkroom for official paper business. But Patrick agreed to let me use it for practice since I have experience developing pictures."

"You do?" Cate raised her eyebrows.

He shrugged. "Sure. I used the darkroom in high school all the time."

"Shady Springs High has a darkroom?"

He pushed her shoulder lightly. "We have to have somewhere to develop pictures of all our livestock for the auctions, you know."

"Seriously?"

"No. I mean, probably." He laughed. "I always just used it for school projects. But I wouldn't be surprised if there were some kids who used it for their Future Farmers of America stuff."

"Well, how about you show me what you've got, Mullins."

Henry grinned and pushed the door open. The familiar tangy scent of chemicals wafted through the air. "Do you want to help me?" He turned to her, eyebrows raised.

She gave a half smile. "Sure."

Cate's passion for learning was one of the things he loved about her.

Woah.

Henry turned back to the camera and pretended to concentrate deeply as he let that thought penetrate. He was falling in love with Cate. There was no way he could let her know that—not if he ever wanted a second date.

"We have to load the film in the dark." In one hand, he held the developing tank. In the other, he clutched the camera. "Can you turn off the lights for me?"

"Okay." *Click.*

Cate's breathing reverberated in the quiet room. "How long does this usually take?"

"You scared?" Recalling years of muscle memory, he slid the film into place, securing it in the tank.

"It is a little creepy." Her voice barely rose above a whisper. "You almost done?"

Henry crept to the place where he thought Cate was standing. "Yes."

She let out a yelp. *Click.* The overhead lights flashed back on.

"Ouch." Henry squinted, his eyes protesting the sudden brightness.

"Serves you right for scaring me like that."

"The whole process takes about thirty minutes." He measured the first chemistry and preset his timer, turning it on as soon as the developer touched the film. Cate had questions about everything, and he was happy to share what he knew. He showed her how to agitate the film and explained the purpose of each liquid he poured into the tank.

Few things in life came easily to Henry, but he loved everything about photography. A bubble of pride swelled in him as he watched Cate's eye light up with interest.

When the last timer rang, Henry opened the tank. "Now we can take a look at the negatives." He held out the strip for Cate to examine. "What do you think?"

Cate squinted at the tiny images until a slow grin spread over her face. "I think you're an amazing photographer." She tilted her head and pointed at the shot he'd snapped of her. "I look happy."

"Are you? Happy?" His stomach twisted in knots. He wasn't usually this blunt with anyone. Something about Cate made him brave—and a little bit stupid. Gently, he attached the negatives to a clothesline on the wall.

"Very." Her voice was breathy.

His heart pounded.

"Cate?" He reached out to tuck a strand of hair behind her ear, his thumb lingering on her cheek far longer than he intended. Something like a magnetic force pulled her to him.

She took a step closer. "Henry?"

"May I?" He searched her face. More than anything, he wanted to kiss her.

"Yes," she whispered, and closed the space between them.

Henry shut his eyes and took it all in. The feel of Cate's soft lips on his, the smell of her vanilla shampoo, the sound of her breathing, the pulsing of his heart.

Pulling back, he gazed into her eyes. Henry was falling in love with Cate. He knew it with absolute certainty.

He kissed her again, with more urgency and more passion.

Cate pulled away next and grinned up at him. "Should we be kissing in the *Talon* darkroom?"

"Definitely not." He squeezed her shoulders and gave her one more peck on the lips. "Right."

Pointing to the film drying on the clothesline, Cate asked "Don't I get my picture? As a memento?" She pouted a little, and the sight tempted Henry to plant another kiss on her lips.

Smiling, he winked. "Not until those dry and I can make prints. But for now, I need to clean up."

Henry's gaze flitted over to Cate every few seconds as he returned the bottles and tank to their proper places. His lips buzzed with the memory of her kiss. His heart beat erratically, overwhelmed by the closeness of her.

"All done." He made a show of dusting off his hands, then motioned to the door.

Cate sighed as she looked at him. "I've never realized this about you."

"What?" He let his fingers run up and down her arm.

Taking his hand, she pulled his focus back to her face. "You see so much, Henry." She gestured to his photos. "You see me more than I knew."

He smirked. "Now you see me, too, I guess."

She laughed. "I guess so."

"May I walk you over to your dorm?"

Henry laced his fingers through hers. They still had time before the night was over, and he wanted to savor every minute.

The night air was cool as they stepped out of the Student Center and toward the front lawn.

"Want to swing?" A white swing sat empty beside the path. He hopped in and patted the seat.

Giving in, Cate rolled her eyes and sat down. "This is two swings now."

Henry smiled to himself as he kicked out his feet. She was counting.

"Cate, I'd like to go on another date. I have to work the next two days, but maybe next weekend?"

The quiet lasted a long while, but Henry didn't mind waiting.

"Okay."

He breathed a sigh of relief. "Great."

They swung a bit more.

Henry cleared his throat. "I'd like something else too."

"What's that?" She tapped her feet on the ground, stopping the swing.

"I'd like to go out again the next week, and the week after that." He took her face in his hands. "Please, Cate?"

"You know how I feel about relationships in college." She shook her head, and Henry's hands fell.

"I promise I won't get in the way."

With a deep sigh, Cate began to swing again.

"I like you, Henry, I really do. But let's just take it one date at a time."

His heart sank, but he wasn't beaten yet. While Cate wasn't ready to commit to anything, he knew he wasn't in competition with anyone else. As long as he could get her to keep saying *yes* to dates week after week, he just might wear her down.

Henry stood and held out his hand. "Let's get you back home."

They walked together in silence, their hands clasped. Henry swung his arms.

Sure, he couldn't tell her yet that he loved her. And he couldn't call her his girlfriend. But Henry had kissed Cate Hodges that night, and nothing was going to keep him down.

26

PRESENT DAY

"Are you at work right now?"

"Yes, but I only have a few more minutes of paperwork." Catherine pulled the phone away from her face to double-check the caller ID. Why would Henry be calling?

It had been almost a week since they'd last spoken, and she'd replayed their conversation in her head a million times. *I was too harsh with him. Maybe I'll get the chance to apologize now.* Some time and distance had tempered her anger. Henry had not actually been drinking. As far as she could tell, he'd been living right for years now and was committed to sobriety.

"Okay, let me know when you leave." The call went dead.

How strange. Catherine wrapped up the files she was working on and said good night to the RN. "I'll see you tomorrow, Shari. Let me know what you hear about your mother."

Shari grimaced and patted Catherine on the arm. "Thank you. We should get the test results back next week."

Catherine smiled at her coworker. "I'll be praying for you." And she really meant it. Whether she was praying for Shari's mom's biopsy or a man's heart murmur, the day always went smoother when she made a point to pray for her patients and coworkers.

Shari squeezed her arm. "Thank you. I'll see you later, hon."

"Have a good night."

Catherine clicked on her recent calls and dialed Henry's number on her way downstairs. "I'm headed out to my car. What's up, Henry?"

"I'm in the lobby. Where can I meet you?"

"What? Why are you here?" In all her years in Kansas City, Henry had never once visited her.

"I'll explain it all in a minute."

She gave him directions to the spot where she'd parked her car. A sense of doom wrapped around her chest. *What's going on?*

Catherine had just placed her handbag inside her car when she heard footsteps beside her. Henry was approaching, and he wasn't alone. A young man carried a manilla envelope beside him.

She gave what she hoped was a friendly smile, although her stomach was churning.

"Are you Catherine Mullins?"

"Yes." It came out more like a question than a statement. She looked back and forth between Henry and the strange man.

He handed the envelope to her. "You've been served."

Taking the envelope from him, Catherine's knees weakened. She held onto the side of the sedan for support. "Henry?"

Henry turned to the young man. "Thank you. That's all."

The man nodded once and walked away.

Henry's face was grim, but he didn't look apologetic or sympathetic. "I wanted to be here to tell you in person. I would have given the documents to you myself, but the lawyer said it had to be either by certified mail or a 'process server.'" He used air quotes and rolled his eyes as he said it.

"I don't understand." Catherine sat in the front seat of her car.

"I thought a lot about what you said the other night. After the engagement party." Henry stepped closer. He wrung his hands. "If you are really finished with us, with this ..." He gestured between them. "Then it's time to make it official."

She couldn't speak.

"I guess I thought you'd be happy. Or at least relieved. We're finally getting a divorce."

A divorce.

It wasn't like she'd never wanted one. Back when Henry first left, she'd even made an appointment with a lawyer. But then she found out how expensive it would be. Add to that the possibility of going to court and dragging Maddy through the whole process, and Catherine had decided there was no real rush.

But after over a decade of separation, Catherine had pushed a divorce to the back of her mind, almost out of the picture. She'd never entertained the idea of getting remarried.

"Why now, Henry? I'm not looking to get married again. I haven't even been on a date."

"Maybe not, but you deserve to. I was the one who left. I was the one to commit adultery. You shouldn't have to live alone forever for my sake."

A sudden thought occurred to her. "Are you dating someone?"

"No! That's not it at all." Henry stepped back, shaking his head vigorously, and Catherine believed him. He ran his fingers through his hair. Still thick after all these years. "I told you. If you've really decided that there's no chance of us ever getting back together—"

Catherine frowned, and Henry must have taken it as a confirmation.

"Then this is the next logical step. We need to get a legal divorce."

"What will this do to your business?"

"Nothing, I don't think. I haven't really considered that."

She was surprised his studio wasn't the first thing on his mind. "Isn't that photography business your whole life now?"

"No, it's not. You and Maddy have always been the most important thing to me. That's why I'm trying to set you free." He sighed. "This is for your own good, Catherine."

He hardly ever used her full name, and it shook her. Catherine knew what Henry was saying made sense. Logically. So why could she not wrap her heart around it? Why did she feel as though her whole world had fallen out from underneath her?

"There's no rush." His voice was softer. "Look over everything and make sure it looks good. We don't have shared assets anymore. Not since you sold the house. There's no money to divide up. We're just making something official that's already been true for a long time."

He was right. She knew he was right.

Catherine cleared her throat. "Thank you, Henry." She looked up. "And thank you for delivering these in person. I appreciate it."

In different times, she might have asked where he was staying or if he had dinner plans. But she didn't want to know. All she could think to do was wave goodbye and close her car door. She checked to make sure the way was clear and drove home, the distance between her and Henry growing with every mile.

* * *

"I'm sorry, what, now?" Madeleine's mouth hung open. "You and Dad aren't divorced?"

Catherine grimaced. She wiped the condensation off her sweet tea glass on the side table, delaying eye contact. She hated feeling like she'd been keeping secrets from Maddy, and these were some whoppers. First, that she and Henry were still married. And second, that he'd served divorce papers a few days ago. Catherine wanted to come to terms with the news herself before telling Maddy and Clara in person. Her quick weekend trip to Shady Springs seemed like the perfect time.

Madeleine turned to Clara, beside her in the front flower bed. "Did you know about this?"

Clara made a face. "It's been so long, I'd forgotten they never made it official." She wiped her hands on her pants and reached for another daffodil bulb. "So, you're finally getting a divorce. It must feel good to put that chapter to a close."

"It should." She'd meant the words to come out more confidently, but they betrayed her inner turmoil.

"But ...?" Clara waited, eyebrows raised.

"But it feels all wrong. Like he's rejecting me and leaving me all over again." She frowned and looked at her feet under the porch swing. What did she expect after speaking to Henry the way she did at the engagement party? She couldn't have it both ways. Either she risked betrayal and pursued a relationship with Henry, or she protected her heart and officially ended their marriage. If only the decision were that simple.

"Oh, honey." Clara stood to join her sister. "Don't look at it that way. You said, didn't you, that he still loves you? He's trying to do the right thing."

"I know, I know." Catherine furrowed her brow. She leaned into her sister's shoulder as Clara joined her on the seat.

Madeleine returned to the chore at hand of placing bulbs, fat end down, into the holes Clara had dug. In the early spring, the front yard would be covered with daffodils. Catherine was of the mindset that there were already plenty of bulbs scattered all over the property, but Clara insisted she needed more flowers surrounding her trees and mailbox.

"What about that time we went to the big office and you and Dad signed some papers?" Madeleine pursed her lips in thought.

"There was a fish tank. And a nice lady gave me some hard candy."

Catherine reached into the dark corners of her mind for a forgotten memory. "Do you mean the realtor's office? When we sold the house?"

"Oh, that must have been it." Maddy's frown deepened. "So, you guys are actually married?"

"Legally, yes." Catherine's gaze met Maddy's. "But in every other way, our marriage ended eleven years ago. You had to go through all the heartbreak just as if we *had* gotten a divorce."

Pain was written across Maddy's features. This all must come as a huge shock to her.

The bulbs were all planted, and Madeleine began patting the ground gently. "What now, then? Are you going to end things for good?"

Catherine cleared her throat. "That seems best." She nodded and pushed the swing lightly. Now that she knew where Henry stood, she needed to move forward with her life.

Clara bit her lip and stared out over the lawn. "Not if neither of you want it."

"What do you mean?" The swing halted, Catherine's feet planted firmly on the porch floor.

"You're obviously struggling with the idea of getting a divorce. And we all know Henry is still in love with you. So …" Clara twisted her lips in a small smile. "Maybe you should stay married."

Madeleine looked at her mother, her brow furrowed and her mouth forming a perfect *O*, as though seeing her for the first time. "Mom, are you in love with Dad?"

Catherine gasped quietly. "I—I shouldn't be talking to you about these things. I'm not being a good mother." Her eyes stung as she picked up her glass from the table and stood to leave. "I'll clean up the dishes and get started on supper."

Inside the house, Catherine placed the glass on the counter

and pressed her palm to her face. She leaned against the kitchen wall, far from Maddy's probing gaze. It was embarrassing enough to be rejected by Henry. Again.

But to share her heartbreak and humiliation with her sister and daughter was more than she could bear. Catherine had honestly thought, for a moment, that maybe she could have love again. Maybe she could open her heart to a perfectly imperfect love and find some happiness with Henry.

And then her dreams had all come crashing down. Again.

A life with Henry wasn't meant to be. She knew that now. So, she would do what she always did when life threw her a curve. She would pick up the pieces of her shattered dreams and work harder to build what she could out of what was left.

Catherine could count on God, on her sister, and on her daughter. She could not count on Henry anymore. Or even herself.

27

FEBRUARY, FRESHMAN YEAR

Henry ran his finger along Cate's cheek. He could stay in this moment with her forever.

They'd had a mild winter with no threats of snow or even ice. It was as if the warmth in Henry's heart had thawed the whole state. Even in February, the weather was nice enough to picnic on the front lawn for lunch. And that's just what Henry and Cate did as often as they could. Although Cate had become more and more busy with club activities, and Henry had picked up extra hours at work to save for a car, they were usually able to meet for the occasional meal and at Wednesday Bible study at the Coopers' house.

After an excruciating winter break at home in Shady Springs, Henry had made plans to go on a Spring Break mission trip to New Mexico with Cate.

Cate smiled back at him. "Have you turned in your final payment for the trip?"

Henry sat straight. "Oh, I forgot to tell you. Someone from church made an anonymous donation."

"Really?"

He still fizzed with excitement when he thought about it. "One of the elders called me last night. They sent the check to the school, so I'm good to go."

"That's wonderful!"

Raising money for the trip had been incredibly difficult. Not because people didn't want to give him money, but because he didn't want to ask. Then Cate had helped him to see things in a different light.

"You're providing them with an opportunity to give and serve the Lord." She'd told him many times. So many, that he was finally able to believe it.

"Now we just have to make it to March eighth." It couldn't come fast enough.

Tracy walked up the path and plopped down beside Cate. She took a sip of a soda she carried. "Are you two going to Hadie Sawkins week?"

Henry's brow furrowed as he looked across the blanket at Tracy. "What's that?"

"It's like Sadie Hawkins week, but backward. The guys ask the girls out."

"So, it's just like every other day."

Tracy huffed at him. "Except they're going to have activities. All leading up to Valentine's Day. A movie night, and a concert, and Twister in the student center."

Henry wiggled his eyebrows at Cate. "Sounds scandalous. Wanna go?"

Cate laughed. "Sure, Henry. As long as I don't have too much homework."

It was another semester and another round of Honors classes. But this time they were taking Old Testament, which was proving to be much more difficult. With a harder professor too. Dr. Grieburn, or Greybeard, as they referred to him.

"We'll have a reading assignment for Greybeard. But I think

I could pencil you in for an hour or two." He smirked and squeezed Cate's hand. "But not tonight—I've got work."

"We have a meeting tonight, anyway." Cate gestured to Tracy with her fork.

Tracy gave them both a pointed look. She'd been giving them a hard time about excluding her from conversations lately. "I'm going with Frank, if anyone cares."

Henry did a double take. "Pardon?"

Tracy stared him down and enunciated her words slowly. "Frank Thomas asked me out, and I said yes."

Henry looked from Tracy to Cate, hoping for backup from his girlfriend. Or whatever she was. "Isn't it a little soon? You and Jason just broke up."

Tracy rolled her eyes. "Henry, we broke up months ago. Last semester."

"So, you're going out with my roommate? He and Jason are friends, you know." Barely, but still. First, his best friend, and now his roommate? Didn't she know any other guys?

Tracy waved her arms out. "Look around. Everyone here is friends." She sighed and her expression softened. "Besides, I heard Jason has already gone on two dates with Molly Perkins."

Henry had heard that too. From Jason.

Cate cut in. "Frank is a nice guy. I'm sure you'll have fun." Her look to Henry clearly said she'd like him to change the subject.

"Should we head out?" It was about time for Henry's next class.

"Oh, all right." Cate held out a hand to Henry.

Henry pulled Cate up first and then Tracy. They shook out the blanket Henry had indefinitely borrowed from Frank and dusted off their pants. Tracy busied herself with something in her purse while Henry stole a brief kiss from Cate. He tugged on one of her curls. "See you later?"

His stomach fluttered when she looked back into his eyes. "Later, Henry."

* * *

"You've got to do something more than just take her to the Student Center for Valentine's Day." Jason leaned against the counter Henry was wiping down with a cloth.

"I know, but I don't have the cash for anything big. Christmas almost broke me." Henry nudged Jason's elbow away so he could finish cleaning. "The whole reason I want a car is to take Cate around. And the whole reason I can't afford a car is because I want to take Cate around."

"Hmm."

"Hey, follow me." Henry stepped toward the tables to clean off trash and spilled food.

"It seems like you're working all the time now."

"And you're either away at games or practice all the time." Henry knew Jason couldn't help being busy. But he missed his friend.

"I'm here now, aren't I, Cinder-fella?"

Henry shot him a teasing glare. It was pretty cool of Jason to hang out with him while he scrubbed tables and swept floors in the cafeteria. It was not cool of Jason to call Henry "Cinderfella," but he'd take what he could get.

"What are you doing with Molly for Valentine's Day?" Maybe his friend would have some ideas he could steal.

"Dinner and flowers. Can't go wrong with a classic."

"Yeah. I wish I could do that for Cate."

"How much can you spare? Surely you have *something*."

"I've got ten bucks cash, but I was going to use that as gas money for when we go back to Shady Springs next weekend."

Jason held up a finger. "Number one, you don't have to pay

me. Number two, you have the wrong date. It's not next weekend."

Henry winced. "I've got to remember to add that to my calendar."

Jason kept going. "And number three, you don't have to come home with me."

"You know your mom doesn't want you driving alone."

Jason shrugged and waved away his concerns.

"Besides," Henry said. "It's no trouble at all, especially if I get to crash at your place." If Henry had his way, he'd spend as little time as possible at home. But Mrs. Jones had practically begged Henry to ride with Jason so he'd have some company when he drove to Shady Springs for his parents' twenty-fifth anniversary.

"So, back to you and your problems." Jason tossed a wad of paper napkins into a trashcan. It was a beautiful shot, of course. The guy had skills. "Molly works in the education workroom. You can grab some construction paper, cut out some hearts and write her a poem. It'll be half the price of a card and twice as many brownie points."

Henry frowned. "But I can't write poetry."

Jason rolled his eyes. "Then copy down some Shakespeare or something. Then buy her some flowers with what you've got left."

"Chocolate. I think she'd like chocolate more."

"Fine, chocolate."

Henry tapped his finger over his mouth. "Okay. I like it."

"Hey, Mullins!"

Henry turned to see his supervisor, Dana, standing with her hands over her hips.

"Stop yacking and get back to work."

"See ya later." Jason waved and grabbed a couple of cookies off the tray on his way out the door.

Cate deserved a fancy dinner and a massive bouquet of flowers. If he ever graduated from college and owned his own business, then someday he'd have that kind of cash. The trick was getting Cate to stick with him that long.

Thank goodness for friends like Jason. Henry didn't know what he would do without him.

28

FEBRUARY, FRESHMAN YEAR

"Are you sure you're okay going without me?" Henry paced the floor of Jason's dorm room.

"Yes, a thousand times, yes." Jason gripped him by the shoulders, forcing him to be still. "It's only three hours. I'll be fine."

Henry rubbed the back of his neck. "Your mom really wanted me to come with you."

"My mom would agree with me that you'd better jump on this chance to take Cate to her spring formal."

Henry couldn't help but smile at the anticipation of an evening spent with Cate. He'd be in a suit and tie. She'd be in a beautiful dress. He was fuzzy on the rest of the details, but he knew it would be the closest he'd get to a nice date this side of graduation.

"I can't believe I got my dates mixed up." He'd been working extra hard to stay on top of his schedule. But with work and class assignments and everything else, he'd written Cate's club formal down on the wrong weekend. He'd only realized his mistake that morning when Cate reminded him to pick her up at five-thirty.

"It happens to the best of us." Jason effortlessly pulled a duffle down from the top shelf of his closet. "I'll tell Mom you'll make it up to her somehow. Dad knows I'll be fine, of course."

"Thanks, J." Henry rested on Raymond's bed while Jason dumped his hamper of dirty clothes into the bag. "Don't forget nice clothes for the anniversary dinner."

"I've got church clothes in there, I'm sure." But Jason reached for a tie and some black socks and shoes. He threw those in with the clothes and then stepped into the adjoining bathroom.

"By the way, thanks for the advice for Valentine's Day. Cate loved the card I made. Oh, and tell Molly I said thanks for the help."

"Oh, um. I probably shouldn't."

"Why not?"

"Things with Molly have cooled off a little."

Henry sat up straight. "What happened?"

Jason walked out of the bathroom carrying a brown bag, which he threw on the growing pile. "It's hard to explain." He shoved the mass down and pulled on the duffle's zipper. "You know how you and Cate seem perfect for each other?"

"You should tell *her* that." After about six months of dating exclusively, Cate still refused to commit to anything serious or call herself Henry's girlfriend.

"She'll come around. You guys are the real deal."

"So, what does this have to do with Molly?"

Jason faced him and grimaced. "Listen, you have to promise not to tell Raymond or any of the other guys."

"Of course." Now his interest was piqued.

"She wanted …" His face turned a bright shade of red. "She wanted to do some stuff that I didn't think we should do yet. You know … physically."

Henry's eyebrows shot up. "Wow. She seemed so nice."

"She is nice. She's very nice."

"Don't worry, I'm not going to go around sullying Molly's reputation."

"I know." But Jason looked relieved. He turned back to the duffle bag. "Molly called me a prude. I think she was embarrassed, you know? Like she felt rejected because I didn't want that. I mean, I do *want* it, it's just—"

"Not yet."

Jason sat on the bag and pulled the zipper the rest of the way closed. "It's important to me, to wait until marriage. I want to find a girl who's even more committed to Jesus than she is to me, and I just haven't found her yet."

"What about Tracy?"

Jason shrugged. "Tracy's still a little immature. But maybe in a couple years ..." His gaze roamed out the window then returned to Henry suddenly. "You know what? You can tell Raymond. I want him to know how I feel about spiritual stuff. Just, leave out Molly's name maybe."

"I'm sure they know how you feel. You guys have spent all that time together in Bible study and on the court."

"I hope so." Jason furrowed his brow. "You know, though, don't you?"

"Yes, Jason." Henry smiled at his best friend. "I know how you feel about Jesus."

Jason gave a short nod. "Cool." He loaded the bag on his shoulder. "Have fun tonight." He pointed a finger at Henry and gave him a stern look. "But not too much fun."

Henry raised his hands in surrender as he followed Jason out of the room. "Not too much, I promise." He chuckled. "Drive safe, J."

"Thanks, buddy."

* * *

Cate stepped in the dorm lobby and Henry's jaw dropped. "Wow."

She wore a dress with long sleeves made of lace and some kind of shiny fabric. Her curls were pinned up in a fancy hairstyle that showed off her face. The dress and Cate's smile glowed.

The pale pink color of her gown was so light, it almost looked white. What might Cate look like on her wedding day in a beautiful lace dress? And what lucky guy would get to meet her at the end of her walk down the aisle? Just like he waited for her on that night?

"You look amazing." Henry forced himself to snap out of his admiring reverie.

"You look pretty great yourself." Cate slipped her hand into his. She looked over her shoulder to where Tracy walked down the hall. "Is Frank outside?"

"Yes, he's got the car running."

"Tracy, you look very nice." Henry held the door open for the two girls.

Tracy smoothed her hair a bit. "Thanks, Henry. You're too sweet." She climbed in the passenger side of Frank's car.

Henry held open the door for Cate and ran around to join her in the back. "We're all here and ready to go."

"Anyone have a problem with some a cappella music?" Frank shot a hopeful look over his shoulder.

"What else have you got?" Tracy rifled through the cassette tapes sliding around the floorboard.

They were able to agree on some old rock tunes and settled in for the drive east on the interstate.

The dinner took place at a country club twenty minutes away. Daffodils were blooming in the flower beds, and the trees were showing buds. Spring break and a whole week with Cate was just around the corner.

Henry was careful to cut his steak into small bites and watch the people around him to figure out which fork to use. He was not used to rubbing shoulders with the country club set. Some of his classmates had been around wealth their whole lives and were comfortable in this world. The light clinking of silver against china around him and the soft piano music in the background reminded Henry that he was far from home.

Cate, with her soft curls and dress the color of a flower blossom, fit in seamlessly. Henry longed for a place in her life. He wanted to be her other half, to attach himself to her rising star. If only she would allow him, he'd try every day to give her all the things she wanted. Space to be herself, and a soft place to land at the end of the day.

Henry was content to watch and listen as Cate chatted happily with her club sisters. They regaled the table with stories of pledge week, most of which he'd heard a dozen times already. After supper, they sang their club songs and gave their dates handmade gifts.

Henry hadn't been expecting to receive anything. He was still learning all of Cate's club traditions.

"Open it up." Cate handed him a wrapped box.

"What is this?" He didn't wait for an answer before slipping his finger through the paper.

A sense of déjà vu hit him as he opened the cardboard box. He pulled out wad after wad of pink tissue paper. There was a pink card with cookies and candies.

"Look on the outside."

The box was addressed to Catherine Hodges.

"Is this your care package?"

"No, read the card."

He opened up the card and pulled it down again. "Am I going to get in trouble for reading this like last time?"

"No, goofball. Just read it."

Dear Henry,

I know how much you like to open care packages, so I made

one just for you. It's a lot like that first box, the one that brought us together, but this one I'm gladly giving away.

These past few months have meant so much to me. You've taught me that traveling the journey of life with friends is much better than going it alone.

So, here's what I want to ask. Will you go on a date with me this weekend? And next weekend? And the one after that? Will you be my boyfriend?

All my love,
Cate

Henry blinked twice. Did he read that right? Did she love him?

Henry didn't wait to ask, he just planted a kiss on her, right then and there. In front of all her friends and their dates. All of Kappa Rho could watch him. He didn't care.

"Thank you. I love it." But Henry hoped that in his eyes she could see what he really wanted to say. *I love you.* That would have to wait until they were alone.

"So, is that a *yes*?"

"Yes, Cate Hodges." He kissed her again, quickly.

Tracy giggled beside them. "Hey, you guys. Save it for the wedding."

Cate blushed, but Henry swelled with pride. Let them talk. Cate Hodges was his girlfriend.

29

FEBRUARY, FRESHMAN YEAR

Henry floated all the way home, across campus in Frank's car, into his dorm lobby.

But something inside of him burst when he saw his friend Leon at the front desk. His face was drawn, and his lips pinched together as he handed Henry a slip of paper. "Henry. I've got a message for you. Your mom wants you to call. She sounded worried."

It took a minute for the information to sink in. Why would his mom be calling? He stood, gaping, until Frank pushed him toward the door to the stairwell. "I'll make sure he calls her."

The phone only rang once before his mom picked up. He didn't even think about the long-distance charges they were building up.

"Hello?"

"Mom? What's going on?"

"Oh, Henry. Listen, I can't talk long. Your dad is home. But I wanted to let you know. It's Jason. He was in an accident this afternoon."

"What?" The walls and floor swam around him. Henry held on to the phone as he fell down to his bed.

"Honey ..." His mom took a breath. She hadn't called him that since he was little. "He didn't make it."

The phone slipped out of his fingers.

Someone, probably Frank, picked up the phone and said goodbye.

Henry's vision blurred. His body felt numb.

"No."

Henry blinked until the room returned.

Frank's arm slipped around his shoulders. "She said to tell you that the funeral will probably be next weekend."

Henry shook his head.

"Whose funeral, Henry? What happened?"

He felt like throwing up. He couldn't say the words. "J—"

"Not Jason, right?"

Henry shook his head before he realized what he was doing. "Jason." He nodded once, slowly.

"But how?"

"Car accident."

Frank squeezed him tighter. "I can't believe it. He was ... I just talked to him the other day. When was that? Last week in the cafeteria. He was ... I can't believe it." Frank slumped over, his head in his hands.

Henry slid down to the floor.

"We have to tell the girls." Frank paced the room. "Tracy and Cate will want to know."

Henry nodded but didn't get off the floor.

Frank's legs stopped, but he shook nervous energy from his hands. "We can't go over there right now. It's too late. But we can call their room. Do you know their room number?"

He thought he did, but he couldn't bring it to mind. He'd been there once or twice when they opened up the girls' dorms. He could see the room in his memory, but the numbers were fuzzy. Henry pointed to the shelf above his desk. "Directory."

Frank snapped his fingers. "Right, I'll just look it up." He pulled down the thin Freshman Directory and flipped through the pages. He held his finger on a picture of Cate. "Do you want to make the call?"

He shook his head. He couldn't even move his legs, let alone make a phone call.

Suddenly, he could move his legs and he needed to be sick. Henry ran to the toilet.

When he came back to the room, Frank was on the phone.

"Yes, I'll let you know when we find out ... Sure ... Well, I knew you would want to know ... Sure, that's a good idea." Frank looked at Henry and then back to the phone. "I'll ask him ... Okay, see you tomorrow."

Henry climbed under his covers.

"You okay?"

"Yeah. No. I don't know."

"Tracy thought we could all drive over to Shady Springs for the funeral. Do you think we could stay at your place?"

Henry shot up on his elbows. "No, that won't work. Not my place."

"Do you know of anyone else we could stay with? We can't exactly stay with Jason's family."

Of course not. They'd have enough going on without hosting extra guests.

"I'll find someone from church. I'll figure it out." All Henry wanted in that moment was to be left alone. He rolled over.

Frank nodded. "Sure. We'll figure something out."

Henry squeezed his eyes shut. *Jason is gone. Jason is gone. Jason is gone.*

Maybe his mom was mistaken. Maybe when he woke up in the morning, he'd find out it had all been a big misunderstanding.

"I'm going down to the lobby. I need to go for a walk or something." The door clicked shut as Frank left the room.

Henry curled his knees up against his stomach, not caring

about the permanent wrinkles he was allowing to take over his one good suit. He pushed back the wave of nausea sweeping over him again. A thought occurred to him. *It was supposed to be me. It should have been me.*

* * *

The next week blurred together into one hazy memory. Henry made it to class and ate the occasional meal, thanks to Frank, but he had no recollection of what his professors said or what food he'd eaten. He managed to ask Dana for time off work in the cafeteria. And he found a couple from the church in Shady Springs who would let Frank and the girls stay with them when they all came for the funeral.

Somehow, he made it to the visitation Friday night at the Wilson-Hopkins funeral home in Shady Springs. He hugged Dale and Nancy Jones wordlessly. Every time he opened his mouth to say something, whatever words he could think of rang hollow in his head. How could he possibly comfort them?

"Thank you for coming, Henry." Nancy squeezed his forearm. "You meant so much to him."

Henry nodded, pushing down the lump in his throat.

"You were a good friend to our boy." Dale clapped him on the back and cleared his throat.

He joined his friends in line. Cate pulled him tight and leaned her head against his shoulder.

"I'm sorry, Henry. I know this must be so hard for you."

His arms twitched involuntarily, jostling Cate's head. "Hey, let's get out of here."

"And go where?" Frank looked around.

The room was packed with people, most of whom Henry had known since he was in kindergarten. "I don't know." He only knew he couldn't face another conversation right then. He needed to get his feet moving. "Let's go to the park. It's just down the street."

Frank turned to the girls. Tracy shrugged and Cate gripped Henry's hand in hers. They pulled on their jackets and pushed through the crowd toward the doors outside.

On the way, Henry was stopped by no fewer than four people telling him how good it was to see him or how sorry they were about Jason. Henry didn't look up, just muttered a "thank you" to everyone.

At long last, the doors opened, and he gulped in a breath of fresh air. The crowd was gone, the tight wall of people left behind at the funeral home. But a buzz of nervous energy still built inside his chest. He walked faster and faster. Maybe if he walked fast enough, he could chase away the dread and panic simmering inside of him.

"Wait up!" Cate's feet slapped on the pavement behind him.

Henry slowed, but his blood pressure continued to rise.

Cate grabbed his hand. "Hey, there. Are you all right?"

Of course, he wasn't all right. His best friend was dead. Jason. The guy who'd practically adopted him into his family. Who brought him to Christ. Who taught Henry he could be more than his dad, or anyone, had ever thought he could be. Jason loved him when even Henry had thought of himself as nothing.

He waited to speak until they'd crossed onto the gravel of the playground. Then he slumped into one of the black swings. It let out a high-pitched squeal as the rusted metal chain strained with his weight. He pushed off of the ground and into the air.

Cate sat on the swing beside his. Frank and Tracy lingered on the sidewalk.

"It was supposed to be me. I should have been with him."

"What do you mean? We were at the dinner that night."

"I told Jason's parents I would ride home with him. I could've stopped the accident, or at least stopped Jason from getting killed."

"You could've stopped the drunk driver from crashing into him?" Cate raised one eyebrow, skeptical.

"Maybe I could have seen it before he did." Henry pushed himself higher and higher.

"Henry, if you'd been there, you and Jason would *both* be dead, and I'd be even more devastated than I already am. You can't know what might've happened."

"Then at least he wouldn't be alone." And at least Henry wouldn't be left behind.

"He's not alone. I know you don't believe that. And we'll all be together again someday. This wasn't the end for Jason—only the beginning of something new."

"But why would God take him away? Why not me?"

Cate halted and looked up at him, but Henry continued to push himself farther and farther away from the ground.

"It doesn't work like that. We all die someday."

"But he had so much more to give. He knew so much more about the Bible and about God. He led a Bible study. He was a better friend and a better person than I could ever be."

"Then why did he pick you for his best friend? If he was such a great guy, what does that say about you?"

Straightening his legs, Henry stopped pumping and thought about Cate's question. "Honestly, I never could figure that out."

Cate grabbed the chain of his swing. He spun out of control for a moment before meeting her. She pulled his shoulders toward hers.

"Henry, when I look at you, I see someone who is smart and sweet and passionate. You've never known your own worth, but I see it. And Jason saw it. If you can't love yourself right now, let me love you."

Henry covered her mouth with his. And for a moment, he was able to forget Jason and forget the restless, angry feeling growing inside of him. For just an instant, it was Henry and

Cate. But reality hit him, and he pulled away from her just as quickly.

"I can't." He needed space. From Cate and from his friends. From school. From himself. "I need to go home." He walked out of the park before Cate could protest. He called over his shoulder. "I'll see you guys tomorrow."

He could barely hear Cate call after him as he took off toward home.

30

FEBRUARY, FRESHMAN YEAR

Henry hadn't been to many funerals. He supposed that was a blessing. Jason's was nice, as far as those things went. There were a lot of people there. Brother Reed said some good things—at least that's what Frank said afterward.

"I think Jason would've liked it," Frank spoke softly. "A lot of people are going to miss him."

Henry nodded. He looked down at his tie. How ironic that he'd been wearing that very suit and tie the night Jason died. It was his nicest outfit, despite the lingering wrinkles, and he'd wanted to honor his friend. He just also happened to wear that suit to every nice event, including Cate's formal.

He couldn't get his mind around Jason's death. He'd seen the body. He heard the eulogy. But he still expected his best friend to come bursting in through the church doors. Wouldn't that be a great joke? Henry could picture him cracking up about how he'd fooled everyone.

Cate wrapped her arm around Henry's shoulder and leaned in close. The scent of vanilla should have comforted him, but it was almost cloying instead. He felt hot in the overcrowded auditorium.

"Let's head out." Henry stood, grabbing Cate's hand. He pulled her toward the exit in the corner, the one no one else had thought to use. He breathed deeply in the fresh air. It was almost cold outside, and the sky was overcast, but the breeze felt good.

"Are you all packed?"

"What?" His tone was harsher than he'd intended. He pulled his lips into a half-smile but knew it had fallen flat by the look on Cate's face.

She pointed toward the parking lot. "We've got Frank's car loaded up and ready to go. We can stay as long as you need, but Tracy and I wanted to be back for church in the morning. We volunteered to work in the nursery before ..." Before Jason died.

It wouldn't take long for Henry to pack. He'd only brought a few things and his laundry. But he didn't want to leave Shady Springs. How could he go back to class and work and have weekend dates with Cate? How could he pretend like everything was normal when his whole world had been shaken?

"I'm not going back."

Frank's expression was full of concern and pity. "But we only have one more week until spring break. Can't you stick it out for a few more days?"

"I can't. I don't even remember what happened last week. I'll call the school and ask if I can be excused. I'll make it all up when I get back."

"What about the mission trip?" Cate rubbed her thumb over his hand.

Henry jerked involuntarily. He'd forgotten their hands were linked. He muttered an apology but shoved his hands in his pockets. "Can you tell them I can't go?"

"But—" Cate stammered and shook her head. "You already paid for it. What about your anonymous benefactor? Won't they be disappointed?"

"Honestly? I'm pretty sure it was Mr. and Mrs. Jones who

wrote the check." Of all people, he was sure they'd understand. "Besides, Halloway can just put it toward someone else. That's why we funnel all the money through them anyway, right? Because college students are unpredictable. Life is unpredictable."

Cate bit her lip. "I was really looking forward to this trip. We need you for our team. Who will take your part in the skits? Or the puppet show for the kids?"

"I'm sure you'll find somebody who can do it better than I can."

Cate flung her hands in the air. "So that's it? You're going to stay here and ... do what exactly?"

Henry shrugged. He didn't have a clue. "I just know I can't go back. Not yet."

Tracy pulled her friend's hand. "Just let him stay, Cate. He'll be okay."

Her stare pierced him for a long while, then she nodded once. "We'll see you in two weeks then?"

"Yes." Henry gave her a small smile. "I'm sorry."

Cate sighed and crossed the space between them. She gave him a soft kiss, cupping his chin in her hands. "I love you."

She held his gaze a moment, waiting. Henry opened his mouth, expecting to say it back. He'd been waiting so long to tell Cate he loved her and to hear it in return. But all he said was, "I'll see you in two weeks."

Something in Cate's eyes went cold as if a small part of her was now locked away. She gave him a tight-lipped smile and ducked into the back of Frank's car.

Frank embraced him in a brief but firm hug. "You need a ride home?"

"No, I'll walk. But thanks."

"You need me to do anything? Mail you some of your stuff?"

Henry shook his head. The picture of receiving a box in the

mail from Frank, like a reverse care package, almost made him laugh. "Thanks, man. You're a good friend." Henry was struck with another thought. Frank was his new best friend now. His belly grew cold with the reminder of what he'd lost.

He waved after the car as Frank drove away. *Now what?*

* * *

The house was empty when Henry returned. He wandered into the kitchen but found he wasn't hungry. Walking to the living room, he sat on the couch but didn't have the energy or motivation to pick up the remote. He wound his way across the house to his bedroom and lay down, his eyes wide open, and stared at the ceiling. Rolling his head to the side, he looked at his desk.

In two neat piles sat all of his laundry, washed and folded. Henry sat up. Either he'd lost more time than he thought, or his mom had done all of his laundry for him.

She'd come through for him in a lot of ways in the week since Jason's accident. She made multiple phone calls to Henry's dorm to let him know about the funeral and visitation. She cooked an actual meal for him on Friday night. And now this.

The side door creaked open.

"Henry? You in here?"

He padded down the hall to the kitchen. "Hi, Mom."

She wore a navy dress he hadn't seen in years. He checked the clock. Normally she wouldn't be getting home from work this early. Wait, wasn't it Saturday?

"Mom, did you go to the funeral?"

She looked at him like he had three heads. "Of course I did. He was your best friend. Didn't you see me there?"

"No, I'm sorry." Henry would be surprised if he remembered anything from that funeral by the end of next week. It was already slipping away from him.

A sudden panicked thought eclipsed all others. What if memories of Jason slipped away too? What if he couldn't hang on to the one thing he had left of his best friend?

Henry sat with force in the closest chair he could find.

"Everything okay?" His mom ruffled his hair then patted his head. Her touch was awkward and stilted, rusty from lack of practice. She sat beside him at the table.

He rested his forehead on his hands. "Sometimes it doesn't feel real. And then it feels too real." He looked at her for help. "Does that make any sense?" He was afraid that nothing he did or said had any logic or rationality behind it.

His mom placed her hand on his. She squeezed it, and her mouth lifted on one side. "I know what you mean. Jason's death really hit home for me too."

Waiting for her to explain, he held her gaze.

"It could have been you, Henry."

He dipped his chin. She'd had the same thoughts he had. "It *should* have been me."

"No, you don't understand." She held his face in her hands. "I could have lost you in that car too. I could have lost my son just like Nancy and Dale did." Breaking contact, she brushed a tear from her cheek.

Henry appraised his mother in a new light. He'd never thought his parents would miss him if he left. They'd certainly shown no signs of missing him when he left for college. But his mother's revelation made him question that.

Clearing her throat, she leaned back. "Your father and I ..." She sighed. "We fell in love very young. He was always my first love. But you were my second." Her smile was like sunlight breaking through the clouds. "And it scared Bobby to see how much I cared about you. For some reason, it's always been a competition with him. He was so jealous if I ever talked to another boy when we were in school." Her eyes clouded with memory. "One time, I did it on purpose, to punish him for something he'd said. That poor boy had to go to the emergency room with a broken nose." She shook her head, snapping back to reality. "But never again. I couldn't let that happen again."

"Why did you stay with him? After he did that?"

"Because I love him." She looked at him as if it were that simple. "And he loves me. I'd never find someone else to love me as much as he does."

"Maybe not, but you could've tried. You could've found someone to love you better. Someone who wasn't so possessive and jealous. Who wouldn't treat his own son like garbage."

His mother clasped her hands on the table. "I'm sorry for that, Henry." She looked up from her hands and into his eyes. Her gaze bored into him. "I'm not stupid. I've seen what he put you through. Your dad may not understand why you had to leave, but I do."

Henry ran his fingers through his hair and pulled at the ends. "I was doing well before—" The words wouldn't come at first, but he forced them out. "Before Jason died. But now I don't think I can do it. I think I've ruined my chance to escape this place."

"Have some patience, son. He just died. Take time to grieve and then finish strong."

Maybe she was right. But it was so hard to see past each day. Time after Jason seemed to warp and stretch in the strangest ways.

"What do I do now?"

"I'll tell you what *I'm* going to do. I'm going to be grateful for more time with my boy. And I'm going to look after the parents who *did* lose their son in a car crash." She stood, picking up her purse. "I told Nancy we'd bring by a casserole later. You should come with me."

"You made a casserole?"

She shrugged. "I guess I have hidden depths."

Henry laughed. It was quiet and not much more than a breath of air. But it was the first time he'd laughed since Jason died.

He didn't know if Nancy and Dale would want him around. But he resolved to go with his mom when she delivered dinner. Maybe he didn't have Jason anymore, but he still had the Jones family. They were the closest he could get to having his friend around. And maybe they'd want to talk to him too.

31

APRIL, FRESHMAN YEAR

Henry was failing. There was no way around it. He'd been back at Halloway for a few weeks now, and every class was the same. He'd missed too much time, and his mind was too muddled.

He slammed his notebook down. In the hushed library, it sounded like a slap. Henry held his head in his hands and tugged at the ends of his hair.

This was his one chance to get out of Shady Springs, and he'd blown it.

At the time, coming to Halloway had seemed like such a great choice. He had a good scholarship, he'd be able to study the Bible with other young Christians, and—best of all—he'd get to be with his closest friend and spiritual mentor. But now Jason was gone. And he was left alone, drifting through his first year of college without an anchor.

If Henry couldn't pass his classes with at least a B, he'd lose his scholarship. And after flunking out of Halloway, he didn't imagine any other universities in Arkansas would give him a scholarship, either.

Maybe Dad had been right. He should've joined Uncle Jimmy and become an electrician.

Henry sighed loudly. Someone shushed him from another study carrel.

"Hey there."

He popped his head up to see Cate standing beside him.

"I thought you might be here." She squished into the tiny space, resting against the desk.

He could have scooted over to give her room, but he was more than a little irritated to be interrupted. Truth be told, something about Cate's presence annoyed him. No, not annoyed. It provoked him.

Every time she was close to him, he was at war with himself. Part of him longed for her nearness and thrilled at her touch. The other part of him recoiled with guilt. What right did he have to be happy with Cate when Jason was dead? *It should have been me. Jason had so much left to live for. I should have been the one to die.*

Henry shook his head to clear the voices away.

He'd been putting it off long enough. It was time to talk to Cate.

"Listen, there's something I've been meaning to talk to you about."

Her face fell. "Do we have to do this now? Today?"

"Yes." He filled his lungs and steeled his nerves. "Remember what we said at the beginning? About no distractions?"

Cate nodded, her mouth set in a straight line.

"I'm not doing well." In more ways than one, if he was being honest. "I need to take a step back."

"From me?" Her voice rose, and she seemed almost surprised by the sound. She looked around, making sure no one was disturbed.

"From you, from the newspaper, from anything that isn't work or school." He waved his notebook. "I have to spend all my time studying, or I'm going to flunk out of my classes and lose my scholarship." Saying it out loud made him even more anxious.

Cate stood, her whisper intense and pleading. "I can help you, Henry. I don't have to be a distraction." She rolled her eyes. "We already don't spend any time together nowadays. I don't see how I could be keeping you from your work."

"I'm sorry. I need to focus on finishing the semester right now."

"Don't you think your problems might be caused by the fact that you're grieving and depressed? Your best friend just died, and you're blaming *me* for everything."

Henry's chest tightened, and tension spread across his shoulders. Cate knew how to push his buttons better than anyone else. His voice came out in a staccato, like punching the keys on his old typewriter. "I *know* my best friend just died. And of course, I'm grieving." Henry fumbled for the words. How could he possibly explain the turmoil inside of him? "I don't expect you to understand. I know you've had a pretty great life. But I *need* to finish my degree. I *need* to get out."

Cate took a step back. "How can you say that? Jason was my friend too. And maybe I don't have a monster for a father, but I've lost people before. I lost someone that day too."

Someone shushed her.

Cate pursed her lips and shushed back angrily.

"What am I doing? Fine." She no longer bothered keeping her voice down. "I'm not going to stand here and grovel for you to take me back. If you want to break up, so be it. Have a nice life."

Her words shoved him back in his chair.

He hadn't expected Cate to be happy about breaking up, but he didn't think she would fight with him either. Or *for* him? Was she fighting *for* their relationship?

And if Cate was fighting for him, who was he fighting for?

* * *

"We need to talk."

Henry gulped. Tracy Van Horn was making a beeline straight for him, and she didn't look happy.

"Can this wait? I'm not supposed to talk to friends while I'm working."

"It won't take long." She propped her hands on her hips. "I'd just like to know what kind of nerve you think you have. Breaking up with Cate on today, of all days."

Henry gripped the mop in his hands. His gaze darted left and right, checking for Dana or someone who might yell at him for slacking off. Someone who might save him from this confrontation.

Tracy snapped her fingers in his face. "Hey! Look at me!"

Henry furrowed his brows. "I'm sorry. What do you mean, today of all—"

His mouth hung open. Dread washed over him.

"What is the date?"

Tracy gave him that look that all women give. Eyebrows raised, head slightly tipped. The one where they know they're right. Like satisfaction mixed with condemnation mixed with righteous anger. "April first."

The dread closed in on him. "It's her birthday."

"That's right."

"I broke up with her on her birthday." Henry grabbed the closest chair and sat down before he could pass out on the floor.

"Bingo."

"Oh, Tracy. What have I done?"

Tracy seemed a bit flummoxed. Perhaps she hadn't expected her chastisement to work so well. She sat next to Henry and rubbed his back. "Hey. Nothing that can't be undone."

"I was planning to do something nice for her birthday. I was going to buy her those chocolates she likes. Maybe take her out to a movie or dinner."

"You still can." Tracy's voice was gentler. "Just go tell her you're sorry for whatever insane idea got into your head. Tell her you take it all back. She's angry, but she'll understand. We've all been a little crazy lately."

Could he take it all back? Did he even want to?

Henry shook his head in his hands. "No. I can't take it back. We need to break up."

"Then you really *are* crazy." Tracy yanked her hand away from his back. "If you can't see how perfect you two are for each other, you've completely lost it."

"Maybe I have." Henry sighed. "I've been a total jerk, but maybe that's for the best."

"What do you mean?"

He looked up at her through his fingers. "I can't be the man she needs, and maybe I never could be." He sat up straighter. "I was never good enough for Cate. If she sees how much better she is without me, then she can move on without any regrets."

"Henry." Tracy leveled her gaze at him. "What are you talking about? Cate loves you. And you love her. You need her right now more than ever."

"I used to see her, Tracy. I used to notice every little detail about her." He closed his eyes. He could conjure her face in his mind. He could still see the hurt written all over her when they'd broken up. "But today, I didn't even remember her birthday."

"We're in agreement that forgetting your girlfriend's birthday is a bad move. But that doesn't mean you need to throw in the towel."

"No, it's not just that."

"Then what, Henry? Because none of us understands you right now."

"My grades are terrible, I can't be a good boyfriend, I can barely sleep. I feel like I'm drowning."

Tracy gripped his wrist so hard it almost hurt. "Then let us help you. Let your friends be there for you."

Henry tugged his arm away. "I need to be alone."

She stood. "Alone is the last thing you need right now."

"I have to get back to the way things were before Jason …"

"Before he died?"

"No, before I even met him."

Tracy took a step back, then two more. She furrowed her brows and opened her mouth, then turned on her heels. She marched out of the cafeteria.

Good, Henry thought. *She's better off without me. They all are.*

32

PRESENT DAY

Catherine grinned at the unexpected sight of her daughter waiting at the table with two steaming cups of rooibos tea when she got home from work.

"Hi, sweetie. I didn't know you'd be in town today."

"Hey, Mom." She pushed up from the table and approached as if to give her a hug.

Catherine held up her hands and backed away. "Let me shower first, please. It was a rough day."

"Sure thing." Maddy stepped back to allow Catherine to pass into the hallway. "Just don't take too long. Your tea won't stay hot forever."

"I'll hurry."

After thirty minutes and one quick trip back to the microwave for the cup of tea, Catherine and her daughter settled in on the living room couch.

Maddy pulled Catherine's "box of memories" from the floor and into her lap. The two of them had taken to calling it that as they revisited the objects and mementos from college and Catherine's relationship with Henry. "Mom, I want the rest of the story you promised me."

"Oh?" Catherine had thought they were finished looking through everything, so she'd put it back in the closet. Apparently, Maddy wasn't done yet and had retrieved the box.

"About you and Dad."

"I already told you everything."

"Almost. You told me about how you two met, about your first kiss, and about your first Valentine's Day." She slid a photograph out from the top of the box. Four faces smiled up at the camera.

"What do you want to know?"

"Everything. But tell me about this picture first. Who are the other two people?"

Catherine scanned the picture and a smile crept over her lips. "That's Tracy, my roommate. You met her a long time ago. When you were little."

"And the boy?"

Catherine brushed her thumb over the photograph. "That's Jason Jones. He was your dad's best friend."

Maddy squinted as she examined the picture again. "You mean the son of Nancy Jones? That Jason?"

"One and the same."

Madeleine looked at the young man again. "He looks nice."

"He was very nice." In the photograph, all four of them were squeezed onto a picnic blanket. Jason's arms were thrown around Tracy and Henry. His smile was open and unguarded. Catherine's heart squeezed at the memory. It still hurt after all these years.

"Were you close?"

Catherine's eyes lost focus as she retreated to a distant memory. Blinking, she took a breath. "Yes. We were good friends. I was devastated when he passed away during our freshman year." She looked at Madeleine. "But your father …" She shook her head. "I thought he'd never be the same again."

The clock in the living room clicked the seconds away as

Catherine gathered her thoughts. "We broke up for a while after Jason died. I don't know if I ever told you that." She looked up at Madeleine, but her gaze shifted away again. "He always withdrew, your father, when he felt overwhelmed. Instead of reaching out for help, he'd retreat until he felt it was safe to come out again."

"How did you end up getting back together?"

A slow smile stretched across her face. "The mailbox."

"The mailbox?"

"Remember, I told you we shared a box?"

Madeleine nodded.

"Well, your father wasn't the only one to intercept some letters."

"You stole his mail?"

Catherine's hands shot up defensively. "I didn't *steal* them. I didn't even read most of them. I just wanted to make sure he was okay."

Maddy cocked an eyebrow and leveled her gaze at Catherine.

"Okay, I also wanted to know if he was dating someone else." Catherine smirked. "I know I shouldn't have done it, but I was desperate and young and not always very smart."

"If they weren't from a girlfriend, who were the letters from?"

"Nancy Jones, mostly." She smiled again. The thought that she'd suspected Nancy was a girlfriend always made her laugh. "He'd started writing her letters almost every week and checking in on her whenever he was in Shady Springs. She became like a second mother to him. And Dale was like the father he never had."

"I thought he did have a father."

"Not in any real way. He never had a man he could look up to until Dale."

"So how did the letters get you back together?"

Catherine grimaced. "He caught me. And it wasn't pretty at first."

"But you learned to trust each other again?"

She nodded once before looking down at the picture in her hands. "I thought we did. But then when times got tough again …" She drifted off and her gaze wandered to the photos on the wall. There were a few of the two of them together and a lot of Madeleine when she was younger, but none of Henry. "He took himself out of the picture."

"Mom? What happened back then?" She bit her lip. "I mean, I know he cheated on you and started drinking a lot, but I don't understand why."

Catherine sighed. She set the photograph down on the side table. She'd been avoiding this conversation, and Maddy was right that she hadn't told her everything. "It all started when his parents passed away. Do you remember that?"

Madeleine furrowed her brows. "Only a little."

"You were only three when your Grandpa Mullins died and five or six when Grandma passed. Well, you know he never had a great relationship with them, but he did patch things up a bit before Grandpa got sick. That's why we moved back to Shady Springs in the first place. It's funny, he spent so much time trying to get out of Shady Springs only to end up there anyway."

She'd thought Henry was crazy at first when he suggested moving home. After years of running away, he'd gone straight back to the place he'd been trying to get away from. But the move had allowed Henry to have some closure, and Henry's connections in town had provided him with his very own photography studio.

"He wanted to forgive his parents?"

She nodded. "I think he succeeded, but it was very difficult. Grandpa Mullins was a mean man and a bad father when your dad was a boy. Dad struggled so much with self-esteem because his father always told him he wasn't good enough."

"So, he had a hard time after they died?"

"Yes, but he also struggled with depression. He was in denial about it at first, but he just pushed everything down. And he kept pushing and pushing. He poured himself into his photography business and into volunteering at church. Those are good things, of course, but they didn't take away the hurt. When he finally started drinking, it was to self-medicate, I think. And when I got upset about it, and he couldn't take life at home anymore, he found someone else."

Maddy reached out a hand to Catherine. They clung to each other for a while. Even though they'd traveled together through those difficult times many years before, talking about it all felt a bit like cleaning a wound. When Maddy was little, Catherine had cleaned her cuts and scrapes with hydrogen peroxide. It had burned, and Maddy would squeeze her hand while the chemical did its job. But then the pain was over, and the wound was clean. And Catherine knew the pain was worth the end result.

Maddy frowned. "I'm sorry, Mom. I wish I could have been there for you back then."

"That's not your job. You were too young. Besides, I had Clara."

"You should've had more support."

"Well, I had that falling out with Nancy. And then, no one at church knew what to do with me. A single mother who was enduring a scandalous breakup." She attempted a good-natured shrug, but the truth was that the scorn she'd endured at church had been almost as painful as the breakup itself.

"But now you've forgiven Nancy and Dad?"

"I know it seems nearly impossible. And it feels that way some days." Catherine folded her hands. "It's not me that's doing the forgiving, really."

"What do you mean?"

"If I were relying on my own power, I would fail. But if I allow God to work through me, then I can forgive them."

Madeleine looked down at the box on the floor, but she didn't pull anything out. "If you had another chance with Dad, a fresh start, would you take it?"

Catherine stared back at her for a moment, her lips parted. The seconds ticked away. She looked down at her hands. She'd thought the answer would be *yes* until Henry had asked for a divorce. But now ... "I don't know."

"What if he's changed? He's been sober for years and going to meetings every week. He has a therapist and prescription drugs for his depression now. He's even found a good church home in Fayetteville."

Catherine leaned back on the couch. She still didn't understand how digging through ancient history would help Maddy with her present-day situation.

She'd been working so hard to close herself off to Henry, but she wanted Maddy to be able to move on from the past and start living her own life. And maybe she needed to do the same. If she kept hiding the truth from her daughter, no one would benefit. "How do I know he won't leave me again?" There it was—the heart of the reason she hadn't ever tried to get back together with Henry.

Maddy paused, then looked her mother in the eye. "I guess you'd just have to trust him."

Catherine returned her gaze. "That's what I'm afraid of."

Maddy grabbed her hand and held it tight, almost like she was squeezing the truth from her mother.

Staring back at Maddy, Catherine took a breath. Her defenses crumbled. "Okay, if I'm being completely honest with you, then yes." Catherine raised her gaze to the ceiling, unsure if she could bare her heart while looking into her daughter's eyes. "If I had a chance for a fresh start with your dad, I'd take it. In fact, I had planned to suggest just that before he asked for a divorce. But now, it's too late."

"Maybe not, Mom."

Catherine squeezed Maddy's hand back. "It's too late for me, sweetie, but it's not too late for you. You and A.J. could have a beautiful life together if you took him back."

Maddy pulled her hand away. "I don't think so, Mom."

"I do. I think the real explanation for why you keep asking me for stories is because you're looking for a reason to marry that man. You know it's the right choice, but you're too afraid."

Maddy shifted away on the couch. "No, this is for the best. A.J. is better off without me."

"No, he's not, and you aren't better off without him, either." Catherine turned her knees into her daughter's. "Love is worth the risk, Maddy. On the other side of an ugly breakup, I say it. On the other side of a tragic death, Aunt Clara says it. If you take a chance on love, you will never regret it." She slipped her hand into her daughter's. "We aren't meant to walk through life alone. God made us for love and companionship. You have an amazing man who loves you and wants to be with you. Don't waste that precious gift."

Maddy squeezed her eyes shut. Catherine knew she could only make one last attempt to get through to her daughter before she shut down. "Will you promise to think about it?"

She nodded and lifted her gaze. "I will if you will too."

Catherine blew out a breath. Fine. If it would get her daughter to come to her senses, she would entertain thoughts of Henry. "Okay, I will."

Now, how am I supposed to keep up my end of the deal?

33

AUGUST, SOPHOMORE YEAR

The auditorium smelled the same way it had during Henry's freshman year. The faint scents of old songbooks, wood and paint from the sets of past plays, and a couple thousand pairs of sneakers. It was the second day of school, but it was Henry's first time trying to find his chapel seat.

The very first chapel of the year was always convocation. A parade of teachers in regalia marched down the double aisles, followed by students carrying flags from every state and country represented in the student body that year. It was a moving sight to behold, but the chapel checkers never kept attendance on that first day, and Henry had watched from a back seat before leaving early.

He checked the index card where he'd written his chapel seat. 315S. The 300s were in the center of the building. He mentally sang through the alphabet as he passed each row and excused himself as he climbed over a few laps to get to seat 15.

Henry froze at a familiar sight. Curly brown hair pulled into a high ponytail. He attempted to slide into his seat without making eye contact, but she turned as soon as he got close.

Cate's mouth hung open. Then she shut it with such force,

Henry imagined it must have hurt a little. Her lips tightened into a straight line.

He offered a shrug and a smile. "I forgot that we picked our chapel seats together last year."

She gave a curt nod. Almost too quiet to hear, she muttered, "You seem to forget a lot of things."

Henry winced. He still felt awful for the way he'd broken up with Cate last year. Only four months ago, but it felt like another lifetime.

So much had happened the rest of the semester and over the summer. He'd buckled down and scraped by with three B's, one C, and one A. Just high enough to keep his scholarship. On the advice of a professor, he'd taken Calculus at the nearby community college in June so he could spend the time needed to focus on his coursework while he was away from distractions.

He and his mom had gotten into a routine on days she had to work. He'd drop her off at the school office, then drive the hour to Bentonville and arrive just in time for class at nine. When class let out around noon, he'd eat a sandwich and spend two hours working on homework before driving back to pick up his mother.

When he wasn't driving back and forth to Bentonville, he was working. He baled hay with a buddy from high school and worked the counter at Mike's Diner in Shady Springs on weekends. The pay was good enough that he was able to buy an old sedan from one of the elders at church. It was fire engine red and sturdy enough to get him from Shady Springs to Halloway University without worry. He loved it.

When he was inside that old car, he felt for the first time that he had a space of his own. It didn't belong to his parents. He didn't share it with a roommate. Every inch of that vehicle belonged to him. The feeling was exhilarating.

Henry longed to talk to Cate about it all. About the A he got in Calculus. About the tenuous friendship he'd formed with his own mother. About the car.

There was something else too. Over spring break and with increasing regularity, Henry had started visiting the Jones family. At first, he just went to check on them and tell stories about Jason. Then, he started going for lunch after church every Sunday morning. During the summer, he'd come over for dinner and game night every Friday evening. He even started bringing his mother on the weekends his dad wasn't around.

Nancy Jones had asked him to write and call every week since she wouldn't get to see him while he was away at college. Henry had agreed and had sent off his first letter that morning. Not as exhilarating as a car, but joyous all the same, was the steady reminder that his existence mattered to someone. Nancy and Dale had unofficially adopted him into their family. Not as a replacement for Jason, but on his own merit. Because grieving together was better than grieving alone.

Henry shifted his eyes toward Cate. He wanted to share all of that with her. And he wondered about her too. She'd been hoping to work at a church camp over the summer, but he didn't know if she'd done that or something else. Had she started dating someone new? Maybe one of her fellow counselors, someone tall and tanned. Probably a lifeguard.

He lasered his focus on the speaker on stage. The student association president was making announcements, and then someone else led a prayer.

Last year, Cate hadn't wanted chapel seats together. They weren't officially a couple until well into the spring semester, and she'd wanted to sit with her club sisters. When he finally talked Cate into picking these chapel seats, he'd imagined holding her hand during the prayers and whispering to each other during announcements. Maybe she'd lean her head on his shoulder or she'd elbow him to stay awake during a long chapel talk.

One of his friends from the newspaper, David, got up to lead singing. When they stood for the first song, Henry did his level best not to bump or jostle Cate. His fingers almost brushed hers as he reached for a songbook.

When he flipped to the hymn David called out, his heart leaped to his throat. Six hundred forty-six, "It is Well with My Soul," Jason's favorite song. Henry swallowed past the lump in his throat. He hadn't heard these words since Jason's funeral.

Out of the corner of his eye, he could feel Cate's stare boring into him. His cheeks burned, but he didn't want her comfort or her sympathy. He just needed to power through the song.

At first his voice came out like a whisper, but then it got stronger. Only once did he almost choke up when he remembered how Jason's voice always sounded a bit like a toad when he sang the low notes.

When the song ended, everyone sat back down. The speaker got up to give the chapel talk. And then they were dismissed. Henry bolted as quickly as he could out of the auditorium. Now he wouldn't have to endure chapel with Cate until tomorrow morning.

This was going to be a long semester.

* * *

"Why do you have my mail in your hand?"

"What?" Cate's cheeks flushed a bright pink. She turned the envelope in her right hand over to the front. "Oh, I'm sorry. This looks like it's yours. I must have grabbed it by accident."

Henry could practically feel smoke billowing out of his ears. "Except you didn't come from our box. You had that in your hands when you walked in the Student Center."

Her face turned an even darker shade of crimson. "Right, I just realized I had grabbed the wrong mail and was bringing it back."

Henry narrowed his eyes. "How long have you been reading my mail, Cate?"

Her mouth closed and opened wordlessly. She cleared her throat and tried again. "What?"

"I said, how long have you been stealing and opening and reading my mail?"

The irony was not lost on him. He knew how hypocritical he sounded. He'd accidentally picked up an entire package of hers the year before. And Jason had eaten some of its contents. But she'd been furious with him when the shoe was on the other foot. Shouldn't she know better? Hadn't they both learned from their mistakes?

Cate hung her head. "Only a few weeks. I just wanted to make sure you were okay."

"A few weeks? Cate." He shook his head, at a loss for words. It was late September, and they'd only been in school for a month now. Had she been stealing his mail this whole time? The letters he'd gotten had been a little crumpled, but he'd chalked that up to careless mail sorters.

"I know, I know. I'm so sorry."

Henry turned on his heels. He couldn't bear to be around her one more second. He couldn't even begin to think about what it was going to be like to share a mailbox with her for three more years. A growl rumbled in his chest.

Cate grabbed his arm. "Wait, please."

A different feeling bloomed in his chest. His arm warmed where she held it. Something in him longed to embrace her again. He pulled his arm free but didn't walk away. Slowly, he turned to face her.

"I didn't read them all. Just a couple. And this time, I honestly didn't mean to take the letter with me."

"It doesn't matter, Cate."

"What I did was wrong, but I need to know you're okay." She bit her lip and then spoke again. "Are you? Okay?"

Henry closed his eyes for a moment. He remembered the look on her face when he'd broken up with her. She wore the same sad expression now. It killed him to know he was the one hurting her.

Besides, hadn't he been wishing for the chance to talk?

He nodded his head toward the coffee shop at the front of the Student Center. "Have you had breakfast yet?"

She widened her eyes, surprised. "No, I haven't."

Henry walked away again, but this time, Cate followed. He slowed his steps so they could walk together.

He grabbed a couple of muffins from the display case and paid for them with his credit balance. "Blueberry still your favorite?"

Cate nodded and took the muffin from his outstretched hand.

They found an empty booth and sat across from each other.

"I've been wanting to talk to you for a long time."

"Me too," Cate said.

Where to begin? "I heard you went on a couple of dates with Thomas Weiss." That was not what he'd meant to say, but once the words left his mouth, he needed to know her response. His heart hammered in his chest.

"It didn't really go anywhere." Cate unwrapped her muffin slowly, her gaze focused downward.

Henry let out his breath through pursed lips, afraid he'd sigh in relief. He knew that Cate would date other guys someday, but he wasn't quite ready yet.

"Is that what you wanted to talk about?" Cate raised an eyebrow at him. She held a piece of the muffin in her hand.

"No." He blew out another breath. "I wanted to say that I am okay. I wasn't at first. But I'm doing better now." He waved the envelope still in his hand and set it on the table in front of them. "I guess you know I've been writing Jason's mom."

She nodded.

"This summer was hard, but it was good."

Cate swallowed a bite of her muffin and twisted her lips in a small smile. "I'm glad."

The next part was going to be difficult. Henry tapped his fingers on the table nervously. "I'm really sorry, Cate."

To her credit, Cate didn't pretend not to know what he was talking about. She simply took another bite and waited for him to finish.

"I was drowning and didn't know how to save myself. I thought being alone would be better, but it wasn't. In the end, I didn't save myself at all. God guided me through the dark times by using people like Dale and Nancy. Even my mom." He scanned Cate's face for any signs of compassion or empathy. He couldn't read her expression. "I've regretted breaking up with you ever since." He gave a mirthless laugh. "And, to do it on your birthday. That was just the icing on the cake that made me feel like a total jerk."

"You *were* a total jerk." Her gaze bored into him. She stared at him without blinking for a long time. Finally, she looked down at the table. "But I forgive you."

"Really?" His voice came out so quiet and high, it was almost a squeak.

She nodded and crumpled the empty muffin wrapper. "Really. I'd like to be friends again. I've missed you."

Relief flooded him. He wouldn't believe his own ears, except Cate was smiling at him. "I'd like that too." He laughed. "Oh, Cate, I've missed you so much. I want to hear everything about your summer."

"And I want to tell you." She checked her watch. "But right now, we have to get to chapel."

Henry looked around them at the other students packing their bags or walking out the double doors. He quickly stuffed half of his chocolate muffin in his mouth.

While they walked down the red brick path, he devoured the rest of his muffin. He tossed the wrapper in the trash on his way into the auditorium. He happily traipsed down the plush carpeted aisle and gestured for Cate to walk ahead of him through the seats.

Just like the first few days of school, Henry had trouble concentrating on the chapel announcements. But today, it was because he couldn't stop grinning at Cate next to him. His heart was lighter, and the weight on his chest had lifted.

He peeked through lowered lids at Cate's bowed head during the prayer. *Thank you, God, for giving me another chance.*

One of the music professors took the stage to lead some songs. And the very first one they turned to was 646. Henry's chest tightened. He took a deep breath, ready to power through the hymn.

But then he felt something. A smaller hand grabbed onto his left one. Cate's fingers twined through his. He caught her gaze, and she looked just as surprised as he felt. She flinched and pulled back, but Henry tightened his hold. When he smiled at her, she relaxed her shoulders. She gave him a smirk in return.

They both turned to face the songbook in Henry's right hand.

He found his voice growing stronger with each verse and the words rang truer than they ever had. *Whatever my lot, thou hast taught me to say, "It is well with my soul."*

Henry watched Cate from the corner of his eye. He'd been given another chance to hold her hand. Another chance to be a part of her life. And there was no way he was going to waste it this time.

34

PRESENT DAY

"I heard you asked Mom for a divorce."

Henry almost choked on his mouthful of coffee. He pounded on his chest and cleared his throat. "You just cut right to the chase, don't you?" He'd hoped he wouldn't have to talk with Maddy about the divorce, but that had been wishful thinking. Of course, she would want to talk about it. Though he'd assumed she'd only come by to share muffins and coffee and schedule bridal portraits.

Maddy shrugged. "I figure that's the best way to talk to you."

Henry took another drink of coffee. This one went down much smoother. "All right. Yes, I hired a lawyer to put together some papers." He turned back around to his computer. "I thought you wanted to talk about wedding pictures."

She didn't respond, so Henry swiveled back around. Maddy sat fidgeting with the lid on her latte. "I'm not actually getting married anymore, so there's no need for wedding pictures."

Henry was thankful he didn't have any coffee in his mouth that time. "What? Since when?"

"Since a couple weeks ago."

"And you weren't going to tell me?"

Maddy scowled at the cup. "I don't really want to talk about it."

Henry placed both of his hands on the counter between them. "No. If I have to talk about the tough stuff, you do too. Why did you and A.J. break up?"

She threw her hands in the air. "Why would we stay together? Why would anyone get married? If you and mom couldn't make it work when you were so in love, how could I possibly have a successful marriage?"

Taking a steadying breath, he leaned back in his chair. "Do you want to know the reason your mom and I broke up?"

Maddy gave the smallest hint of a nod while she gazed at her coffee cup.

"It's because I always ran away. I never came to your mother with my problems. I always retreated to a corner to lick my wounds and fix my issues." He'd often blamed Catherine's perfectionist tendencies, but he could only find fault with himself now. He had ruined their marriage by trying to walk through life alone instead of together with his wife.

"But isn't that what you're doing now?"

"What do you mean?"

"By filing for divorce, aren't you running away from a relationship with Mom?"

Henry pursed his lips. "We've been separated for a long time. Over ten years. I'm trying to do the right thing by your mom and set her free."

"Is that what you want?"

He raised his shoulders and lowered them again. "I want what's best for her."

"But do you really want to cut all ties with her? Bring lawyers into your relationship? Drag her through this all over again?"

He held up his hands. "Woah. I'm not dragging her through anything. There's nothing left to our relationship anymore." He nodded his head toward Maddy. "Except for you, of course. You will always tie me to your mom."

Maddy took another sip and then twisted her lips in thought. "What if she doesn't want to get a divorce?"

"Of course she does."

"How do you know?"

"She told me we were done. She made it very clear that nothing is ever going to happen between us." He'd been in denial for a long time, but that night in the parking lot after Maddy's engagement party had sealed the deal. Cate wanted nothing more to do with him.

"Maybe she was just upset and said some things she didn't mean in the heat of the moment."

He shook his head slowly. "No. If you'd been there for our conversation, you'd see it the way I do. Your mother is ready to move on."

Maddy blinked slowly and bit her lip. He could tell she was debating what to say next. "Dad. She's still in love with you."

Henry looked into Maddy's eyes for a moment, searching for the truth. "Then why would she say what she did?"

She shrugged. "I think it's been hard for her to forget everything. You were gone for a long time." She added, "And I gather this isn't the first time you've made her feel abandoned."

He rubbed the back of his neck. "I'm sure she's told you lots of things about me."

"Not until recently." Madeleine pressed her hands on the countertop. "I asked her to tell me what went wrong with your marriage. I needed—I wanted—to know, before I committed to getting married myself."

"And what she said made you want to break up with A.J.?"

Maddy leaned away. "No. Mom's been trying her hardest to convince me to stay with him."

"Then why did you do it?"

Maddy's gaze wandered the ceiling. She drummed her

fingers on the counter. "Because I don't know how I could possibly succeed at marriage. How can I give A.J. everything he deserves? How can I protect him from heartbreak? Your marriage, Aunt Clara and Uncle George's marriage, they both ended terribly in a breakup or death."

"You think that everyone raised by a single mom can never have a good marriage?"

"Well, no."

"And you think we should all just live and die alone because marriage is too hard?"

"I guess not."

"And you think that just because you love A.J. and he loves you, that's not enough reason to get married? Even though you can rely on God and the support of the Church through difficult times?"

Maddy rolled her eyes. "I get it, Dad. You can stop."

"No, make me understand. Because it sounds like that's exactly what you think."

She slapped her hands on the counter. "Fine. Maybe you're right. Maybe Mom and Clara are right too. Maybe I'm just a coward."

Henry covered Maddy's hand with his. "No, you're not." He smiled at his beautiful daughter. "No thanks to me, you've grown into an amazing young woman. You're a talented artist, a loving daughter and friend, and a growing Christian. You are all those things, but you are not a coward."

Maddy swiped at her eyes.

"You grew up with a wonderful mother, but you had more than just Mom. You had Uncle George, Aunt Clara, and your grandparents. And now you have a church family in Shady Springs. And a really great guy who loves you."

"He does. And I love him too."

"Then go after him, Maddy."

She chewed on her lip before taking a deep breath. "I should go. I have a lot to get done this afternoon."

"Okay. It was good to see you."

"And Dad?" She hoisted her purse to her shoulder. "Mom loves you. I just know she does. I know her almost as well as I know myself, and I'm telling you, she's still in love with you. And she wants another chance."

Henry swallowed hard as he watched his daughter leave.

Cate loved him.

He swiveled in his chair and let that thought sink in. Cate had seemed upset about the divorce papers, but he hadn't known why until now. What if Maddy was right, and she really did want another chance? What should he do?

Perhaps it was time to pull out the old dating playbook. A lot of time had passed, but maybe Henry could still charm his wife. He wasn't completely sure Maddy was right about Cate's feelings. But if she was, it was worth making a fool of himself for her one last time.

He would give their marriage one more shot before throwing in the towel.

35

PRESENT DAY

"Thanks for coming along with me."

"Of course."

Catherine stretched her neck and rolled her shoulders. She couldn't remember the last time she'd driven from Shady Springs to Halloway, but she was happy to be making the trip with her sister. It was almost like old times, when they were both in college. All of those memories felt like a lifetime ago but also like just yesterday. Especially since reliving all of her stories with Madeleine.

They pulled off the interstate and drove down the main highway through town. Clara rolled her window down and leaned her head out, looking this way and that.

"Do you remember this stoplight being here?"

"No, and they definitely didn't have any of those restaurants."

Their first view of campus was even more changed.

"Are you sure we're in the right place?"

"I wouldn't be, but there's the name: Halloway University. And a giant scrolling LED sign."

"Crazy."

They drove past new apartment buildings, a new health sciences complex, and a new athletic facility. Around each corner was something else to discover.

"It's like a completely different place."

"No, look."

Catherine pointed up ahead on the road. There was the auditorium where they'd attended chapel every day. The business building stood where it had before, albeit with some updates. Then they came to Dr. Cooper's house.

"Ah, now this looks exactly the same."

"Oh, man, seeing this old neighborhood really takes me back."

Catherine could almost see teenaged Henry walking ahead of her on their way to Bible study. She could almost hear his laugh ring out.

Wait.

That wasn't young Henry in her imagination. He was actually here. Talking to Mrs. Cooper in their doorway.

Catherine put the car in park and rolled up the windows. Her stomach flipped in a somersault. She turned to her sister. "This might get weird."

"What, because your soon-to-be-ex-husband is here? And you haven't seen him since he ambushed you in a parking lot and served you divorce papers?"

"Um, yeah."

Clara nodded. "I think we've got this." She hopped out of the car and ran around to Catherine's side. "Come on."

Arms linked, side by side, the two sisters walked up the brick path to the party.

"Is that the Hodges sisters?"

"Sheila!" Clara enveloped Mrs. Cooper in a hug. "It's so good to see you."

Catherine smiled, trying her hardest to focus her attention on Sheila and her sister. *Not* on Henry, still visible from the doorway. Out of the corner of her eye, she saw his form moving through the crowd, and she let out a breath.

"Cate, come here." Sheila gave Catherine a hug. She still smelled like lavender. When Catherine closed her eyes for a moment, she could imagine she was still a college student visiting for Bible study.

As Catherine opened her eyes again, she saw Sheila had changed some in the years that had passed. Her hair was gray and short. Her posture was slightly stooped. Faint wrinkles surrounded her eyes and mouth. But the same sparkle gleamed in her eyes, and Catherine still felt loved and welcomed in her presence.

"Thank you so much for coming. Nathan will be so happy to see you two."

"We were glad we could come."

Another couple of former students walked up behind them.

Sheila squeezed Catherine's hands and looked into her eyes. "Let's catch up some more later. I want to hear all about how you're doing."

Catherine smiled, but a knot of worry formed in her gut. She wasn't sure she could have a heart-to-heart with Sheila Cooper at that moment. Sheila was known for soul-baring conversations, and Catherine didn't want anyone to see inside of her soul right now. Not with the divorce looming and Madeleine's canceled wedding and all the turmoil those two things brought.

Placing her hand in the crook of Clara's arm, she allowed herself to be pulled through the living room.

There were more than a few familiar faces in the crowd. When Clara stopped to talk to an old roommate, Catherine whispered in her ear. "I'm going to grab some refreshments." She slipped through the crowd, trying not to catch any eyes.

It wasn't that she didn't want to talk to any of the people there. The gathering was just too overwhelming. She'd decided to come with Clara to support the Coopers, but she hadn't actually thought through the fact that dozens of her fellow classmates would be there too. It was a Homecoming and a college reunion. And she had not at all prepared for a reunion.

She slunk around the corner, hoping to hide out for a while.

"Cate? Cate Hodges?"

Catherine would know that voice anywhere.

"Tracy?" She almost squealed as she hugged her old roommate.

"I didn't expect to see you here. It's been so long." Tracy squeezed her tight.

Catherine held her friend back at arm's length. "You look great, Tracy. You've hardly aged since college."

Tracy laughed. "You're too sweet."

Catherine looked around the room a minute before she spotted Tracy's husband not far away. "Raymond. How are you?"

A smile lit up his face, and he wrapped his arm around Catherine's shoulders. He still towered above her. A little gray colored the hair around his brown face, but he looked much like the young man she knew all those years ago.

"How have you two been? What are you up to these days?"

Tracy placed her hand on Raymond's back. "We're back here now. Ray got a job as the boys' basketball coach at Halloway Academy about five years ago. And I'm teaching third grade. We're finally in the same school district." Tracy beamed up at her husband.

"Oh, that's wonderful. Those kids are blessed to have you." Catherine had never seen either of them in the classroom, but she knew they both had gentle spirits and servant hearts. "I wish I'd known you were living so close now."

Tracy winced. "I haven't been great about sending Christmas cards or updates."

"And I'm not great about keeping up on social media."

Catherine pressed Tracy's hands in hers. "But we're together now. How are the kids?"

Raymond answered this time. "They're all in high school but our oldest."

"Our baby boy is already in college." Tracy pouted. "They grow up so fast, you know?"

"Oh, I know, believe me." Catherine sighed. "Maddy's left the nest and is out on her own."

Before she could say any more, someone cleared his throat and began talking. An older gentleman Catherine recognized as one of the Bible professors at Halloway stood at the front of the Coopers' living room. "Thank you to all of you who joined us here to honor Dr. Nathan Cooper today."

He went on to talk about all of Dr. Cooper's accomplishments. The distinguished teaching awards, his years of service as the dean of the college and Vice President of Spiritual Affairs. His two children and five grandchildren.

Nearby, Sheila and Nathan Cooper stood, hand-in-hand. Sheila gazed up at Nathan with misty eyes.

When the crowd had finished applauding, Nathan stepped forward.

"When I look out at your faces, all I can say is how grateful I am to have been a part of your lives. My years at Halloway have been an incredible blessing. It is my great pleasure to know all of you." He gestured into the audience. "You've all become such impressive people. Missionaries and preachers, teachers, lawyers, doctors and nurses." He smiled at Catherine. "Award-winning writers, athletes, and artists."

Catherine looked through the crowd to see Henry smiling back at Dr. Cooper. Henry had become an amazing artist and deserved all the praise he got. A glow of pride swelled in her chest. Catherine smiled in spite of herself.

"But the person I'm most grateful for. The one I love with all my heart ..." He turned behind him. "Is my Sheila."

He went on to laud Sheila for her years of support, by working through Dr. Cooper's years of grad school, by hosting hundreds of students in their home, and by providing the emotional support he needed. "Nothing I've ever done has been without her help."

Catherine's heart clenched as she watched the two of them together. *This is what marriage is supposed to be like.* Instead of drawing away from each other when times got tough, Sheila and Nathan had relied on each other and on God.

She looked over at Henry again. His gaze met hers for an instant before she looked away.

Catherine was terrified he'd see her feelings written all over her face. Maddy's question still rang in her ears. *If you had another chance, would you try again?*

Looking at what the Coopers had and thinking about how much she still loved Henry, Catherine could no longer deny the answer was yes. A resounding *yes*.

But Henry had asked for a divorce. He didn't want another chance. He was done. Just like all those years ago, Henry was walking away from her and their marriage.

Catherine couldn't handle being in the house one more second. She slipped quietly out through the kitchen and into the back yard.

She'd only been outside for a minute when she heard footsteps behind her.

"Hey, Cate." Clara pulled her cardigan tight against her chest as she walked closer to her. A breeze blew some leaves through the lawn and onto the benches underneath a tall oak tree.

When she'd been in college, this yard had some swings and a slide. It had been redone sometime in the past couple decades and now blended seamlessly with the small park behind their backyard. There was even a white swing just like the ones sitting on the front lawn of Halloway.

"Are you okay?"

Catherine nodded once but changed her mind and shook her head from side to side. "I didn't realize how difficult this would be."

"How so?"

"I expected to have my life together the next time I saw these people. They're all doing so well. Dr. Cooper is retiring with honors. Tracy and Ray work at the academy and have three beautiful children." She pointed to herself. "And I just got served divorce papers and have been spending the last couple months trying to come to terms with my empty nest. Because I'm too afraid of the past to move forward into the future."

Clara put an arm around her and leaned her head against Catherine's. The sisters were not perfectly matched in height, so it wasn't the most comfortable position. Clara squeezed once then faced her sister. "You know none of them care about that. Especially the Coopers."

"But I let them all down. They invested so much time and energy in me, only to have it all wasted."

Clara clucked her tongue and pursed her lips. Her eyebrows knit together in concern. "Catherine Hodges Mullins, you are not a waste. You're a hard-working and dedicated nurse who saves lives and blesses all your patients. You raised an astounding and beautiful daughter who has surprised all of us with her talent and capacity for forgiveness." Clara placed a hand on either side of Catherine's face. "Do you hear me?"

Catherine closed her eyes and rested in her sister's hands. So much love filled the moment that she didn't want to move, afraid she might break the spell. Finally, she nodded once and Clara lowered her hands.

"Honestly, I feel a little weird in there too." Clara kicked a tuft of grass at her feet. "Last time I visited Halloway, I had George with me. It always feels strange to not have him at my side."

Catherine was horrified. "Oh, Clara, I'm so sorry. Here I was making everything about me." She'd never even spared a moment to think about how Clara might be feeling.

Clara waved away her concern. "No, I didn't say that to make you feel bad."

"Of course not."

"I just wanted you to know you're not alone." She looked up. "And I bet we aren't the only ones feeling wrong-footed."

"You're right." Catherine breathed in the cool air, letting it fill her lungs and give her strength.

"The speeches are about over. I think they're going to announce the scholarship recipients soon."

"I just need a minute."

Clara nodded before heading back inside.

Catherine gazed out at the white swing. The breeze was rocking it to and fro, making it look like someone had only just walked away.

Maddy's question rang out in her head again. *What if you had one more chance?*

36

AUGUST, JUNIOR YEAR

"Almost there."

Cate wiggled in her seat in Henry's sedan. "You know, this isn't a big town. I could probably figure out where you're taking me by counting the miles and remembering the turns." She reached her fingers up toward the blindfold over her eyes, but Henry swatted her hand back down.

"No peeking!" He paused a moment. "Did you? Figure out where we're going?"

"I have a guess or two." Cate smirked under the bandana covering the top of her face.

"Well, keep it to yourself. I'd like to pretend like I've surprised you."

"Oh, being kidnapped and blindfolded by my boyfriend was certainly a surprise." Her voice dripped with sarcasm, but Cate was enjoying herself.

Henry powered off the car. From the sounds and temperature, Cate could tell they were in a shaded and quiet area, which fit with her assumptions for where Henry had taken her.

"Okay. Let me lead you out."

Henry raced around to the other side of the car and held Cate's hands.

"Just a few more steps."

Cate's feet crunched what felt like leaves and acorns scattered along the ground.

When Henry had led her to what he'd apparently deemed just the right spot, he whisked off the mask with a flourish.

"See? We're at River Park. Where we had our first date."

Cate looked around and smiled politely. "Yes, we are." Obviously. What a silly, romantic man he was.

"And I brought a picnic, just like the first time. Except today, I actually bought food from the store."

"Oh, very fancy, Mullins." Her mouth twisted into a smile.

Henry tapped his toes. She could tell he was nervous, but about what she had no idea. He blew out a breath.

Then he got down on one knee.

Cate's lips parted in shock. He wasn't supposed to propose for a few more months at least. This would give them too long of an engagement and did not fit at all with the plan she'd laid out in her head.

But who cared about plans? Cate looked down at the man in front of her. She'd throw out all her carefully made plans for that man, and she'd do it happily.

He'd won her over their freshman year with his handsome smile and his charm. Then he'd won her over again with his love notes their sophomore year. Just like with his blindfolded journey tonight, he hadn't fooled her for a second with his "your admirer" salutation which he'd used to sign each letter. She'd known right away that the messages to her in their mailbox were from him. And with each one, her heart had warmed more and more to him. Until she'd written her own back. "Be my boyfriend?" He'd said yes.

Henry fumbled in his pocket to pull out a ring. A tasteful diamond on a simple gold band.

From behind the bathrooms, Frank and his a cappella quartet walked toward the two of them, humming as they went.

Cate's lip trembled as she recognized the song from the first movie they saw together.

"Breaking up with you was the biggest mistake I've ever made, but it taught me something. Walking the journey of life is so much easier when we walk together. And I've decided that you're the one I want to walk with forever.

"Will you make me the luckiest man alive and marry me?"

She held her hands to her lips as a squeal came out. "Yes!"

Henry grinned as he slid the ring onto Cate's finger. The ring wasn't an exact fit this time, but after it had been adjusted, it would be perfect.

They embraced as they listened to the final chords of the song.

"I love you, Henry Mullins."

"I love you, too, Cate Hodges."

Cate had never been happier in her life and couldn't wait to share her journey with Henry as his wife.

37

PRESENT DAY

Half an hour after the reception, the crowd had thinned considerably. Catherine looked around to see a few of her former classmates talking with the Coopers. She hadn't spotted Henry in a while.

Catherine laughed at a joke Raymond told, but her mind was elsewhere. Some invisible radar inside of her detected Henry's presence nearby. An instinctive, animal part of her could sense him.

He approached and slipped a piece of paper into her hands, but Catherine almost didn't notice it. The surge of electricity from his merest touch had her reeling. Her stomach flipped from the smell of his aftershave and the warmth of his skin.

Bringing her hand closer, she read the paper. *Meet me at our box.*

Catherine had already spent a long time catching up with Tracy and Raymond. They made promises to get together again soon. She waved goodbye to the Coopers, having exchanged phone numbers earlier. They hoped to get together for a chat over coffee before Catherine and Clara headed home that evening.

"I'm going to walk around campus for a bit."

"Do you want me to come with you?" Clara was in the middle of a conversation, but Catherine knew her sister would drop whatever she was doing to make her feel better.

"No," she said. "I won't be long. I'll text you in twenty minutes."

"Okay."

Catherine patted her sister's arm.

The walk to the student center only took about five minutes. From the east side of campus, not much looked different. There was a new science building and a new second-floor walkway. The Bible building had been erected shortly after she graduated and was not really new anymore. For the most part, the red brick structures looked like they did when she was in school.

Somehow, the student center looked very different but smelled exactly the same. There were new restaurants and a coffee shop. The old bowling alley was gone. A fireplace warmed a circle of students sitting at tall tables, and a large television flashed a football game on the wall.

She remembered her old box number, or at least the feel of walking to it. How many steps it took and where she stood in relation to the back wall. And when she turned the corner, she saw another slip of paper.

Meet me where we shared our first kiss.

Catherine should have found all of this irritating. The man who'd served her divorce papers was now attempting to lead her on a romantic scavenger hunt?

But she was intrigued. What did Henry have planned?

The second floor was quiet, but for a handful of students. She asked them for directions to the darkroom, and they gave her blank stares. Thankfully, a professor was nearby and directed her down a hallway.

A white slip of paper was taped to one of the doors.

Meet me at the swings.

Catherine checked the time on her phone. Twelve minutes had passed since she left Clara. She would have to text soon. *Henry better be almost done with this wild good chase.*

And there he was, swinging alone, on the front lawn.

She approached from the side, watching him.

He'd changed so much from the young man she'd met nearly thirty years before. Back then, he'd worn his good looks and charm like a suit of armor. Inside a thin layer of metal plating, he was a scared and lonely little boy who retreated at the first sign of trouble.

Now, he was a middle-aged man. His hair had grayed and his skin had aged with time and sun. He seemed more solid, somehow. He'd gained a little weight, yes, but it was more than that. Catherine got the sense he didn't wear so much armor anymore.

"Hey, you."

Henry gave her a tentative smile. "Care to join me?" He patted the space next to him.

She stopped. This seemed like a test. It all had, really. With each clue, she'd had the chance to turn back. But she'd kept going. Maybe out of curiosity, maybe out of a true desire to reconnect with Henry.

If he was going to make a real effort, she was willing to meet him halfway.

But then, a realization hit her. "This would be our third swing."

Henry smirked. "I believe you are correct."

"Of course, you already proposed to me once, so I guess it doesn't matter."

He shrugged.

She bit her lip. Did she want to turn around? *No. I want to see this through.*

Catherine sat down beside him. Henry kicked his feet and the swing began a slow rhythm.

"I need to text Clara to tell her where I am." Catherine typed out a brief message.

> On the front lawn with Henry. Give me thirty more minutes, plz.

When she'd pocketed the phone, Catherine turned to Henry. "That was quite a hunt."

"Did you like it?"

"I don't know. What was the point of it?"

His face fell.

Her heart twinged at the sight. "I don't mean to hurt your feelings. I just need to know why you're making me revisit all of our old haunts if you're still planning to divorce me."

Henry nodded. "I've been talking to Maddy."

"Me too."

He smirked. "She can be very persuasive at times."

Catherine barked a laugh. "You should have seen her as a teenager." Usually, their daughter used her powers for good, but Catherine remembered a particularly expensive prom dress Maddy had talked her into.

"I should have." Henry looked down at his hands. They gripped the edge of the seat. "I should've been part of your lives, and I can't ever express how sorry I am that I missed all of it."

Catherine nodded. What was there to say? She didn't harbor deep anger toward Henry anymore, but his abandonment still hurt.

"Talking to Maddy reminded me of how much I still love you."

Catherine's breath caught in her throat. He'd already told her he loved her, but she'd assumed all that had changed when he'd decided on a divorce. "Do you?"

"Of course, Cate." His feet skidded the swing to a halt. "I never stopped loving you. Never."

"I never stopped loving you either." There was so much freedom in admitting the truth to him. "And I tried really hard."

He chuckled, but it was a mirthless laugh. "I'm sure you did. I gave you every reason to."

"You did."

As if by an unspoken agreement, they both pushed their feet to start the swing again. Back and forth, back and forth, somewhat like the path their relationship had taken.

"Cate, I know I don't deserve another chance. I know I've broken your trust too many times. But if you have even a shadow of hope, even a seed of love for me, I'm asking you to try again."

"You don't deserve another chance, it's true." She shifted on the seat to face him. "But neither do any of us. You've given me grace for my stubbornness and perfectionism and all of my horribly unattractive traits. So, I want to give you another chance."

Henry's whole face lit up. Even his chest rose visibly.

"But I need to know something," she said. "You told me once that we would walk our journeys together."

He nodded and looked across the lawn as if remembering that day.

"In order for this to work, I need you to promise me we're going to walk through everything together. No more pulling away when things get tough. I go everywhere you go."

Though Henry's expression had softened, he still effused joy and love. "I promise, Cate. If you take me back, we'll walk it all together. Everything. Everywhere. All of it."

Henry slid off the swing and onto one knee. "I had Maddy borrow this for a little while." With his right hand, he pulled out the solitaire diamond on a double gold band from his pocket. The same ring she'd worn for fourteen years before storing it in a box for eleven more.

She'd thought about selling it to a pawn shop or even tossing it in the trash many times. But she'd never been able to part with anything in that box. The memories of Henry and falling in love were too dear and too sweet. They were a part of who she had been and, maybe, who she would be.

Henry looked up at her with love in his eyes. "Cate, will you make me the luckiest man in the world again? Will you still be married to me?"

Cate couldn't help but grin back at him. "Yes, I will."

With a speed that belied his years, Henry leaped up and pulled Catherine along with him, squeezing her in a hug. He pulled back and took her hands in his. The ring still fit perfectly. Catherine breathed a sigh that none of her extra weight over the years had gone into her fingers.

"We can get a better ring now. If you'd like." Henry examined the diamond, turning her hand to catch the afternoon sunlight.

"No. I don't want a new husband, and I don't want a new ring."

Henry pulled her close. "Good."

He leaned down and moved one finger along her cheek, from her ear to her chin. Then he turned her face up to his. "I love you, Cate."

"I love you, too, Henry."

If she'd had any time at all to think, any space left in her brain for something other than Henry's lips, she might have worried about kissing him again. Would their years apart dilute their passion for each other? Had that last brief kiss been a fluke? Did she even remember how to kiss?

But if she'd had a moment to worry, it would have all been in vain.

As their lips met, it was as if they were kissing for the first time again. The familiar buzz of electricity hummed through her body. The warm glow she always felt before returned to her chest. And the taste of Henry on her lips weakened her knees as if she were a college student again.

Except she wasn't.

No, when Catherine kissed Henry again, it was with years of experience behind her. Years growing with Henry and raising their daughter. Years apart from him, learning about her own strengths and weaknesses.

Catherine considered the time ahead of them. The journey would surely be difficult. There were surprises and pitfalls even beyond the struggles they already knew about. She'd be going to therapy sessions and Al-Anon meetings. She'd have to learn how to live with a man again. There were many specifics to be sorted out, but they had time to do it all. As Henry deepened their kiss, she forgot about the details and simply delighted in her husband.

Catherine pulled away from Henry's lips for a moment, only to gaze into his eyes once more. "There's no one I'd rather share this journey with, Henry."

"I feel the same way."

* * *

"Maddy? Are you there?" Catherine and Henry squeezed their faces together as they called their daughter on the video messaging app.

"Hey, you two." Maddy's grin spread from ear to ear. "How's it going?"

"We have some news." Catherine turned to Henry. "You tell her."

"No, you." He elbowed her gently.

"We're staying married!" Catherine showed off her ring to the screen.

Maddy's jaw dropped. "That's amazing! I'm so happy."

Henry placed his arm around Catherine's shoulder. "We wanted you to be the first to know."

"Thanks." Maddy chuckled. She glanced off-screen.

"Oh, sorry, sweetie," Catherine said. "Is now a bad time? We can call back later."

"No, actually—" She whispered something over her shoulder. "Here."

A.J.'s face popped up on the phone. "Hi, there." A goofy grin spread across his face.

Catherine felt a warmth flood her heart. They were back together. "Well, hello, A.J."

Maddy centered herself on the screen again. "We also have some news."

Henry smiled at her. "Oh, really?"

"Really. Two pieces of news, in fact." Maddy held up her own left hand. "We're getting married too!"

"Oh, sweetie. That's wonderful!"

Henry gripped her shoulder in excitement. "We're so happy for you."

"Wait, what's the other news?"

Maddy bit her lip and looked at A.J.

"While we were broken up," A.J. said, "I sent in an early application to Halloway School of Theology."

Maddy interjected. "And he got in, which is really great."

"I start school next August with some leveling work over the summer."

"Congratulations." Catherine could tell that Maddy was nervous about something, but she wasn't sure what. "So why do I sense there's more information?"

Maddy twisted her lips before answering. "We didn't want to be apart for so long during the summer, and once I decided I wanted to get married, I realized I *really* want to marry A.J."

"Plus, we'd already started planning a Christmas wedding," A.J. said.

"So, we decided to bump up the wedding ... to this December!" Maddy held out her hand in a sort of ta-da pose.

Catherine could see her face and Henry's, stuck in matching

stares of shock on the phone screen. If they weren't blinking, they'd appear to be frozen.

"Mom? Dad?"

"Sorry." Catherine sucked in a breath. "You're getting married in less than two months?"

"Yes." Maddy's smile faltered. "We already have the dress and the photographer, so that should help."

"Honey," Henry's voice was much calmer than Catherine's, "we are so excited for you."

Catherine glanced at her husband. How in the world were they supposed to pull off a wedding in only a few weeks? But then she looked at her daughter. Finally, after so much time worrying about the future, her daughter seemed happy. She'd listened to the advice of her parents and taken a leap of faith for the sake of love. A huge leap. Catherine felt a smile lift her lips. "That's right, we're very excited. I'm sure it'll be great. We'll do everything we can to make it the best wedding possible."

Maddy's grin returned. She rested her head on A.J.'s shoulder.

"We sure will." Henry turned to her. "And the best part is, we'll all do it together."

Catherine leaned into her husband's embrace and stared into her daughter's happy face. Henry was right. That's how it would be. They'd figure it all out ... together.

DISCUSSION QUESTIONS

1. Henry is intimidated by his university and his classmates, especially Cate Hodges. If you went to college, do you remember your first semester? What were some of your freshman challenges?
2. Cate is initially resistant to dating Henry. Why do you think that was? Would Henry have convinced you to date him?
3. Henry doesn't want to share his family secrets with Cate. Do you think he should've trusted her sooner? Was he justified in his fears?
4. Dr. Cooper is influential in Henry and Cate's relationship and faith journey. Which teachers of yours were the biggest influence on you and why?
5. Cate and Henry both have childhood and college friends who remain important in their lives. Who is your oldest friend? Do you still keep in touch?
6. Madeleine struggles in her new engagement. How does hearing the story of her parents' relationship help or hurt her?

DISCUSSION QUESTIONS

7. When tragedy strikes, part of Henry's healing process is connecting with the Jones family. Do you have friends outside of your family who have helped you grow?
8. Which part of Henry and Catherine's love story resonated the most with you?
9. Henry and Catherine find meaningful connections in the movie *The Wizard of Oz*. How do the themes of journey and companionship appear in both stories?
10. An inspirational verse for this novel was Ecclesiastes 4:12. What does this verse mean to you? How do you think it might apply to Henry and Catherine's story?

ACKNOWLEDGMENTS

Jeff Montgomery, thank you so much for taking the time to answer my photography questions. You're a rock star. I don't know how you manage to do everything you do, but I suspect time travel might be one of your superpowers.

Caryllee Cheatham, I truly appreciate you talking with me about working for *The Bison* and your college days. I enjoyed reading articles from your time at Harding and your insight into how running a newspaper works.

Thank you to the librarians at the Brackett Library who archived back issues of *The Bison*. I thought I wouldn't enjoy research, but reading through those papers was a delight!

Linda and Heather and everyone at Scrivenings Press, thank you so much for taking me on and giving the Shady Springs series a home. I love working with you in this ministry.

Amy, I thank God every time I think of you. He orchestrated our meeting and has blessed me with your friendship. I feel like you've been holding my hand through every step of this publishing journey, so it's only fitting I get to have you as my editor. Thank you for your wisdom and punctuality and kindness and general awesomeness.

A million thank yous to my husband, Michael, who encourages me, listens to me, and puts up with me. You teach me every day how to be a better version of myself.

To my three children, who just starting reading big books with no pictures, if you ever read this, please know that I love you very much and am thankful to get to be your mom *and* an author. Thank you for understanding when I have to go hide at a coffee shop to write another chapter.

Thank you, thank you, thank you to my friends and family who've supported me and read my books. Thank you for your emails, for stopping me at church to talk about writing, and for sharing my books with your friends. I pray this story is a blessing to you.

Every time I sit down to write, I pray God would guide me and use my words to bless others and glorify His name. I pray that I will always, only, ever glorify Him.

ABOUT THE AUTHOR

Sarah Anne Crouch aims to bless readers with inspirational fiction brimming with heart. The author of A Summer in Shady Springs, "A Sweet Dream Come True" from the Love in Any Season collection, and "Where Love is Planted" from the Love Delivered collection, Sarah writes stories featuring characters growing in love and their relationships with God.

Although Sarah always wanted to be an author, she spent time as a fifth-grade English teacher, earned a degree in library science, and currently makes feeble attempts to corral her children as a stay-at-home mom.

Sarah has lived in many places but calls Arkansas home and draws inspiration from the beautiful surroundings of the Natural State. A graduate of Harding University, she remains actively involved with her alma mater.

Outside of writing, Sarah enjoys reading books, exploring recipes, playing piano music, and cherishing emails from her readers.

MORE FROM THE SHADY SPRINGS SERIES

A Summer in Shady Springs

Book One of the Shady Springs Series

The last place Madeleine Mullins wants to be is back in Shady Springs, Arkansas—the town where her whole world fell apart. But when her beloved Aunt Clara begs her for help, Madeleine reluctantly takes a job painting a mural at her aunt's church. Her plan is to finish quickly and leave her bad memories behind. But the more time she spends with the handsome youth minister and the more she reads her Bible, the more she wonders if she has been wrong about God and the Church all along.

Three years out of college, and A.J. Young still doesn't know what he wants to be when he grows up. He knows he wants to settle down and build a family but hasn't found the wife he'd like to share his life with.

Then Madeleine comes to town. Their friendship buds quickly, although it can never be anything more as long as she isn't a Christian.

An undeniable attraction grows between A.J. and Madeleine, but she's only in town for a few weeks, and he can't date someone who doesn't share his beliefs. How can Madeleine help A.J. discover a passion for the career he's always wanted?

Get your copy here:

https://scrivenings.link/asummerinshadysprings

ALSO BY SARAH ANNE CROUCH

A Match Made at Christmas
A novella collection—includes "A Match of Her Own"
by Sarah Anne Crouch

***A-parent-ly Christmas* (by Amy R Anguish)**—Noel and Joy Davidson didn't mean to separate, but a job promotion and educational opportunities were too much for their marriage to withstand. Now, it's Christmas and their son Andy wants them together. Between his mischief, an unexpected snowstorm, and the holiday spirit, they're remembering why they first wanted to be together. But which one will give up their dream for the other?

***A Match of her Own* (by Sarah Anne Crouch)**—Victoria Wood is torn between elation and devastation now that her sister is married and gone. When she realizes her sister's best friend is alone and best-friend-less on Christmas, she knows just what to do. Set her up with a boyfriend! But pesky Jared Knight keeps getting in the way. Jared can't date Victoria—she's too immature—but he can't convince his heart to move on. How will he keep Victoria from ruining everyone's love lives? When will she realize her perfect match is closer than she thinks?

Jingle Bell Matchmakers **(by Lori DeJong)**—When country music star Aubrey Mayfield is lured home after years away, she's bewildered when she and ex-fiance-now-widowed-dad Cody Lansdale keep finding themselves in the same place at the same time. As they become reacquainted, however, old feelings stir. Aubrey's at a crossroads in her career and is contemplating a change. But when a chance at headlining her own tour takes her back to Nashville, Cody realizes her dreams may once again come between them. Unless God, with a little help from the Jingle Bell Committee, has a better plan.

The Santa Setup **(by Heather Greer)**—Turning friendship into love takes magic. Good thing Nicholas Eckert and Julie Clarke work at Christmas Wonderland. The attraction brims with holiday magic, not to mention four teenage elves determined that Mr. and Mrs. Claus stop playing a couple and become one. The teens will need more than mistletoe to pair up these two. Julie is seeing someone, and Nick won't risk their friendship for possible love. Only the elven employees' outrageous antics stand a chance of setting up Santa in time for Christmas.

Get your copy here:
https://scrivenings.link/amatchmadeatchristmas

* * *

Love Delivered

A novella collection—includes "Where Love Is Planted"

by Sarah Anne Crouch

***Romance at Register Five* (by Amy R Anguish)**—Mack McDonald isn't happy about the Grocerease app coming to his grocery store. But he's committed to the sixty-day trial period, and braces himself to lose money. Kaitlyn Daniels loves how the Grocerease app helps her make ends meet so she can assist her mom, the reason she moved to small Sassafras, AR. Mack and Kaitlyn struggle to overcome differing opinions on the perks of the app. But if they don't, it could keep them from something even better.

***Where Love is Planted* (by Sarah Anne Crouch)**—Ivy Aaronson is surrounded by family at their flower shop in West Texas—just the way she likes it. But she's given up hope on ever finding a man who understands her choices. When attorney Grant Keller orders flowers for his mother, Ivy wonders if maybe there are indeed some considerate men left in the world…until she finds out Grant's relationship with his parents is less than ideal. How can Ivy ever find love when every man she meets puts career over family?

***Sweet Delivery* (by Heather Greer)**—After winning Cake That, Will Forrester thinks his Pastry Perfect Baking Dreams have come true. The sweetness fades when a chain bakery moves to town, and Will must adjust his plans to keep his customers. Hiring Erica Gerard is one of those changes. As they work together, Erica challenges Will and offers new ideas to improve the bakery. Soon, Erica and Will start bringing out the best in each other. But Erica harbors a secret, and if it's discovered, Will might never be the same.

***The Mermaids, the Ex, and USSS* (by Rachel Herod)**—Braig Sanborn is the most loyal employee the United States Shipping Service has ever seen, which is why he agreed to transfer across the country with only a few weeks' notice. Bailey Bivens is so busy planning a friend's wedding, she didn't expect to fall for the carrier who delivers packages to her house. When they both find themselves in too deep, will they agree the relationship was doomed from the start?

Get your copy here:
https://scrivenings.link/lovedelivered

* * *

Love in Any Season

A novella collection—includes "A Sweet Dream Come True"

by Sarah Anne Crouch

***Spring Has Sprung*(by Regina Rudd Merrick)**—Laurel Pascal, Assistant City Manager of Spring, Kentucky, is tasked with organizing the town's beloved Daffodil Festival, and she's not happy. An allergy sufferer all her life, she dreads the season from the first Daffodil bloom in the yard to the last coat of pollen on her car. Newcomer Dr. Owen Roswell volunteers to help, and soon finds that not only does Laurel need his expertise as an allergist, but help in appreciating the season she's obligated to celebrate.

What does he want more—for Laurel to fall in love with his favorite season? Or him?

***The Missing Piece* (by Amy R. Anguish)**—Beth Norton and Tommy England grew up together with best-friend moms who had a love of quilting and a business celebrating the craft. When high school ended, though, so did Beth and Tommy's friendship.

When Tommy moves back after seven years and his mother's death, he can't understand why Beth is so angry with him. Helping Beth and her mother stabilize the finances of the business, they're forced to work together. As Tommy sorts through his mother's things, he finds an unfinished quilt, and it turns into a joint project.

With each stitch taken, they work toward more than just a completed blanket.

***A Sweet Dream Come True* (by Sarah Anne Crouch)**—Isaac Campbell is living his dream of running an ice cream shop but fears he won't last past the first difficult year. Mel Wilson is a busy single mother who longs to be a chocolatier but is too afraid to turn her dreams into reality.

When Mel and Isaac meet at Bestwood, Tennessee's fall festival, it seems like divine providence. But once Mel agrees to help Isaac bring in customers by selling her chocolates at his shop, she realizes how challenging running a business can be.

Can Mel and Isaac trust in God's provision and make a leap of faith?

Will their partnership end in disaster, or will it be a sweet dream come true?

***Sugar and Spice* (by Heather Greer)**—Emeline Becker, owner of Sugar and Spice Bakery, loves New Kuchenbrünn, except for the gingerbread. As the only bakery, she supplies the annual Gingerbread Festival with the one treat she can't stand. It's gingerbread everywhere.

Things get worse when Ryker Lehmann is hired as the festival photographer. He was her secret teen crush, her sister's boyfriend, and witness to her worst humiliation. Plus, he broke her sister's heart and bruised hers when he left town after graduation. Now, he's back in town, determined to fix their friendship before the festival ends.

With gingerbread and Ryker together, can Emmie make it through the festival with her mind and heart intact?

Get your copy here:

https://scrivenings.link/loveinanyseason

* * *

Stay up-to-date on your favorite books and authors with our free e-newsletters.

ScriveningsPress.com

Made in the USA
Columbia, SC
09 March 2025